FRIGHT TRAIN

edited by

THE SWITCH HOUSE GANG

An imprint of Haverhill House Publishing

TABLE OF CONTENTS

FRIGHT TRAIN

INTRODUCTION

"Three a. m. That's our reward. Three in the morn. The soul's midnight. The tide goes out. The soul ebbs. And a train arrives at an hour of despair...."
                    --Ray Bradbury, Something Wicked
                                This Way Comes

There is something inherently creepy about trains. Don't think so? Anyone who has ever been awakened late at night by a distant train whistle knows there is no lonelier sound. It is a mournful howl from a soulless traveler on a night journey to destinations unknown.

Writers have long known the macabre romance of trains. Charles Dickens' story *The Signalman* is considered a classic of horror. Robert Bloch, author of Psycho, wrote of *The Hellbound Train* in the fifties. Manly Wade Wellman wrote about *The Little Black Train*, which comes for a sinner's soul. Clive Barker took us for a ride on *The Midnight Meat Train*.

This anthology came about because co-editor Tony Tremblay and I were having a social-media discussion of horror stories involving trains. We said we'd enjoy writing that kind of story, and writer/publisher John McIlveen joined in and said he would publish such a book if we could get enough stories. The following summer at the Northeastern Writer's Conference, aka Camp Necon, we firmed up the plans and were joined by Scott Goudsward as third co-editor.

We decided to call ourselves The Switch House Gang, after the small buildings where manual track switches were housed. Those switches were used to direct trains to different sets of tracks, sending them to varying locations. That's what we hope to do with this book. Send readers on many dark and dangerous journeys.

We wanted a wide range of stories, and we got them. They vary from Victorian-era ghost stories to contemporary chillers to dark fantasy. Some are just plain creepy. One or two are humorous. Many are terrifying. None are boring.

Anyway, the conductor keeps glancing at his watch. Your seat is waiting. Don't worry about the shadows in the car or the strange looking passengers. You don't need a ticket. Just a willingness to travel to places unknown.

Charles R. Rutledge
Atlanta Georgia. 2021

When I was a young boy, my friends and I would bike to a freight train depot located in the bowels of Manchester, N. H. , my hometown. Our parents would ward us off the area, telling stories of a hobo jungle on the far side of the depot. They'd spin yarns of how the hobos would entice kids into their camps and then do unspeakable things to them.

While our parent's efforts to keep us safe had some effect, it wasn't enough to keep us away. We kept to the main areas, away from the hobos (which we had never seen, by the way), watching the trains either speed by or park for loading.

It was the speeding trains that captured our attention. We would put pennies on the track; the weight and locomotive power of the trains would crush those pennies and elongate them into ovals. Occasionally, my parents would find one of those coins in my bedroom with Abe Lincoln's thinned head stretched to about twice its length, and I would get another *talking to.*

When those trains barreled by, I watched in fascination. The ca-chunking and whine of the wheels, the turbulence strong enough to ruffle my hair, and the ground rumbling beneath my feet—all left two lasting impressions on me: awe and fear.

When I was in high school, I had a friend named Ed Cooper who loved trains. He would take me to different locations around the state where we'd sit on the grass and watch locomotives thunder by until they vanished around a bend or were reduced to a small dot on the horizon. Ed always had a notebook with him and would diligently record the numbers of all the engines that labored along those tracks. When he was older, Ed wrote a book about trains and the men who worked them.

So, yeah, trains have been a part of my life since I was old enough to ride a bike. That awe and fear of them I mentioned had taken up residence in a small corner of my mind, always reemerging when I crossed a railroad crossing or hopped onto a subway. As a writer, there was no way I was going to pass up this opportunity to write a horror story and edit an anthology about trains.

As Charles mentioned above, the tales in Fright Train are varied, but man, they are all so damn good. I would like to thank *The Switch House Gang*, all the authors who participated, and Haverhill House Publishing for contributing to this labor of love. I hope you are ready for some great storytelling; if so, then...ALL ABOARD!

Tony Tremblay
Goffstown, N. H. 2021

Like most people who live in or near a metropolitan area, I'm more than acquainted with trains. One of the "joys" of living in Haverhill, Massachusetts, is having a rail line that runs through the town into Boston. After a quick car drive to the local train station, it takes me about an hour of riding the rails to get to the city. An hour might seem long, but due to traffic, it could take at least twice that if I drove it (longer if the Red Sox, Celtics, or Bruins are playing). When arriving in Boston, the train lets me off at North Station. It's centrally located; you either walk or hop on a commuter rail to get where you need to be.

When visiting relatives in NJ, I remember (like Tony) putting pennies on the tracks in the morning and then returning after lunch to search for the squished coins. More often than not, the coins were gone when we got back. When we did find them, not one was remotely like the other. Each one of the stories in this book is like those coins—no two are alike. They are unique, ranging from gothic beauty to in your face horror. Skip around, read the stories in any order you like, but make sure you read every word, as each story is an amazing work of fiction.

It was such a privilege to be included in this anthology and work with Tony and Charles. See you when the whistle blows.

Scott T. Goudsward
Haverhill, MA. 2021

WEIGHTLESS BEFORE SHE FALLS

Bracken MacLeod

for Jennifer McMahon

"You know how you let yourself think that everything will be all right if you can only get to a certain place or do a certain thing. But when you get there, you find it's not that simple."

--Richard Adams, Watership Down

The distant hills along the horizon were autumn painted, red and yellow and orange; bright color spreading into the valley in a carpet of brilliance that reminded her of Fiver's apocalyptic vision of Sandleford Field. New England in October was a sanguineous landscape. The scene crawled along, gliding slowly under billowing white clouds that barely moved against the blue sky behind. A river wound along, lacerating the scene, sparkling in the early day's sunlight, glinting striking white like broken glass. A house nestled in the trees: white siding, green roof. Dark windows. No movement, other than to glide past with everything else resolute in its place as the train sliced through the countryside.

The rhythmic sound of steel wheels on rail like a mother's heartbeat against an infant's ear—*tchuk-shuk tchuk-shuk*—settled her nerves, lulling her to a near calm she hadn't felt in so long the sensation was as much a stranger to her as feeling whole. She left her headphones hugging her neck, enjoying the ambiance of the train. In the city, she rarely took the clamshells off. Why would she want to hear car horns honking, drivers shouting criticisms out windows at each other that would be reflected back to them by the next light? The thunder of busses and garbage trucks, motorcycles driven by men much too old for their performative toughness—half of them lawyers, anyway. No. Who wanted to hear any of that shit? Not her. But the sound of the *train*. That was just all right. She could listen to it all day. Except, she knew undisturbed peace wasn't in her future.

Enjoy it while you can.

She dared close her eyes and wait. It wasn't long before

"Excuse me, do you mind if I sit here?" The man in the aisle gestured at the seat facing hers. He wore a sport coat and jeans, but not a casual tweed sport coat with the elbow patches like her dad. No, this was a suit jacket, dark blue and almost shiny. Its formality contrasted with his faded dungarees. He wore it naturally, though it didn't look good, not to her. She shrugged, knowing he wasn't about to accept a refusal. The act of asking was obligatory, yet meaningless, like saying, "How are you doing?" when greeting someone. No one ever listened for an answer; it was enough to have ritually uttered the words. He was already bending to take the seat as she shrugged her assent. He smiled. Their car was empty. So many unoccupied seats. Though she wanted to return to gazing out at the landscape, he continued looking at her, forcing her attention.

"You know, I know you."

"Yeah?"

"I've... seen you in the waiting room at Counselors' Co-operative." He laughed, trying to feign nervousness. "No one in the lobby ever says anything to each other. We're there, hanging out before our appointments, and trying not to make eye contact. It seems, weird, you know? Not to even say 'hi. '"

She knew. She recognized him—seen him there more than a few times. He wasn't as shy as he claimed. Others would come in and try to find a seat in the waiting room, far from anyone else. Protected in a bubble of short distance. They'd stare at their phones or thumb through an old copy of *Psychology Today* or *People* from the rack on the wall until they were called. Even when it was a couple in for counseling, they wouldn't talk to each other. The unspoken decorum of the therapists' waiting room was to save conversation for the clock. For behind a closed door. Odd little cream-colored noise machines sat on the floor outside of each of the offices, droning on in a pink noise monotone, obscuring the tears and confessions, raised voices and recriminations on the other sides of doors while people in the lobby waited their turn to peel back the bandage, show their wound some sunlight. Silently waiting helped further the illusion of not being seen in this place of vulnerability. Not being exposed as one of the broken. Except this man. He'd come in and sit, not looking at a device or a magazine, but staring ahead into the room, looking around like it was a dentist's office, and he was waiting to compare smiles with other patients. She'd started staggering the days of her sessions with her therapist to try to avoid seeing him. He showed up on Thursdays, she'd try a Friday. He came on Friday, she moved to Wednesday. Despite her efforts to add an element of randomness into her schedule—and the difficulty it caused her at work—she still saw him there.

And now here.

"Okay," she said.

"I'm Allan, with two L's two A's, like Edgar Allan." He smiled. A smug look like he was trying to show how much he knew about her from her black clothes, her dark mien. "It's nice to meet you."

It doesn't matter, she reminded herself. "Alice," she said, not shaking his proffered hand.

"Alice. *Very* nice to meet you. It's funny," he said without waiting for any sign she was interested in more than introductions. The sound of her name on his voice felt bad, like touching her tongue to rust. Bitter and metallic, not quite like blood, but close enough. "To run into you here, I mean. I see you around town too. Your look is... pretty distinctive; you're a hard person to miss, you know." She was aware. She'd seen him too, though he stood out less than she did, she always knew when he was near. "You like to walk," he said. She did. The time alone felt good, especially after spending a shift with customers who treated her like one of the weird things they stocked in the store instead of a person.

"I don't have a car," she replied.

"I figured. Ripton isn't that big, but still. You've got to clock the miles on your tracker." He glanced at his expensive smart watch, ignoring the fact she wore strings of black beads around her wrists, but no devices. "I know I'd like to spend more time out of the car than I do, but you know how it is. I've got client meetings all over the place, and if I walked between them, I'd be out of a job."

She knew he was expecting her to ask what it was he did. She didn't care. Whatever it was, it gave him the freedom to be out of the office all day in his car. He drove a BMW. It didn't have a name like Legacy or Intrepid or anything. It was a something series—X9 or whatever. She didn't care about cars, though she knew his by sight. It was some color between brown and red that the dealer probably had a fancy name for instead of maroon. The car had big black wheels you could see the brakes through and thin tires. She thought they looked like sci-fi wagon wheels. The thing was always shiny clean, even when there was salt on the roads, or it had rained. At a distance, it looked to her like a blood clot with headlights.

The slight side to side motion of the train increased a little and she felt slightly queasy. Though he was the one facing backwards, he seemed unperturbed by the motion. She took a deep breath and let it out slowly. His cologne didn't help settle her tummy.

"Anyway, I've seen you around town, but never got the chance to say 'hi' until now. You always seem to vanish every time I think we're going to the same coffee shop or something." He laughed again. Forced.

"Right?" she said. "I guess I've seen you around too." She didn't mention that when she did, she usually darted off into someone's yard or through an alley he couldn't follow her down. Nearly every time she saw the clot coming toward her, her guts seized and she tried to vanish, but in a way that wouldn't make it *look* like she was deliberately avoiding him. She didn't want to follow that timeline to its end.

He smiled broadly at the admission that he hadn't escaped her notice. "What luck we're on the same train, then. Where are *you* headed?"

"Vermont."

"Well, yeah. Me too. Stowe, specifically. I have a ski cabin up there. I take a few days every fall to go up and unwind before winter gets its hooks in."

"You have a nice car. Why don't you drive?"

His smile faded a little. "It's part of getting away. I work in my car, so when I travel for relaxation, I like to take the train. I'll get a ride share whenever I need to go in town, but most of the time I just hang out at the cabin. You know, cook, listen to

CDs, get a taste of the good life, if I was set enough to retire and be a homebody-slash-ski-bum." Big smile.

"It's too early for skiing."

"You have to open up the house ahead of the season. Get it ready. That's what I do. Get everything set up so I can escape whenever I want and hit the slopes when the powder does come."

It was bullshit. They both knew it. He was on the train because she'd dropped her unsecured phone in the waiting room when she got up to go into her session the week before. He'd had an uninterrupted hour with it. Looking through her photo gallery, texts, Instagram. Her e-mails. He'd seen her e-receipt for the ticket she'd bought on the Nor'Easter Line to West Hall, Vermont. She'd have bought a ticket all the way to Ashford, but West Hall was far enough, so she tried to save a little money. Neither of those towns were anywhere near Stowe. But here he was. On *her* train.

After her session, she'd come out to find her phone sitting on the children's table in the waiting room instead of on the floor under her seat. She'd called up the app that would take a selfie every time the device was woken up. Her face was first. Taken just now. She deleted the picture, and the man's countenance slid into view. His eyes wide and lips pursed in a look of delighted surprise she assumed came from finding no security code enabled on the wakeup screen. That face made her shudder. She took a look at the battery icon. It had been at seventy-two percent when she went in and now was sixty. She deleted the picture, disabled the selfie app, and reactivated her unlock code.

She sat there gently rocking in her seat as the train seemed to pick up speed.

tchuk-shuk tchuk-shuk tchuk-shuk

Her stomach in knots, wondering what to do next. She wanted to glance at the clock on her phone. But, knowing what time it was wouldn't help. She had to do this by feel.

Here he sat with her in the empty train car, his salesman's smile so broad she could see the dark hole where the molar behind his right canine should've been. "What are the chances, right?" he said. "I know you're thinking, 'why sit right here when this whole car is empty, except for the two of us?'. It's just, when I saw you, I felt like I had to stop. I see you in the Co-op and all around town, and I think, *there's* somebody who looks interesting. Somebody who knows what it's like."

"I don't."

"Or… at least gets it. We both go there to get help with our problems. We talk to people we barely know to try to gain some insight into why we are the way we are. They know all about us, but they don't *know*. Not the way you and I do." He tilted his head a little to accentuate his feigned uncertainty with his prepared monologue. "My bet is, you probably feel a hell of a lot more in tune with my feelings than Bob or Holly. You see Holly, right?"

She nodded.

"Is she good?"

Alice shrugged. "I guess so. She gets me, I guess."

"But not a hundred percent, am I right?" He pointed to her shirt. It read, *LOVE ME LIKE MY DEMONS DO!* She didn't answer and he didn't pause. "Bob is okay. He hears what I'm saying when I tell him how…."

"You don't have to—"

"It's okay. I can talk about it now," he said, ignoring her subtle plea to please not overshare. Then again, she knew what he was about to say was almost certainly a lie, like everything that'd come before. Sure, she saw him in the waiting room often enough. But she never saw him go in or come out of Bob's office. For all she knew, maybe Bob was just a friend, and Allan with two L's and two A's dropped in from time to time for lunch or something else.

He continued. "Since my dad passed, I... the old man was a son of a bitch—always hard on me—but I guess, he was still my dad, right? I'm sure you get it."

He'd taken a stab. A pretty safe one, she thought. Daddy issues seemed likely for her. Either abusive or absent. Too harsh and out of touch with the way she looked, the things she liked. But her dad was all right. It wasn't him that'd sent her to therapy.

Allan sat there waiting for her to answer, letting the silence lengthen to an uncomfortable duration, one he was counting on her to fill. So, she did. "Holly gets me okay. She helps. But, you know. It's hard. My problem is..." she let the sentence dangle. Like she felt: hanging at the end of a hook.

"You can tell me." He leaned forward as if to say, it's safe for you to whisper it. No one in this empty train car will hear but me.

"Complicated," she finished.

He sat back, a trace of disappointment in his voice. "I'm sure it is." His face darkened. He looked so subtly frightening no matter his expression, but now there was nothing understated about him. Her heartbeat quickened in time with the train.

tchuk-shuk tchuk-shuk tchuk-shuk

"No one believes me," she said. "Not even Holly. But you will. Right?"

"Of course, I will."

She looked at her hands in her lap. Her bag under them. Inside was her notebook, allergy meds, makeup, wallet, and phone. That last was in the front pocket, just under her hands. Useless. There wasn't a soul on Earth she could call to fix the situation she'd gotten herself in. She knew that would be the case beforehand, being in motion, on the train, but she'd done it anyway, because of all the times she'd ducked him on the street as he passed her in the clot, she knew she wouldn't elude him forever, and the one time she didn't would be the end of her problems. Of everything. Forever.

His eyes shifted to the bag. She could see him thinking things through. Whether to take it from her. He stayed still, knowing he could reach it before she could pull a Taser or pepper spray out of the zippered main compartment. She had neither. Just an inhaler. That wouldn't do shit. He wasn't a cosmic spiderclown in the sewers. He was a *real* monster. She went on.

"Holly gets it. I mean, she understands how I *feel*, but I know she doesn't *believe* me, no matter how much I prove it to her."

He leaned forward again, trying to force closeness. To disarm. "You shouldn't have to prove a thing." He put his hand on her knee. Her stomach lurched, and the back of her throat burned. This gentle resting of a hand on her, the first of many touches. None of which she'd consent to. None of which he cared to seek permission for. She wanted to jump up and run right then.

Not yet. It's not time yet.

She said, "Yeah, well, I get why she can't. It's... a thing that's... hard to swallow."

His eye twitched. She pretended she didn't see it. "What is it?"

She took a deep breath. "I kind of... can see the future."

He sat back in his seat, smile broadening, even though it

was a slip in his caring persona. He was laughing at her on the inside and couldn't hide it. "It can feel like that, but self-fulfilling prophecies—"

"See? You don't believe me either."

His brow furrowed but the unkind smile lingered like the last vision of the Cheshire cat. "I do! I mean, I want to understand, it's just—"

"Weird, right? I know. I have real *visions* of the future. I see things before they happen. It's not like, *knowing* what's definitely going to happen. But I know when something is, like, so possible it might as well've happened already."

"That's... different."

"How?"

"It's..." he seemed to be searching for words, genuinely intrigued by her delusion. Delayed, but not derailed, from his true intent. "A lot of people are good at putting together pieces of predictive information. Hell, that's how traders on Wall Street make a living. They study what's happening in the market and make predictions about where to put their clients' money. Lots of people do it. Horse racing betters and people like that." It was the first thing he'd said to her that wasn't rehearsed.

"It's not the same. Like, I knew you'd be on this train."

"Yeah?" His face dropped into that darker expression again as she reminded him why he was there. "How'd you know that?"

She shrugged again. "Just knew it. Same way I knew when you were following me in your car. I saw it, and then it happened."

His face reddened, fists balling up. "So, I've been *following* you, have I?"

"But I can change things. I know what, and kind of when,

depending on how close. I know that when you're driving up on me, I better get lost."

"Or what?"

"And I know when you're in the office before I go in, or if you're coming in while I'm waiting. I mean, I don't know a lot of things, but big strokes. Like, I know this train is going to crash."

His eyes widened with amusement. "It is, is it?"

She nodded, clutching her bag tighter to her abdomen. "Uh huh. Right now, the driver or conductor or whatever, is passed out. I don't know why. He's drunk or epileptic—I guess if he was epileptic, they wouldn't let him drive trains—anyway, he's lying on the floor in the engine compartment and we're going to be going too fast for a curve coming up."

The man looked out the window at the increasingly blurry landscape, his brow furrowed. Not wanting to believe her, but feeling that creeping certainty settle into his mind like seeing someone in a dark mask standing at the back door. *They're coming in,* a person in that situation would think. And they'd know that even though the door was locked, it was true because normal people's houses weren't impregnable. Not like castles, no matter how much anyone liked to think of them like that. A broken window next to a doorknob, and he was in. Faster than you could get to a phone and dial for help. Much quicker than you could reach the gun with the trigger lock on in your nightstand all the way at the other end of the house. He'd be in. And then reality would change. The thought was like that. The speeding landscape, the feeling of increased velocity in his body was a man in a dark mask outside the window, looking in at him.

She knew the sensation exactly. "I feel like I'm already dead and I'm just waiting for time to catch up to me," she'd said to

Holly, thinking of the man driving the clot. The one who was going to kill her. He was going to do it on a Tuesday afternoon. Snatch her in his car and take her home. She ducked into a hardware store and hid. He was going to do it on a Friday evening on her way home from work. Same idea, except this time, he wanted to take her to the park. She lit in between that pizza place and the Haitian church. And again, on a Saturday. And again. Until she didn't see a way out.

And then, she dreamt the train. And the driver. And the river.

"You're full of shit." He stood up, rocking on his feet as the train swayed from side to side. He reached over and grabbed her arm, pulling her up out of her seat. She resisted him, but he was bigger. The bones in his hand popped, he squeezed her wrist so hard. Loud enough she heard it over the sound of the tracks.

tchuk-shuk tchuk-shuk tchuk-shuk

The car swayed again and he took an awkward step into the aisle, holding on to her as if she could keep him from falling.

"Not yet," she said.

"Fuck you! I've been waiting for this for a long time. You have nowhere to disappear to this time." He yanked the bag from her hands and dragged her away from her seat into the aisle, toward the bathroom at the end of the car. He jammed the door open revealing a space not much bigger than an airplane toilet, but big enough for two people. Big enough for him to close his hands around her neck and watch her face turn red as autumn and then purple over his white knuckles, see his own face in the mirror over her shoulder. His ecstasy reflected behind her while her tongue stuck out, her eyes bugged, her voice a whisper as she asked him to please stop. And he wouldn't. He'd squeeze until he felt that pop, until it felt right, until he felt her weight in his hands pulling down and the tightness in his pants lessen. Oh God, why hadn't he ever done one in a mirror before?

He shoved her into the bathroom, she fell and hit her back against the sink. He smiled at her pained wince, and took a step into the room toward her. Maybe she wanted to die sometimes, but not like this. She reared up with a knee and kicked at him with her boot. "It's not time yet!" He staggered back into the wall opposite the bathroom door, slipping on the corrugated metal floor in his nice smooth-soled shoes. Before he could get his feet under him, she slammed the door and latched it.

His cries on the other side were deranged, but muffled. So soft confined in her box swathed in the sound of steel wheels on rails like a pulse in her ears.

tchuk-shuk tchuk-shuk tchuk-shuk

He banged on the door. Kicked it. He had to know she couldn't outwait him; he could just sit down and bide his time until she had to emerge. But he believed her that time was fleeting.

And then it happened. To Alice, it felt like being at the apex of an imminent drop. So slow, but pulling at your stomach with the promise of descent. A pause before the fall. Like being in the front car of a rollercoaster going over the first rise.

She braced herself, sitting on the toilet, pressing her hands to opposite walls and her feet against the sink. It wouldn't help, but it was better than standing in the aisle near the door between cars, where there was only open space and metal and window to break against.

The car tilted and the soothing rhythmic churn of the wheels stopped.

tchuk-______

She felt a kind of sick weightlessness. Her body lifting from the seat despite her best effort to stay braced. She dared close her eyes and listen.

A groan of metal, long and elegiac. And somewhere in another car, the screams of other people headed north for vacations, romantic getaways, and just the thrill of a train ride during leaf peeping season. A population she'd increased by two, knowing what would happen. Hoping it would happen, because she didn't know any other way to stop the *other* outcome. The other vision where, instead of gazing through a window at hills and rivers and lonely houses, she was trapped in the dark of a car trunk. The luxurious cargo space of a BMW X9 or whatever. Until that sudden bright white of the lid opening and nothing more after that.

Weightlessness became sudden embodiment. The feeling of a hard surface against her, breaking, bruising. She, bleeding. The ring and the pain and the sensation of a sudden stop and a slower renewed descent. And that new sound. Water.

She fumbled with the latch on the door. The bolt slid, but the door stayed shut. Bent in its frame. Stuck in place. She braced herself and shoved at the hinged middle. It hurt so much. Her shoulder. A rib too, she thought. It was hard to get a deep breath. She soldiered on and pushed until it gave. And then gave again a little more. Until she could shimmy out.

The ever-tilting car gave her aid, and she fell from the bathroom into the aisle landing heavily in the angle between floor and wall.

It was dark. She couldn't see the man. Maybe she'd heard him hit the floor. Maybe she heard something else, but it satisfied her either way. Because she knew what she knew. What the vision had given her. Blood rolling over bright New England hills, and a train slipping off its tracks into the rushing river below. And him, no longer in her dream. Unable to dream of killing her.

Water rushed in through the gaps in the door. She reached for the emergency handle on the passenger window above her. Freeing it to a cascade of bracing water that battered her with frigid violence, shoving her away from the opening.

Just like the vision.

She held on to a seatback and waited for the car to fill enough she could swim out. Finally, when it seemed like her last chance, she took as deep a breath as she could and ducked down under the rising water to pull herself out of the car, into the river, swimming for the bright sparkles of sunlight on the surface, thinking only of the dream.

And the headline in it

FEW SURVIVORS OF TRAIN DERAILMENT IN VERMONT

THE RHYTHM OF GRIEF

Mercedes M. Yardley

A man is listening to a train. His old hands had put it together and created that heavy heartbeat that thrummed along the tracks. It takes him back, and he tastes fire and steel and everything that made his blood pump faster. He remembers being a little kid, running around in his short knickers and blowing on a wooden whistle, mimicking the trains as they lumbered by. His mama squalled at him some for being too close to the tracks, but didn't she know, didn't she know, didn't she know that these steel giants had some kind of rhythm, some kind of power that made him dance.

"It makes me alive, Mama," he had said, and received a swat on the behind for it.

"You're too close to the tracks," Mama told him.

He was too close to the tracks, then on the wrong side of the tracks. Next he worked on the tracks, came full circle, and was too close to the tracks again.

When the trains rumbled by, his grim apartment shook. It started low and quiet, like a woman's growl, but it soon became a full-throated thing. The leaves on his plants quivered. His walls were bare except for that old picture of Jesus Christ his wife insisted he keep up. His holy eyes watched him walk around the room and when he was so old he was mostly confined to his bed, they watched him there. Christ trembled and stared and every now and then the trains shook

Him so hard that God himself fell from the wall and onto the ground and it was the Crucifixion all over again.

"'S'all right, Christ," the man reassured him. "You've seen worse and I reckon I have, too. This train is born of grief and power and when I die, it's gonna be to the sound the train makes." It will shake his soul up to heaven or grind it down to hell, but whichever way he goes, the old man knows it will be a right ride.

The picture of Christ is on the floor and the man can't summon up the strength to get out of bed and pick Him up right now. He'll just lean on back and listen to the train. Christ watches him from the floor, understanding. He knows what it's like to be done for the day.

In the distance, stars fall.

A woman is sitting on a train. Faith has red hair, stunning beauty, and eyes that see far more than most. She is holding a glass bowl in her hands with something that looks like yarn inside. But it isn't yarn; it's a container of spider webs, and she weaves them deftly with her fingers while she studies the other passengers on the train.

They all have their heads down in the way people have learned of late. They look at phones and devices, with earbuds in their ears. They consume podcasts and music and audiobooks. They fill their ears and minds and souls with noise, noise, noise, because it's easier than listening to the quiet. The quiet makes you think. It makes you realize, and realizing hurts. Faith knows this pain, this deep ache that eats you from the inside out. It gnaws at your organs and pulls the air out of your lungs. It puts its mouth to the holes in your bones and sucks out the marrow, until your body folds and collapses. Head down, shoulders rounded. The body can't stand up on its own anymore, straight and tall, because it has been so hollowed by grief. You simply take a seat on the train and let it carry you away.

So it's best to listen to the news and watch the digital videos, because it's easier than listening to the wind blow through those hollow bones like a flute.

Faith continues to knit the webs together, her long fingernails flashing in the low glow of the gaslights. Spiders spill from her bowl and run across her skin, living jewels that adorn her fingers. They provide her with more spider silk. They provide her with a pattering sensation on her body that brings her back to the present, back to the now, and tethers her here in this place instead of allowing her to drift off into the ether. They wave their legs with the rum-rum-rumble of the wheels.

Her sharp eyes rest on a blonde man. His hands are quiet in his lap, his head bowed. He's wearing running shoes and something about them brings up an image of him in Faith's mind. He wore similar shoes in his youth. He wore them to pieces, grinding the rubber down and pushing his toes through the leather. He was fast and light on his feet, legs flashing in front of him and taking him to the edge of the desert. No, further. They took him farther than he ever intended.

The man raised his head and met her eyes.

"We're on quite an unusual train," Faith said.

The man watched her knit. "They're very nice," he said, and nodded at the spiderwebs. "What will you do with them when you're done?"

Faith shrugged. "Many things. They can be a shroud. They can clot blood. I can make a veil or a mask or something that glitters and shines to decorate this car. I'll know what to do when I'm finished."

The man listened politely, but his mind was far away. Faith had a sense that he was always thinking about something else. Someone else.

A woman sat on the seat next to him. She had fine bones and fine features and a fine way about her. She held the man's hand and stared into his eyes, but he couldn't see her. The man's gaze fluttered back to the floor.

The woman turned to Faith. "His name is Tom," she said, and leaned against his shoulder. "I miss him. *We* miss him." She gestured at the tall, dark-haired man that sat in the seat across from this man, this Tom. The dark-haired man jiggled his leg impatiently. Faith could see that this man had a smile that was easy most of the time, but it was missing now.

"Tom," Faith said.

Tom looked up in surprise.

"How do you know my name?" he asked

"Your wife told me."

Tom's face did all of the things faces do whenever Faith mentioned a departed loved one. He rainbowed through the emotions. His expression was shocked and then soft and then broken and then wistful. His wife and best friend blinked in tandem with the motion of the train.

"She's here. Your friend, too. They're always here. They're always by your side, but right now you're not where you're supposed to be," Faith said. Tom watched her spin, spin, spin the spiderwebs until they became something firm, something tangible.

"A noose?" he asked.

"Or a rope to pull you out of the abyss. This is a train for the dead, and you're still very much alive. There will be plenty of time to join them in the future, when the time is right."

Tom thought of his kids. He thought of his job. He thought of his wife and his best friend and how he was straddling the worlds of the living and the dead. It was too much.

"What do I do?" he asked. He looked out of the train window. Stars began to fall from the sky, burning like meteors and chiming like old clocks. They lit up the dark sky. It was unspeakably lovely and horrifying all at once.

His wife kissed his cheek. His best friend rested his hand on Tom's shoulder.

Faith handed him the rope. It could anchor him to life, to the real world.

His wife put her forehead against Tom's. Her dark lashes fluttered as she closed her eyes and whispered.

"Get off the train."

░░░░░░░

A woman stands in front of a train.

Her name is Laura and she's seen some darkness. She's had bad days and worse days and sometimes those days all blend together until she can't tell one from another.

She's standing at a bend in the tracks. It's high on a bridge and it's a special place where college kids go to test their bravery. They test their trust and their love and their commitment for living. Three people have died here and two have lost limbs. Several have lost friends and lovers, because not everyone can stand and face an oncoming train. Some turn and run, and somebody very special is left behind. Life is like that.

These are the rules:

Never come to The Bend alone. Always have somebody

who has been here before with you. Their job is to keep you from panicking and jumping in front of the train.

Only face the train in the dark.

Wear tightfitting, dark clothes. You don't want to be seen by the engineer. If you wear something light that flies up around you, you might look like a ghost.

▦▦▦▦▦

Laura had been to The Bend before. She knew to tie back her dark hair so it didn't blow into her eyes and blind her. She knew how to crouch on the bridge so it looked like the train was coming, was coming, was coming straight for her before it suddenly shifted away. Everything rocked and creaked and the ground moved beneath her like the sea. The headlight from the train blinded her and then left her in absolute blackness, and the sound was so loud that she couldn't hear herself scream. The first time, the noise and fear and light and movement were so intense that it shocked everything inside of her. *Run,* her soul cried. *Run,* her body shouted. Synapsis fired and her legs kicked and she tried to flee, but her friend Merrilee held her down.

"No," Merilee shouted into her ear, and Laura could barely hear her over the wailing of the world shutting down. "Don't move." Merilee wrapped her arms around Laura and they cowered down like baby rabbits while the train roared past. Then it was gone, its taillights glowing like dull hellfire as it disappeared.

"Are you all right?" Merrilee's voice was calm, but her eyes studied Laura intently. "The first time can be...a bit much."

Laura's heart, always weak and irregular on its own, stopped its faltering beat. From that moment on, somehow it beat in time with the train, with the rhythm of the wheels against steel. Her eyes were wild with shock, her body flushed with adrenaline, but somehow, for the first time, things seemed clear.

At least, for a while.

Now, years later, it was time to break the rules.

Laura stood alone on the tracks and looked at the stars. They were bright and beautiful and peered back at her with interest. What was she going to do, they wondered? She seemed so different from the last time they saw her here.

"Things didn't go as I planned," she told them. "I expected so much more."

They understood. They understood. The cosmos was big and it was great, but even as awesome as it was in its grandeur, the small, little lives of ordinary humans were so fascinating in their intricacy. Plans derailed. Hopes realized and then shattered. Wants that became great vacuums in their souls.

"I thought if I just came back to the place of my childhood," Laura explained to the stars, "everything would make sense. But it doesn't."

They nodded their heads, chiming. One burned bright and fell at Laura's feet. It was a celestial diamond.

The tracks vibrated. The train was coming. Another star gasped and also fell.

Laura didn't know whether to close her eyes or watch the sky. One last decision. She blinked and was surprised to feel tears run down her face.

"Laura."

Laura glanced at the stars in surprise, but they weren't speaking. They were roiling in the sky, excited and anxious, but the voice wasn't theirs.

"Laura."

Laura turned her head to see Merilee pressed against the stone of the bridge. Her face was white and her eyes were far too large. They fairly seemed to burn with the stars themselves.

"Merilee, what are you doing here?"

"I knew you'd be here. I came to stop you."

The sound of the train. Its whistle blew, far down the tracks. It passed the vacant lot and the old tattoo parlor. The railroad crossing arms went down, protecting the streets. It was coming. It was coming.

"I wish you hadn't," Laura said. Another star fell and singed her cheek. She put her hand to her skin, dreamily surprised at the pain. "Please go."

"I won't," Merilee said. She looked down the line and saw the train come into sight. "Get off the tracks," she said, and grabbed at her friend, but Laura stepped out of reach.

Her tears were flowing freely now. The stars themselves were weeping, hurling themselves from the heavens. They were ground under the wheels of the train. They pattered to the ground and started small fires. The train wailed. The stars joined in.

The headlight blinded Laura, and suddenly it was too much, it was too *much,* and the stars and the noise and the shake, shake, shaking of the ground under her feet made her go wild, and she remembered Merilee holding her safe and securely on her first time at The Bend, and she threw her arm out toward Merilee now.

Merilee was right there, and she grabbed Laura's hand to pull her from the tracks. The train roared by and they both fell to the ground. Merilee put her arm over Laura's head and they shut their eyes. The night was full of screams and memories as the cosmos plummeted around them.

"It's okay. It's okay," Merilee said. The train was long gone, just a sound disappearing into the dust. The women sat up, still holding hands.

"It's hard," Laura said simply.

"I know," her friend assured her. "But it won't always be this hard."

A final star fluttered from the sky like a piece of confetti. Merilee opened her mouth and caught the star on her tongue. It chimed.

THE SIGNALMAN

Charles Dickens

'Halloa! Below there!'

When he heard a voice thus calling to him, he was standing at the door of his box, with a flag in his hand, furled round its short pole. One would have thought, considering the nature of the ground, that he could not have doubted from what quarter the voice came; but, instead of looking up to where I stood on the top of the steep cutting nearly over his head, he turned himself about and looked down the Line. There was something remarkable in his manner of doing so, though I could not have said, for my life, what. But, I know it was remarkable enough to attract my notice, even though his figure was foreshortened and shadowed, down in the deep trench, and mine was high above him, so steeped in the glow of an angry sunset that I had shaded my eyes with my hand before I saw him at all.

'Halloa! Below!'

From looking down the Line, he turned himself about again, and, raising his eyes, saw my figure high above him.

'Is there any path by which I can come down and speak to you?'

He looked up at me without replying, and I looked down at him without pressing him too soon with a repetition of my idle question. Just then, there came a vague vibration in the earth and air, quickly changing into a violent pulsation, and an oncoming rush that caused me to start back, as though it had force to draw me down. When such vapour as rose to my height from this rapid train, had passed me and was skimming away over the landscape, I looked down again, and saw him re-furling the flag he had shown while the train went by.

I repeated my inquiry. After a pause, during which he seemed to regard me with fixed attention, he motioned with his rolled-up flag towards a point on my level, some two or three hundred yards distant. I called down to him, 'All right!' and made for that point. There, by dint of looking closely about me, I found a rough zig-zag descending path notched out: which I followed.

The cutting was extremely deep, and unusually precipitate. It was made through a clammy stone that became oozier and wetter as I went down. For these reasons, I found the way long enough to give me time to recall a singular air of reluctance or compulsion with which he had pointed out the path.

When I came down low enough upon the zig-zag descent, to see him again, I saw that he was standing between the rails on the way by which the train had lately passed, in an attitude as if he were waiting for me to appear. He had his left hand at his chin, and that left elbow rested on his right hand crossed over his breast. His attitude was one of such expectation and watchfulness, that I stopped a moment, wondering at it.

I resumed my downward way, and, stepping out upon the level of the railroad and drawing nearer to him, saw that he was a dark sallow man, with a dark beard and rather heavy eyebrows. His post was in as solitary and dismal a place as ever I saw. On either side, a dripping-wet wall of jagged stone, excluding all view but a strip of sky; the perspective one way, only a crooked prolongation of this great dungeon; the shorter perspective in the other direction, terminating in a gloomy red light, and the gloomier entrance to a black tunnel, in whose massive architecture there was a barbarous, depressing, and forbidding air. So little sunlight ever found its way to this spot, that it had an earthy deadly smell; and so much cold wind rushed through it, that it struck chill to me, as if I had left the natural world.

Before he stirred, I was near enough to him to have touched him. Not even then removing his eyes from mine, he stepped back one step, and lifted his hand.

This was a lonesome post to occupy (I said), and it had riveted my attention when I looked down from up yonder. A visitor was a rarity, I should suppose; not an unwelcome rarity, I hoped? In me, he merely saw a man who had been shut up within narrow limits all his life, and who, being at last set free, had a newly-awakened interest in these great works. To such purpose I spoke to him; but I am far from sure of the terms I used, for, besides that I am not happy in opening any conversation, there was something in the man that daunted me.

He directed a most curious look towards the red light near the tunnel's mouth, and looked all about it, as if something were missing from it, and then looked at me.

That light was part of his charge? Was it not?

He answered in a low voice: 'Don't you know it is?'

The monstrous thought came into my mind as I perused the fixed eyes and the saturnine face, that this was a spirit, not a man. I have speculated since, whether there may have been infection in his mind.

In my turn, I stepped back. But in making the action, I detected in his eyes some latent fear of me. This put the monstrous thought to flight.

"You look at me," I said, forcing a smile, 'as if you had a dread of me. '

'I was doubtful,' he returned, 'whether I had seen you before.'

'Where?'

He pointed to the red light he had looked at.

'There?' I said.

Intently watchful of me, he replied (but without sound), Yes.

'My good fellow, what should I do there? However, be that as it may, I never was there, you may swear.'

'I think I may,' he rejoined. 'Yes. I am sure I may.'

His manner cleared, like my own. He replied to my remarks with readiness, and in well-chosen words. Had he much to do there? Yes; that was to say, he had enough responsibility to bear; but exactness and watchfulness were what was required of him, and of actual work--manual labour he had next to none. To change that signal, to trim those lights, and to turn this iron handle now and then, was all he had to do under that head.

Regarding those many long and lonely hours of which I seemed to make so much, he could only say that the routine of his life had shaped itself into that form, and he had grown used to it. He had taught himself a language down here--if only to know it by sight, and to have formed his own crude ideas of its pronunciation, could be called learning it. He had also worked at fractions and decimals, and tried a little algebra; but he was, and had been as a boy, a poor hand at figures. Was it necessary for him when on duty, always to remain in that channel of damp air, and could he never rise into the sunshine from between those high stone walls? Why, that depended upon times and circumstances. Under some conditions there would be less upon the Line than under others, and the same held good as to certain hours of the day and night. In bright weather, he did choose occasions for getting a little above these lower shadows; but, being at all times liable to be called by his electric bell, and at such times listening for it with redoubled anxiety, the relief was less than I would suppose.

He took me into his box, where there was a fire, a desk for an official book in which he had to make certain entries, a telegraphic instrument with its dial face and needles, and the little bell of which he had spoken. On my trusting that he would excuse the remark that he had been well-educated, and (I hoped I might say without offence), perhaps educated above that station, he observed that instances of slight incongruity in such-wise would rarely be found wanting among large bodies of men; that he had heard it was so in workhouses, in the police force, even in that last desperate resource, the army; and that he knew it was so, more or less, in any great railway staff. He had been, when young (if I could believe it, sitting in that, hut; he scarcely could), a student of natural philosophy, and had attended lectures; but he had run wild, misused his opportunities, gone down, and never risen again. He had no complaint to offer about that. He had made his bed and he lay upon it. It was far too late to make another.

All that I have here condensed, he said in a quiet manner, with his grave dark regards divided between me and the fire. He threw in the word 'Sir' from time to time, and especially when he referred to his youth: as though to request me to understand that he claimed to be nothing but what I found him. He was several times interrupted by the little bell, and had to read off messages, and send replies. Once, he had to stand without the door, and display a flag as a train passed, and make some verbal communication to the driver. In the discharge of his duties I observed him to be remarkably exact and vigilant, breaking off his discourse at a syllable, and remaining silent until what he had to do was done.

In a word, I should have set this man down as one of the safest of men to be employed in that capacity, but for the circumstance that while he was speaking to me he twice broke off with a fallen colour, turned his face towards the little bell when it did NOT ring, opened the door of the hut (which was kept shut to exclude the unhealthy damp), and looked out towards the red light near the mouth of the tunnel. On both of those occasions, he came back to the fire with the inexplicable air upon him which I had remarked, without being able to define, when we were so far asunder.

Said I when I rose to leave him: 'You almost make me think that I have met with a contented man. '

(I am afraid I must acknowledge that I said it to lead him on.)

'I believe I used to be so,' he rejoined, in the low voice in which he had first spoken; 'but I am troubled, sir, I am troubled. '

He would have recalled the words if he could. He had said them, however, and I took them up quickly.

'With what? What is your trouble?'

'It is very difficult to impart, sir. It is very, very difficult to speak of. If ever you make me another visit, I will try to tell you. '

'But I expressly intend to make you another visit. Say, when shall it be?'

'I go off early in the morning, and I shall be on again at ten to-morrow night, sir. '

'I will come at eleven. '

He thanked me, and went out at the door with me.

'I'll show my white light, sir,' he said, in his peculiar low voice, 'till you have found the way up. When you have found it, don't call out! And when you are at the top, don't call out!'

His manner seemed to make the place strike colder to me, but I said no more than 'Very well. '

'And when you come down to-morrow night, don't call out! Let me ask you a parting question. What made you cry 'Halloa! Below there!' to-night?'

'Heaven knows,' said I. 'I cried something to that effect----'

'Not to that effect, sir. Those were the very words. I know them well. '

'Admit those were the very words. I said them, no doubt, because I saw you below. '

'For no other reason?'

'What other reason could I possibly have!'

'You had no feeling that they were conveyed to you in any supernatural way?'

'No. '

He wished me good night, and held up his light. I walked by the side of the down Line of rails (with a very disagreeable sensation of a train coming behind me), until I found the path. It was easier to mount than to descend, and I got back to my inn without any adventure.

Punctual to my appointment, I placed my foot on the first notch of the zig-zag next night, as the distant clocks were striking eleven. He was waiting for me at the bottom, with his white light on. 'I have not called out,' I said, when we came close together; 'may I speak now?' 'By all means, sir. ' 'Good night then, and here's my hand. ' 'Good night, sir, and here's mine. ' With that, we walked side by side to his box, entered it, closed the door, and sat down by the fire.

'I have made up my mind, sir,' he began, bending forward as soon as we were seated, and speaking in a tone but a little above a whisper, 'that you shall not have to ask me twice what troubles me. I took you for someone else yesterday evening.

That troubles me. '

'That mistake?'

'No. That someone else. '

'Who is it?'

'I don't know. '

'Like me?'

'I don't know. I never saw the face. The left arm is across the face, and the right arm is waved. Violently waved. This way.'

I followed his action with my eyes, and it was the action of an arm gesticulating with the utmost passion and vehemence: 'For God's sake clear the way!'

'One moonlight night,' said the man, 'I was sitting here, when I heard a voice cry "Halloa! Below there!" I started up, looked from that door, and saw this someone else standing by the red light near the tunnel, waving as I just now showed you. The voice seemed hoarse with shouting, and it cried, "Look out! Look out!" And then again "Halloa! Below there! Look out!" I caught up my lamp, turned it on red, and ran towards the figure, calling, "What's wrong? What has happened? Where?" It stood just outside the blackness of the tunnel. I advanced so close upon it that I wondered at its keeping the sleeve across its eyes. I ran right up at it, and had my hand stretched out to pull the sleeve away, when it was gone. '

'Into the tunnel,' said I.

'No. I ran on into the tunnel, five hundred yards. I stopped and held my lamp above my head, and saw the figures of the measured distance, and saw the wet stains stealing down the walls and trickling through the arch. I ran out again, faster than I had run in (for I had a mortal abhorrence of the place upon me), and I looked all round the red light with my own red light, and I went up the iron ladder to the gallery atop of it, and I came down again, and ran back here. I telegraphed both ways, "An alarm has been given. Is anything wrong?" The answer came back, both ways: "All well. "'

Resisting the slow touch of a frozen finger tracing out my spine, I showed him how that this figure must be a deception of his sense of sight, and how that figures, originating in disease of the delicate nerves that minister to the functions of the eye, were known to have often troubled patients, some of whom had become conscious of the nature of their affliction, and had even proved it by experiments upon themselves. 'As to an imaginary cry,' said I, 'do but listen for a moment to the wind in this unnatural valley while we speak so low, and to the wild harp it makes of the telegraph wires!'

That was all very well, he returned, after we had sat listening for a while, and he ought to know something of the wind and the wires, he who so often passed long winter nights there, alone and watching. But he would beg to remark that he had not finished.

I asked his pardon, and he slowly added these words, touching my arm: 'Within six hours after the Appearance, the memorable accident on this Line happened, and within ten hours the dead and wounded were brought along through the tunnel over the spot where the figure had stood. '

A disagreeable shudder crept over me, but I did my best against it. It was not to be denied, I rejoined, that this was a remarkable coincidence, calculated deeply to impress his mind. But it was unquestionable that remarkable coincidences did continually occur, and they must be taken into account in dealing with such a subject. Though to be sure I must admit, I added (for I thought I saw that he was going to bring the objection to bear upon me), men of common sense did not allow much for coincidences in making the ordinary calculations of life.

He again begged to remark that he had not finished.

I again begged his pardon for being betrayed into interruptions.

'This,' he said, again laying his hand upon my arm, and glancing over his shoulder with hollow eyes, 'was just a year ago. Six or seven months passed, and I had recovered from the surprise and shock, when one morning, as the day was breaking, I, standing at that door, looked towards the red light, and saw the spectre again. ' He stopped, with a fixed look at me.

'Did it cry out?'

'No. It was silent. '

'Did it wave its arm?'

'No. It leaned against the shaft of the light, with both hands before the face. Like this. '

Once more, I followed his action with my eyes. It was an action of mourning. I have seen such an attitude in stone figures on tombs.

'Did you go up to it?'

'I came in and sat down, partly to collect my thoughts, partly because it had turned me faint. When I went to the door again, daylight was above me, and the ghost was gone. '

'But nothing followed? Nothing came of this?'

He touched me on the arm with his forefinger twice or thrice, giving a ghastly nod each time: 'That very day, as a train came out of the tunnel, I noticed, at a carriage window on my side, what looked like a confusion of hands and heads, and something waved. I saw it, just in time to signal the driver, Stop! He shut off, and put his brake on, but the train drifted past here a hundred and fifty yards or more. I ran after it, and, as I went along, heard terrible screams and cries. A beautiful young lady had died instantaneously in one of the compartments, and was brought in here, and laid down on this floor between us. '

Involuntarily, I pushed my chair back, as I looked from the boards at which he pointed, to himself.

'True, sir. True. Precisely as it happened, so I tell it you. '

I could think of nothing to say, to any purpose, and my mouth was very dry. The wind and the wires took up the story with a long lamenting wail.

He resumed. 'Now, sir, mark this, and judge how my mind is troubled. The spectre came back, a week ago. Ever since, it has been there, now and again, by fits and starts. '

'At the light?'

'At the Danger-light. '

'What does it seem to do?'

He repeated, if possible with increased passion and vehemence, that former gesticulation of 'For God's sake clear the way!'

Then, he went on. 'I have no peace or rest for it. It calls to me, for many minutes together, in an agonised manner, "Below there! Look out! Look out!" It stands waving to me. It rings my little bell----'

I caught at that. 'Did it ring your bell yesterday evening when I was here, and you went to the door?'

'Twice. '

'Why, see,' said I, 'how your imagination misleads you. My eyes were on the bell, and my ears were open to the bell, and if I am a living man, it did NOT ring at those times. No, nor at any other time, except when it was rung in the natural course of physical things by the station communicating with you. '

He shook his head. 'I have never made a mistake as to that, yet, sir. I have never confused the spectre's ring with the man's.

The ghost's ring is a strange vibration in the bell that it derives from nothing else, and I have not asserted that the bell stirs to the eye. I don't wonder that you failed to hear it. But I heard it.
'

'And did the spectre seem to be there, when you looked out?'

'It WAS there. '

'Both times?'

He repeated firmly: 'Both times. '

'Will you come to the door with me, and look for it now?'

He bit his under-lip as though he were somewhat unwilling, but arose. I opened the door, and stood on the step, while he stood in the doorway. There, was the Danger-light. There, was the dismal mouth of the tunnel. There, were the high wet stone walls of the cutting. There, were the stars above them.

'Do you see it?' I asked him, taking particular note of his face. His eyes were prominent and strained; but not very much more so, perhaps, than my own had been when I had directed them earnestly towards the same spot.

'No,' he answered. 'It is not there. '

'Agreed,' said I.

We went in again, shut the door, and resumed our seats. I was thinking how best to improve this advantage, if it might be called one, when he took up the conversation in such a matter of course way, so assuming that there could be no serious question of fact between us, that I felt myself placed in the weakest of positions.

'By this time you will fully understand, sir,' he said, 'that what troubles me so dreadfully, is the question, What does the spectre mean?'

I was not sure, I told him, that I did fully understand.

'What is its warning against?' he said, ruminating, with his eyes on the fire, and only by times turning them on me. 'What is the danger? Where is the danger? There is danger overhanging, somewhere on the Line. Some dreadful calamity will happen. It is not to be doubted this third time, after what has gone before. But surely this is a cruel haunting of me. What can I do?'

He pulled out his handkerchief, and wiped the drops from his heated forehead.

'If I telegraph Danger, on either side of me, or on both, I can give no reason for it,' he went on, wiping the palms of his hands. 'I should get into trouble, and do no good. They would think I was mad. This is the way it would work:--Message: "Danger! Take care!" Answer: "What danger? Where?" Message: "Don't know. But for God's sake take care!" They would displace me. What else could they do?'

His pain of mind was most pitiable to see. It was the mental torture of a conscientious man, oppressed beyond endurance by an unintelligible responsibility involving life.

'When it first stood under the Danger-light,' he went on, putting his dark hair back from his head, and drawing his hands outward across and across his temples in an extremity of feverish distress, 'why not tell me where that accident was to happen--if it must happen? Why not tell me how it could be averted--if it could have been averted? When on its second coming it hid its face, why not tell me instead: "She is going to die. Let them keep her at home"? If it came, on those two occasions, only to show me that its warnings were true, and so to prepare me for the third, why not warn me plainly now? And I, Lord help me! A mere poor signalman on this solitary station! Why not go to somebody with credit to be believed, and power to act!'

When I saw him in this state, I saw that for the poor man's sake, as well as for the public safety, what I had to do for the time was, to compose his mind. Therefore, setting aside all question of reality or unreality between us, I represented to him that whoever thoroughly discharged his duty, must do well, and that at least it was his comfort that he understood his duty, though he did not understand these confounding Appearances. In this effort I succeeded far better than in the attempt to reason him out of his conviction. He became calm; the occupations incidental to his post as the night advanced, began to make larger demands on his attention; and I left him at two in the morning. I had offered to stay through the night, but he would not hear of it.

That I more than once looked back at the red light as I ascended the pathway, that I did not like the red light, and that I should have slept but poorly if my bed had been under it, I see no reason to conceal. Nor, did I like the two sequences of the accident and the dead girl. I see no reason to conceal that, either.

But, what ran most in my thoughts was the consideration how ought I to act, having become the recipient of this disclosure? I had proved the man to be intelligent, vigilant, painstaking, and exact; but how long might he remain so, in his state of mind? Though in a subordinate position, still he held a most important trust, and would I (for instance) like to stake my own life on the chances of his continuing to execute it with precision?

Unable to overcome a feeling that there would be something treacherous in my communicating what he had told me, to his superiors in the Company, without first being plain with himself and proposing a middle course to him, I ultimately resolved to offer to accompany him (otherwise keeping his secret for the present) to the wisest medical practitioner we could hear of in those parts, and to take his opinion. A change in his time of duty would come round next night, he had apprised me, and he would be off an hour or two after sunrise, and on again soon after sunset. I had appointed to return accordingly.

Next evening was a lovely evening, and I walked out early to enjoy it. The sun was not yet quite down when I traversed the field-path near the top of the deep cutting. I would extend my walk for an hour, I said to myself, half an hour on and half an hour back, and it would then be time to go to my signalman's box.

Before pursuing my stroll, I stepped to the brink, and mechanically looked down, from the point from which I had first seen him. I cannot describe the thrill that seized upon me, when, close at the mouth of the tunnel, I saw the appearance of a man, with his left sleeve across his eyes, passionately waving his right arm.

The nameless horror that oppressed me, passed in a moment, for in a moment I saw that this appearance of a man was a man indeed, and that there was a little group of other men standing at a short distance, to whom he seemed to be rehearsing the gesture he made. The Danger-light was not yet lighted. Against its shaft, a little low hut, entirely new to me, had been made of some wooden supports and tarpaulin. It looked no bigger than a bed.

With an irresistible sense that something was wrong--with a flashing self-reproachful fear that fatal mischief had come of my leaving the man there, and causing no one to be sent to overlook or correct what he did--I descended the notched path with all the speed I could make.

'What is the matter?' I asked the men.

'Signalman killed this morning, sir. '

'Not the man belonging to that box?'

'Yes, sir. '

'Not the man I know?'

'You will recognise him, sir, if you knew him,' said the man who spoke for the others, solemnly uncovering his own head and raising an end of the tarpaulin, 'for his face is quite composed. '

'O! how did this happen, how did this happen?' I asked, turning from one to another as the hut closed in again.

'He was cut down by an engine, sir. No man in England knew his work better. But somehow he was not clear of the outer rail. It was just at broad day. He had struck the light, and had the lamp in his hand. As the engine came out of the tunnel, his back was towards her, and she cut him down. That man drove her, and was showing how it happened. Show the gentleman, Tom. '

The man, who wore a rough dark dress, stepped back to his former place at the mouth of the tunnel!

'Coming round the curve in the tunnel, sir,' he said, 'I saw him at the end, like as if I saw him down a perspective-glass. There was no time to check speed, and I knew him to be very careful. As he didn't seem to take heed of the whistle, I shut it off when we were running down upon him, and called to him as loud as I could call. '

'What did you say?'

'I said, Below there! Look out! Look out! For God's sake clear the way!'

I started.

'Ah! it was a dreadful time, sir. I never left off calling to him. I put this arm before my eyes, not to see, and I waved this arm to the last; but it was no use. '

Without prolonging the narrative to dwell on any one of its curious circumstances more than on any other, I may, in closing it, point out the coincidence that the warning of the Engine-Driver included, not only the words which the unfortunate Signalman had repeated to me as haunting him, but also the words which I myself--not he--had attached, and that only in my own mind, to the gesticulation he had imitated.

WEEPING WATERS

Lee Murray

Tangiwai
24 December 1953
10:15 pm

Rawiri Temera jerked upright on the leather bench seat, the hairs on his neck prickling. The 626-night express rattled rhythmically on the tracks, a slow and steady lullaby. His fellow passengers bobbed their heads in sleep—even the children, which was no small feat given it was Christmas Eve. Across the aisle, a boy lay with his head in his mother's lap and his thumb in his mouth, and beyond the slumbering pair, in the orange glow of the carriage light, his reflection stared back from the window. On the other side of the pane, the mountains were invisible in the darkness.

Everything's fine.

Except it wasn't. Something was wrong. Temera slipped his hand inside his cotton shirt to the flattened pūrerehua-bullroarer at his throat. Clasping the wooden instrument, Temera reached out with his soul. No one answered.

What woke me?

He glanced at the carriage clock. A quarter past ten. They weren't long out of Taihape township, then. Probably somewhere near Tangiwai. Still several hours until he reached his stop at Huntly. He should go back to sleep. If there *was* something wrong, he might see it in his dreams, where his spirit-guide—his friend, the morepork-ruru—could reveal it to him.

Who was he kidding? Even with the little owl's guidance, messages from the spirit world were always so obscure. That was the trouble with his gift—it was a feast or a bloody famine—either everything spoke to you, or nothing at all. It was as annoying as spending a night with a hungry mosquito.

Temera's old mentor, when he'd been alive, had counseled patience. "Learning to use your gift isn't like training to be a plumber," Mātua Rata had told him a decade ago, when Temera was only twelve. "It's not like you start with a washer, slip in an O-ring, and you're good to go. The ways of seeing are different for all matakite, sometimes for different situations. You have the makings of a powerful seer, Rawiri, but even the best fisherman doesn't catch a tuna without a little waiting. Take your time; you'll find a way." He'd cuffed Temera on the shoulder and taken back his cigarette. Temera missed the old man. Truth be told, he missed the cigarettes, too.

The train groaned softly, the forward coupling grinding as the KA949 locomotive took the bend. *Damn.* There it was again. That prickling on the back of his neck, and it had nothing to do with the scratchy wool of his suit. Arching his back, he twisted his torso left and right, trying to shake off some of the unease.

Someone else was awake. He hadn't noticed her before. Older than Temera, the woman was sitting alone at the rear of the car. She wore a cream dress and matching chiffon scarf, and although her hair had been pulled into a bun at her nape, a day of travel had allowed a few unruly wisps to escape.

Lifting his hand, Temera acknowledged her with a wave that said, "Look at us night-owls still awake, aye?"

But the woman didn't wave back. Instead, she turned away to press her forehead to the window.

Idiot. You've only gone and made her feel uncomfortable, too.

Why *were* his nerves jangling? Was it because the train was passing through the central plateau region right under the noses of the great mountain warriors of the Kāhui Tupua? Those fellows had been bickering over the affections of the beautiful mountain of Pīhanga since practically forever. Perhaps it was their grumbling he could sense. Or, maybe it had nothing to do with their centuries-old feud. Maybe the mountain-gods were miffed because just yesterday the newly crowned white queen had arrived in New Zealand with her duke for her first royal tour. Temera had heard rumblings from Māori elders about the visit. Things like the organizers weren't being properly respectful of tribal differences. That her coming was an evil omen: an *aituā*.

Well, if the mountains' unrest was the cause of the bad karma, he only had to wait another half hour until the train had left the region on its journey up the country. *Perhaps then I'll be able to get some sleep…*

The carriage door opened, letting in a gust of keen air. Temera shivered as a woman entered from the car in front. Her hair was wild, dark tendrils clinging to her face after being buffeted by the wind as she'd passed between the coaches. She paused a moment, her eyes darting around the carriage, as if she were searching for someone.

She marched over and thrust her face into his. "You! I've been looking for you. You have to save my daughter," she said.

What? Who was this woman? Temera shrunk backwards on the bench seat. "Your daughter? Why? What's wrong? Where is she?"

"I don't know. I've lost her. They've *taken* her. Please help me. Help me find her," the woman's voice rose to a shriek.

Temera glanced around, expecting her shout to have woken the other passengers, but lulled by the gentle sway of the train, they slept on.

Shuffling sideways, he slid off the seat to stand in the aisle. "Maybe I could fetch the conductor for you?" he said. "I'm sure they have procedures for children who go missing on the train. Perhaps, your daughter was over-excited, what with the trip on the night express and it being Christmas. You should have seen the little boy over there earlier, he—"

"No!" She put her hands on her head, clutching at her hair. "Mary didn't go missing on the train. She ran away."

Temera frowned. The woman wasn't making any sense. One minute the child was kidnapped and the next she'd run away? More likely she'd wandered off to explore the train while her mother was dozing.

"Look, she won't have gone far. There can't be more than a dozen carriages on this train," Temera said, gesturing to the bench. "Why don't you take a seat here and I'll get—"

"Not the conductor," the woman pleaded. She clasped her hands together, imploring him. "It has to be you. Please. Say you'll find her!" Suddenly, her mouth went slack and her eyes widened.

Temera turned slowly, following her gaze to the woman at the rear of the train—to the cream dress and unruly hair. He sucked in a breath. Were they sisters? Twins?

He whirled to face the newcomer. It was same cream dress, except the newcomer's had a mud-soaked hem and rents in the fabric. She was missing a shoe too, and an ugly purple bruise was deepening on her temple.

He looked back and forth, comparing the women. The hairs

lifted on his arms. "I don't understand."

"Just promise me, you'll help me look for my daughter. You're the only one who can."

All at once, the train's brakes screamed, the shrill shriek of metal on metal. Temera snatched at the handhold on the corner of the seat.

The newcomer sat down hard, her fingers gripping the seat back. "Too late," she whispered. "We're at the river."

The noise was total. Hurtling into the night, at once fast and also excruciatingly slow, the train lurched. It was derailing. Temera's heart clenched. He clamped his mouth shut, no breath to scream. The train stormed on, groaning as it thundered interminably across the uneven ground. Inside the car, the passengers jolted and rattled like coins in a jar. Luggage tumbled from the racks. Children wailed. The train screeched. For a moment, Temera wondered if they might be slowing...

Then there was a crash, and the train plunged. . . .

Temera fell heavily, pain flaring in his hip as cold and darkness closed in.

▦▦▦▦

Temera gulped a breath before the water—freezing and violent—sucked him down again. Temera flailed in the water. Which way!? His eyes were full of silt. The darkness was complete. The current swirled around him, battering his back and legs with unknown things: some soft, others dull and solid. Something sharp grazed his shoulder and he felt his jacket tear. *Wait, was that a seat?*

He was still in the train: *in the water, yet in the train.* The car might be sinking. He had to get out now. Lungs bursting, he thrashed, grabbed, *snatched* for a handhold. Where the fuck was the wall? His air was almost spent. If anything, he had a minute left. If he didn't find a way out, this carriage would be his tomb.

He kicked out hard, propelling himself forward, sensing something fleshy and fleeting beneath his feet. His fingertips grasped…a rope! Temera grabbed it. Held on. The rope dug into his palm. He was moving! He kicked hard to help his rescuers drag him out. Or had he snagged himself a one-way trip to the bottom of the river? There was no way of knowing. In the darkness, he whispered a karakia-prayer to the gods.

Please. Hurry.

Then he burst onto the surface.

Temera heaved in a breath, tasting mud and dirt and who-knows-what-else. Air never tasted sweeter. He opened his eyes. Through blurred pupils, he glimpsed flickering lights. Still gripping the rope, he struck out in their direction. Frigid water surged around him. He kicked out hard, giving it everything, but dulled with cold and shock, his muscles were as feeble as a newborn's.

Groans and gasps carried over the roar of the current. Other survivors? Or the groans of stressed metal and rush of the river? Temera was powerless to help anyone. He had to reach the bank. If only he wasn't so tired. Whoever his rescuer was, they were tiring too. What if he let go the rope and floated a bit? Just until he caught his breath. He was so cold…

No! He mustn't give up.

Squinting, he fixed on the flicker of the torches. He clutched the rope even tighter and threw himself forward. His feet stumbled, sinking into mud. The bank! He'd reached the edge. With one final push, Temera threw himself out of the water and flopped on the shore.

He must have passed out because when he came to, he was shivering with cold, still lying in the mud. His shoulder was numb. He tried to roll over and sit up, but his hand was caught on something. He blinked, clearing his eyes of grit, then looked down.

His fingers were curled around a scrap of cream chiffon. A scarf. The other end was wrapped tightly around a woman's neck, the knot tightened to a pinched grey ball.

Temera let go and scrambled to his knees.

No, no, no. It was the woman from back of the train. His stomach churning with dread, he scratched at the twisted fabric, pulling it away from her windpipe with clumsy hands. When nothing happened, he lifted the woman's shoulders and yanked the choker over her head, hoping upon hope for the grateful suck of breath.

Come on, breathe dammit!

In the moonlight, the woman lay still, glassy eyes staring up at him, thin lips tinged blue and a dark bruise on her forehead.

Frantic, Temera lay her down, pulled back her chin, pinched her nose, and blew into her mouth. Filled her lungs with air from his own.

Her chest rose. Then fell.

He blew again.

Again her chest rose and fell.

Breathe! Dizzy, he blew again. Nothing. Was her heart still beating? He fumbled for her pulse, but his fingers were like icicles. He thumped her hard on the chest anyway. She didn't respond...

Temera sank back onto his haunches. She was dead. He'd killed her. If he hadn't held on to the scarf, she might have pulled herself clear of the carriage and onto the bank. Had it been her he'd heard gasping? Had she been struggling to get his attention, to free herself, and all the while he'd been slowly strangling her? In his panic, he'd thought of nothing but making it to shore and saving his own miserable soul. Temera drew a deep breath. He dropped his head and covered his face with his hands.

The air stirred as someone sat beside him.

Temera raised his head. It was the woman—not the muddied corpse, but her wairua-spirit.

"You need to get warm or you'll die. There's a suitcase over there," she said. She tilted her head to the left where the sodden luggage lay half-submerged in silt and debris. "Maybe there's something inside it that you can wear."

He hesitated.

"I can't help you I'm afraid; I already tried to open it, but I'm not really here, am I? Anyway, I doubt the owner will mind. Look around. Chances are they're probably dead, too." She smiled sadly.

Temera looked about. She was right: despite the dark, it didn't take much imagination to make out the hulking steel ruins of the train, one of the carriages dashed against the bank and another standing like a boulder in the middle of the river, the current surging around it. The closest of the cars, most likely the compartment Temera and the woman been traveling in, had been cleaved in half like a severed limb, its tendons and vessels trailing in the flooded river. Temera didn't want to think about what might have happened to the other passengers.

"Okay," he said, after a moment. "Warm is good." He crawled up the bank and dragged the suitcase out of the muck. Locked, one corner had been crushed in the disaster. Temera hooked his fingers inside and prized the bag open.

Neatly folded in the bottom were a couple of cotton shirts,

a tie, trousers…a man's sweater. His hands still numb, Temera took off his torn jacket and his shirt and struggled into the sweater, tucking his pūrerehua safely inside the woolen garment. The trousers were too large, but they were dry; he knotted the tie around the waist to keep them up. There were dry socks, too. Carrying them higher up the bank, Temera sat on the grass, and swapped them for his wet ones.

There, that felt better. Maybe there was something else he could use? Returning to the suitcase, he had another rummage. Toiletries. A pair of shoes… Stuffed into the corner of the case and wrapped in thick paper, was a gift. There was a card, but even squinting hard Temera couldn't read it in the dark.

"To Thomas," the woman read over his shoulder, "my favorite boy scout. Merry Christmas, with love from your Uncle Jim."

Temera tore it open. Inside the wrapper was a steel torch. He flicked it on and its yellow light cut through the darkness. Now he could take a proper look at what had happened. He angled the light over the river and up the bank.

He swallowed hard.

It was… awful. Harrowing. Bodies, and parts of bodies, were strewn everywhere. Some half-submerged in mud. Others bobbed on the water.

Temera spotted the boy and his mother a few meters away. By some miracle, they'd been flung out of the carriage together, perhaps when the car had split in half. The miracle hadn't extended to keeping them alive. The woman had landed face down in the shallows, her holiday-best skirt still billowing in the water. Judging from her position, Temera guessed her neck had snapped on impact. Perhaps that was for the best, since one of her arms was missing, severed at the shoulder. Her other arm still grasped the boy, or what remained of him. The child's skull was caved in and his shoulder shredded. Both mother and son's limbs were white, any trace of blood spilled into the river.

The mother's spirit sat up. She dragged the boy from his body and onto her lap, where she cradled him in her arm, speaking softly into his ear. After a moment, a tī-wai-waka cried out, the little bird's calls carrying on the night air, and the pair got up, floating like mist towards the north.

Temera blinked. While he'd seen wairua-spirits departing to join the goddess Hine-nui-te-pō before, on those occasions the deceased had been elders and their deaths expected.

With a start, Temera realized the mother and her son were not the only ones leaving the site of the disaster. All around him, the soft forms of the newly dead were drifting up the bank and into the trees, heading for Cape Reinga at the northernmost tip of the country, to the pōhutukawa tree that marked the stepping off place where they would start their final journey.

At the top of the bank, the wairua-spirit mother stopped. She turned. "Charlotte," she said to the spirit beside Temera. "We're leaving now. You're welcome to travel with us."

The woman—Charlotte—shook her head. "Can't. Not until we find Mary. I have to know she's safe."

The woman pulled her son closer. "If you linger, you could be trapped beside these weeping waters forever."

"She's my daughter," Charlotte whispered.

The mother nodded sadly. "I understand. I hope you find her," she said, then she and the boy melted into the darkness.

"Hey! You!" Replacing the departing spirits, two men emerged on the crest of the bank, the light from their torches slicing through the night-black. "Wait there," they shouted.

Temera shielded his eyes.

Clad in dirty suits muddied at the knees, both men were wearing hats. You didn't come out of a swollen river still wearing a hat, and it was too soon for help to have arrived from town, so they had to be passengers from the train or holiday travelers flagged down on the road. Descending the riverbank, the men stopped briefly at the corpses, one checking the mother and the boy for signs of life, and the other pressing the pulse of the woman whose wairua-spirit was standing alongside Temera.

"You from the train? Are you okay?" the first man said when he reached them.

Temera nodded. "I'm fine. A bit shaken up."

"Arthur Kingswood." The man touched his hand to his hat, probably out of habit. "You were lucky, then."

"Rawiri Temera. No kidding. I was in there." He pointed to the carriage in the river.

"Hell's teeth," the second man said. "You crawled out of *that?*"

Kingswood gave a low whistle. "Yeah, the second-class carriages up front copped the worst of it. It's the lahar; it swept away the bridge and the train cars plowed into the river one after the other. Just some first-class carriages still intact. You're one of the few survivors we've found."

"But he's not wet," the second man said suspiciously.

"I found some warm clothes and this torch in some luggage," Temera said.

The second man narrowed his eyes. He lifted his torch and shone it in Temera's face. It was an accusation, pure and simple.

Temera raised his chin. "I meant no disrespect. I just needed to stay warm," he said.

Kingswood pushed at his companion's hand. "Put the torch

down, Mike. They're just clothes. It's bloody brass monkey weather out here tonight."

Mike sniffed. "Right, well, since our friend is safe and sound, how about he gets his skates on and helps us look for survivors?"

"I'd be happy to—" Temera began, when Charlotte stepped between them.

"No!" she shouted. "You can't. You said you'd help me find my daughter."

"I—"

"I *saved* you," Charlotte said before Temera could complete his sentence. "It was me. *I* pulled you out of the carriage. I could've left you there, could've let you drown! Who knows, I might still be alive. . ."

"You what?" Mike said. It was clear neither he nor Kingswood could see or hear Charlotte.

Temera cleared his throat. He wanted to help the survivors—of course, he did—but there was no one else to help Charlotte. She'd saved his life; he owed her.

"The thing is," he said slowly. "I'm a priest." It wasn't so far from the truth. "If you don't mind, I'd like to stop and say a few words over the dead. Prayers. *Karakia.*" He gestured to the bodies on the shore.

"And where's the sense in that?" Mike snapped. "Until the authorities arrive, we need every able-bodied man looking for survivors."

Kingswood rubbed a hand over the stubble on his chin. "No, I reckon Mr. Temera has a point," he said. "There are plenty of other passengers we can call on to help, folk who haven't taken a dunking in a mangled carriage. Families will feel better knowing someone said a few words over their loved ones in the aftermath of this shitstorm. I know I would."

His companion raised an eyebrow. "But he's—"

"He's a *priest*, Mike, and he's offering to provide solace on a night when there is precious little of it. We'll find some others to help."

Mike shrugged. "Suit yourself."

"Thank you," Temera said.

"Give a shout if you find anyone still alive," Kingswood said, his hand on Temera's shoulder.

"I will," Temera said, but the men were already striding along the shore, the beams of their torches flickering.

Temera crouched over Charlotte's lifeless body. "Why were you on the train?" he asked. "You said you thought Mary had run away. How do you know for sure she was on board?"

Standing above him, wairua-spirit Charlotte wrapped her arms around herself as if keeping out the cold. "Mary told her friend Lila that she was meeting an older man at the station."

"Any chance Lila was lying?

"Lila thought Mary's plan to run away was just a lark, Mary angling for an expensive Christmas present. She didn't think she'd actually do it. Then Mary came to her house to say goodbye. Lila tried to change her mind, but Mary can be stubborn. When Mary left for the station, Lila called me from public phone."

Temera pressed his lips together.

Charlotte's dead eyes flashed. "The girls have been friends since they were seven. That's *six* years, so, yes, I believe her."

"Okay, okay." Temera got up and crossed to the boy, his heart shrinking as he turned the child over. From the front, the boy had looked much as he had while sleeping on his mother's lap on the train, but from the rear the injuries to his cranium were irredeemable, slivers of bone and metal and—part of an umbrella?—embedded in the child's grey matter. Gently,

Temera pulled the child's body up the bank where he couldn't be washed away by the current, sprinkled him with water, then said a karakia-prayer for the boy's wairua-spirit, traveling north with his mother.

What state would Mary be in when they found her? *If* they found her...

"That doesn't explain why you thought Mary would be on the night express," Temera said when he'd completed the prayer. He stood up and trudged through the mud towards the shattered bridge. Kingswood and Mike were long gone now, their torches dimmed by the distance and the debris.

"I gambled," Charlotte said, scurrying after him, her feet gliding over the mud. "I figured whoever had Mary would try to pass her off as his daughter and that he'd want to get her as far away from Wellington as he could—somewhere she wouldn't be recognized. So I asked at the ticket office for last minute fares to Auckland sold to a man and his daughter. Said I was his wife, and since my Christmas shift at Kirkcaldy's had been changed, I was hoping to surprise them. I bought a ticket and got on the train."

Temera was thinking it was a pretty good ploy when a man's wairua-spirit passed them by, nodding briefly at Temera and Charlotte.

"Safe journey, my friend," Temera said.

The spirit gave a wave.

When he'd drifted away, Temera turned to Charlotte. "Obviously, you didn't find Mary on the train."

Charlotte clasped her hands together. "They had to be hiding her because I walked up and down for hours and I couldn't find her anywhere. I would've seen her if she'd been seated in one of the compartments. So I resolved to get out at every station and check the platform, in case they tried to steal away. But then the train crashed…" Suddenly, her eyes grew wide. "That man. I know that man."

She skimmed forward over the mud and hovered near a corpse tangled in a mound of twigs and wires. "It's Mr. Kelly. He works at the grocery store near where I live."

Worked at the grocery store. The man would not be working anywhere ever again. Quite apart from the steel girder protruding from his abdomen, part of his face had been ground away, exposing his cheekbone and a ruptured eye socket. It was a wonder Charlotte even recognized him.

"We should talk to him," Charlotte insisted. "He might have seen Mary."

"I'll try." Temera didn't want to get her hopes up; Kelly's spirit might already have set out on its journey north.

Tucking the torch under his arm, he clambered over the rubble and cleared away some of the debris. He shivered. The girder had run right through Kelly's body pinning him like a butterfly in a museum exhibit. Moving the corpse would require several men.

Winking his ruined eye, Kelly gave Temera a lopsided grin. Then his wairua-spirit shook off a clump of weed, stepped out of its body, and got to its feet. "That was a close call," he said. "Thought I was done for."

Temera gestured to Kelly's impaled corpse. "Sorry."

"Fuck!" Kelly said, jumping off the pile of rubble to the ground. "Fuck, fuck, fuck! No, wait." He paused. "I can't be dead. I can see you. We're talking."

"He's a *matakite*," Charlotte said. "A seer. That's why."

Noticing her for the first time, Kelly sucked in a breath. "Mrs. Hereaka," he said, cringing away from her. "You…you were on the train?"

"I'm looking for my daughter. Mary," Charlotte replied. "She ran away."

Somewhere on the plateau, a tī-wai-waka called, the fantail's song carrying over the roar of the river. A cold wind tugged at Temera's extremities. The little bird was calling to the straggling wairua-spirits, urging them to set out for their final resting place in Hine-nui-te-po's underworld realm.

Charlotte gazed to the north and closed her eyes.

"You should go," Temera said.

She opened her eyes and folded her arms across her chest. "Not until I find Mary," she said.

Kelly snorted. "She'll be dead, too," he said. "Same as us."

Atop the twisted mound of debris, Temera frowned. "Do you know something about this woman's daughter?"

Kelly shrugged. "I know the kid was on the train."

Jumping down, Temera rounded on Kelly. "How? How do you know that?"

Kelly shrugged again.

"How?" Temera demanded, louder this time.

Kelly smirked. "Don't suppose it makes much difference now. What are you going to do? Kill me?" His laugh was harsh. "The truth is, the kid couldn't wait to get away from home, away from *you*." He sneered at Charlotte through the torn muscle of his cheek. "I was going to hook her up with a mate in Auckland. Kid gets what she wants and Robinson gets a nice piece of candy for his establishment. All I had to do was deliver her. It was only fair that I should get a little something for my trouble."

Charlotte rushed at him, scratching at his face with her fingernails. "You sold her, you brute. You sold my baby!"

"Charlotte," Temera said quietly. "He's already dead."

Ducking to avoid her fingernails, Kelly crooned, "Yeah, cut that out, Charlotte, because I'm already fucking dead."

"And yet his spirit is still here..." Temera said.

Kelly's head whipped up. "What's that supposed to mean?"

"You didn't hear the fantail?" Temera asked.

"What fantail?"

"The one calling the lost souls to the north," Temera said.

Kelly's eyes darted about wildly. "What fucking fantail? I didn't hear a ruddy thing."

"Serves you right for selling other people's daughters to strangers," Charlotte said bitterly.

"We need to find her," Temera said. He turned to the dead man. "What compartment were you traveling in?"

"Why should I help you? You're a matakite; work it out for yourself," Kelly said.

"Because it was your fault Mary was on the train in the first place," Charlotte retorted.

"My fault? That's rich, that is,' Kelly snapped. "You should've been a better mother. Then your kid wouldn't have decided to run away on Christmas Eve, would she?"

"Stop it! Both of you," Temera shouted. "Can't you see we're running out of time? If we don't find Mary soon, it'll be too late."

"How long have we got?" Charlotte asked, her face pinched.

"I don't know. The fantail's call is getting fainter."

"What does he mean, too late?" Kelly said. "And what's this about a fantail?"

Charlotte sighed. "It means we'll be stuck here, won't we? Roaming these muddy banks for eternity."

"Bloody hogwash," Kelly said.

"Just tell us where she is!" Temera insisted.

Kelly hesitated. "I don't know," he said finally.

"What do you mean, you don't know?"

"I don't know, okay? I was having a bit of fun with her and

the little bitch bit me on the wrist. She took off. Hid somewhere on the train."

Charlotte gasped.

Temera gritted his teeth. He was tempted to haul the steel girder out of the man's stomach just to drive it in again. "Which direction did she go: forward or back?"

Kelly grinned. "Forward."

Temera's heart skipped. Mary had to be in one of the derailed carriages. He turned and ran, the mud sucking at his legs. His muscles burning with effort, he gave it everything. His shoulder throbbed. He was tired to the bone. All he wanted was to lie down and sleep, but he had to keep going: a girl's life hung in the balance, not to mention her mother's soul.

"Hurry," Charlotte urged.

"What's the point?" Kelly scoffed. "She'll be dead."

"Go on ahead," Temera huffed at Charlotte. "Find her if you can."

Charlotte sped off.

"Good luck with that," Kelly chortled.

The tī-wai-waka trilled again, far away now, the sound fading.

This is crazy. There were six second-class cars. Mary hadn't been in his carriage; Charlotte would have seen her, so the girl had to be in one of the other five. Temera couldn't hope to search them all in time. He had barely enough energy to take another step.

There had to be a better way. He needed to speak to the child and get her to tell him where she was. Not his physical self: Temera could shout all night and Mary might never hear him. He had to speak to her soul. Her *wairua*. But he couldn't wait until Mary was dead. Kelly was right: what would be the point of that?

He had to find her now.

Even the best fisherman doesn't catch a tuna without a little waiting.

Temera stopped running. Had he been in so much of a rush that he hadn't truly listened? Had Mary been calling to him all along? Did that explain his unease? He closed his eyes and listened, straining for a child's voice over the roar of the lahar and the groan of metal. Instead, it was Mātua Rata's voice that came to him, old and mellow: "As well as being a beautiful object," his tutor said, "the pūrerehua's uses are many. The right man can use it to call forth a soul mate, farewell a loved one, even summon the rain...."

Temera pulled the pūrerehua from beneath the borrowed sweater. The wood was warm where the instrument had lain against his chest. He planted his feet in the mud and twirled the string around his head, letting the bullroarer fly. The pūrerehua hummed. Temera closed his eyes and reached into his own wairua-spirit. "Mary! Where are you?"

He spun the pūrerehua and listened.

"Mary!"

"I'm here," she whispered, her voice hollow and distant. "In a box. It's filling with water. Hurry."

Temera's eyes flew open. Still spinning the bullroarer, he scanned the dark water until he spied the crate. Downriver, it was tethered to a girder.

Dammit. How was he going to save her? He'd have to be Superman to swim out there, let alone lift the crate off the girder against current.

He was going to need help.

As the string thrummed, Temera offered up his karakia to the mountain goddess Pīhanga. He called across the plateau to where she towered in the darkness and spoke of lost children and shattered futures—of mud, and of heartbreak. He showed her Mary, trapped in the crate, her face grubby with tears. He poured his soul into the song.

Please. Help us!

Would the mountain hear him? Temera didn't know. He could only twirl his precious bullroarer and sing.

Long moments passed.

Already, so many had perished.

At last, Pīhanga's tears rolled down the mountainside and onto the plateau, and in a final surge, the lahar tore the crate from its tether.

Pulling in his pūrerehua, Temera sprinted along the riverbank, stuffing the instrument into a pocket even as he stumbled over branches to wade into the water. He was almost swept off his feet by the violence of the torrent. He grasped the floating crate and hauled on it with all his might. Fighting the river, his muscles screamed with the strain. Splinters stabbed at his palms. Temera hung on, dragging the crate step by step towards the shore.

Nearly…

A tree trunk rammed against his back. His legs crumpled and he went under. The crate slipped from his grasp.

"Mary!" Temera scrambled to recover, his hands grasping silt and mud. "Mary!"

"Here," Charlotte screamed over the din of the lahar. "She's over here. Follow my voice."

Digging his feet into the mud, Temera lunged forward, his legs burning despite the cold.

"This way!" Charlotte shouted.

The fantail trilled a farewell, as, hands outstretched, Temera followed the dead woman's voice. His fingertips touched wood. Temera claimed it. Then, bracing himself against the tide, he swung the crate like a hammer thrower, taking advantage of the current to land it on the beach.

Lungs heaving, he hauled himself out of the water and, grabbing a hunk of passing steel from the river, used it like a crowbar to prize it open the crate. The girl tumbled out in a wave of water.

Would you look at that? She was a dead ringer for her mother.

||||||||

When he awoke, it was almost dawn, the sky tinged pink on the horizon. Temera sat up. Someone had covered him with a blanket.

"The girl said you fainted after you pulled her out of the river," It was Kingswood. "How did you find her?"

I reached out to her with my soul, Temera thought. Outwardly, he only shrugged. "I heard her crying."

"Well, she's damned lucky you did. Heaven knows how long she'd been clinging to that crate. She's the last survivor. It's only bodies now."

Temera nodded. "Funny thing, turns out, I knew her mother."

"Really?" Kingswood said. Temera glimpsed movement behind him in the shadows. "They're taking Mary to the field hospital at Waiouru. The tractor's just there. You can go with her if you like."

"Can you give me a second?"

"Take your time."

When Kingswood had gone, Charlotte drifted over. "Thank you," she said, her eyes glistening. "You kept your promise."

Temera felt the heat rise in his face. He rubbed his hands

on his knees awkwardly.

Torchlight flickered across the plateau.

"Charlotte, why are you still here? You need to go north to the jumping off place."

"It's too late," Charlotte said, her voice breaking. "The fantail has gone." She straightened her back and gave him a weak smile. "It's okay. Mary's safe; that's all that matters." She tilted her head towards the shore where Kelly was crouched in the mud, trying to open a discarded suitcase. "Figure I'll spend my eternity haunting Kelly. He deserves it."

Temera got to his feet and shucked off the blanket. He lifted his pūrerehua-bullroarer and unraveled the sodden string.

"No need for the fantail," he said, and bracing his feet, he twirled the little instrument above his head until the string was taut and thrumming. "I'll sing you there."

And as the first rays of dawn stole over Pīhanga's snow-cloaked shoulders, Temera began his song.

THE HABIT OF LONG YEARS

Charles R. Rutledge

There were too many vampires on the train. Inspector Ioan Godina rolled his eyes at the motley assortment of Halloween revelers in Bela Lugosi capes, bone white makeup, and ill-fitting plastic fangs. He hoped they were all travelers, though he doubted it. His fellow Romanians weren't immune to Dracula fever. Plus, the train *was* bound for 'Dracula's' castle.

There were plenty of other types of costumes. Men and women dressed as ghosts and witches. A clown or two. There were also quite a few costumes he didn't recognize. Probably based on current American horror films. Godina wasn't a fan of that sort of thing. He saw enough horror in his day to day job as a police inspector.

He was on the trail of one such horror now. Of course none of the partygoers, be they local or visitor, had any idea why he was among them on the Bucharest to Brasov train on Halloween night. The police were keeping the details of the three murders out of the press for now. It was beginning to look like they had a serial killer at work and they wanted to keep that quiet.

Three bodies had been found along this train route. One in Azuga, one in Predeal, and one in Timisu de Jos. Forensics showed none of them had been killed where they had been found. There was no reason to believe the three victims were the only murders. There could easily be more.

It was Godina's theory that the killer was familiar with the Bucharest-Brasov route, possibly someone who frequented the train. He didn't expect to catch the murderer by riding the train, but he was hoping for some insight.

Now that he thought of it, the killings did have one thing in common with the work of a vampire. There was no blood left in the bodies of any of the victims. Of course the fact that their heads had been removed accounted for that. They'd have bled out where they were killed.

Serial murders weren't common in Romania. Godina had been only a boy when Ion Ramaru had been dubbed 'the vampire of Bucharest' after killing four people between 1970 and 1971. More recently, a Romanian auto mechanic had admitted to killing at least two women, and a barrel containing human remains had been found in his home.

Godina wiped the condensation from the window with his coat sleeve and peered out into the night. The train had just left Predeal station, and increasingly heavy snow was falling beyond the glass. He could feel the cold radiating through the windowpane. The cold seemed to bother him more as he approached sixty years.

There weren't many outside lights on this stage of the train ride, and there would be even fewer after they stopped at Timisu de Sus. Most of the route was through mountain country from there until they reached the outskirts of Brasov.

"Looking for something in particular, Inspector?" a voice said from beside him.

Godina spun, startled from his reverie. Someone had taken the seat next to his. His new seatmate was a slender man with close-cropped hair and beard. He looked to be around forty, though he carried a walking stick. Perhaps he had an injury, or perhaps the stick was an affectation.

"Have we met?" Godina said.

"We haven't," the man said. Godina realized suddenly that he was an American, though his Romanian was excellent. "If you're wondering how I knew you were an inspector, your face and demeanor mark you as a police officer, and a veteran one at that."

Godina said, "You are very astute, sir. Do you mind if I ask what you're doing on this train? You're obviously not one of the revelers."

The man smiled. "Let's say I'm here as an experiment in anthropology."

"You are an academic?"

"Retired. I was a professor of British literature. I'm Carter Decamp, by the way."

Godina frowned. "Ah. Literature. You must be here because of Dracula."

"Why would you say that?"

"It is what brings so many people to my country. Just look around you. This train is on its way to Brasov where half these passengers, perhaps you included, will take a bus to a castle claiming association with Vlad Tepes."

Decamp said, "Bran Castle. I've been there. It is not my destination on this trip."

Godina's expression softened. "Forgive me, Mr. Decamp. It is a sore subject with many Romanians. Ask the average visitor from Britain or America what they know of Romania and they will say Dracula. A fiction written by a man who never visited this country."

Decamp said, "You are trapped in the quandary of welcoming the tourist potential of Stoker's work, but still wishing to change the national image of Romania."

"Yes, exactly that."

Godina felt the train begin to slow. They were approaching the station at Timisu de Sus. In focusing his attention on Decamp, Godina hadn't noticed the rising level of noise in the train. The Halloween party was in full swing. People were out of their seats, laughing and chatting, as the train pulled into the small station.

All of that stopped when the doors slid open.

A cold wind, laced with whispering snow, blew into the car. Only two passengers were standing on the platform. The night seemed to gather around them, holding them close, and they brought that darkness with them as they stepped aboard the train.

Once the two newcomers were in the light, Godina could see they were a man and a woman. There was nothing in their features to suggest they were relatives, but there was something about them that made them seem eerily similar. The man, tall and gaunt, had long brown hair, and deep-set eyes. His skin was so pale as to be almost white. The woman's skin was the same, and seemed paler still because of her raven black hair and deep red lips. Both were dressed all in black.

Godina had been a policeman for more than thirty years and all of his instincts were telling him there was something deeply...wrong about this couple. They stood just inside the doorway until the departure chime sounded. As the doors closed and the train moved away into the night, they made their way through the front car, heading toward the back of the train.

As they passed, the man fixed Godina with a cold stare. As Decamp had noted, Godina wore his experience and authority on his face. Had the man realized Godina was with the police? If so his reaction seemed more of a sneer than of concern. The couple slid by, without making a sound. It seemed to Godina that the lights in the car dimmed as they passed.

Godina knew better than to jump to quick judgments. The couple looked sinister, yes, but it was Halloween after all. They didn't seem to be in costume. Their clothing was odd. Almost antiquated. The whiteness of their skin didn't come from makeup. But then he considered the reason he was on the train. He would speak to the pair and see who they were and where they were bound, at least. He was, after all, with the national police force.

Godina started to rise, but felt a hand on his arm.

"Don't," Carter Decamp said.

"Don't what, Mr. Decamp?"

Decamp leaned close. "I agree with you. Those two people have something to do with the recent murders. But confronting them on the train would be a grave error."

Godina took a long look at Decamp. "What do you know about the murders?"

"Very little, other than the basics. Three killings in the last week the police know of. All three bodies decapitated and drained of blood. High probability there have been more murders that haven't come to light."

"This is private, police information. How could you…?"

"I have sources who alert me to this sort of thing. My interest in anthropology is quite specific and rather macabre."

"I'm going to need a better explanation than that."

"Perhaps later," Decamp said. "Right now we need to keep a low profile and not excite the interest of the couple who just got on the train."

"I need to talk to them. If they are somehow connected with the murders, I can't risk letting them get away. You even agreed there is something suspicious about them."

Decamp said, "And I'm telling you that's a very bad idea. It could cost the lives of everyone on this train."

"There are only two of them, Decamp."

"Two is enough. One would be enough."

"You are talking madness."

"Perhaps, but just wait. I think they'll leave the train before it gets to Brasov. You can follow them off and question them then. Safer for everyone on the train."

Godina considered that for a moment. Whatever Decamp's reasons, the man had a point. If the couple were dangerous, it would be best not to confront them on a train crowded with partygoers.

"All right," Godina said. "I will wait. But I want you to know that I'm detaining you as well. If there is an information leak within the police, I need to know who it is."

"I'm fine with that, Inspector."

"Good. I still want to keep the couple in sight. I am going to move further back in the train."

Decamp sighed. "I wish you wouldn't. I think it best the couple don't think you've taken notice of them."

"On this I must insist. I promise you I will not approach them. Can I trust you not to disappear when the train arrives in Brasov?"

"You have my word on that."

"Somehow I think that is good enough."

Godina didn't mention that he planned to use the radio in the engine when he had the chance, to call ahead and have officers waiting in Brasov. He had his phone with him, but there was no cell signal in the mountains. He rose from his seat and with a final glance at Decamp, he started down the narrow aisle toward the door that connected to the next car.

The pall had lifted, and the party mood had returned to the car now that the strange pair had passed. People were laughing and having a good time again. Godina went through the door.

The couple weren't in the next car. That left two more. Godina passed through the revelers, glancing at each seat as he went. When he reached the back of the car he peered through the glass into the third car.

They were there, sitting side by side in the seats nearest the door. Godina couldn't hear anything from the next car through the doors, but he could tell, just by looking, the mood in there was more subdued. People stayed in their seats. Some cast uneasy glances toward the black-clad passengers.

Without warning, the man in black's head swiveled toward Godina and his eyes seemed to spear right into those of the inspector. Godina thought he saw a red glint in those eyes. He stepped backwards quickly, out of the man's line of sight. Godina glanced around the second car. There was one empty seat. He took it.

Godina dug his phone out of his pocket and activated it. No signal, as he had thought. He realized then that he should have gone to the engine and made the radio call before moving to the back of the train. He couldn't risk losing the couple now. He looked back toward the connecting door.

The man in black was standing at the window, looking straight at him.

All of his life Ioan Godina had heard the expression 'blood ran cold', but he had never understood what it meant. Now he did. His entire body felt frozen, held in place by that malevolent stare.

For one of the few times in his police career, Godina wished he carried a firearm. He was cut off from any help, with no way of contacting anyone. The man was still staring at him, and again, Godina thought he saw the eyes gleam red. Then the man opened the door and stepped into the second car.

Again the noise level fell off and Godina became aware that everyone was staring at the dark man. All the Halloween revelers were as still as Godina, their bright costumes, looking cheap and gaudy now in the florescent glare of the unforgiving overhead lights.

The man walked slowly down the aisle, his crimson gaze never leaving Godina. Only now did the inspector realize what he had thought to be a long overcoat was actually a black cloak with a fur collar.

He stopped directly in front of the inspector, the toes of his heavy boots almost touching the tips of Godina's shoes. This close, Godina could smell him. He reeked of turned earth and mold.

The man leaned down so that his face was only inches from Godina. His breath stank and Godina could see his skin was course and pitted.

"You are the police," the man said. His voice was deep. "We will leave the train at the next stop. You will not follow."

Godina tried to speak. He found that his throat was dry and tight. He swallowed. When he spoke, his voice was barely a whisper. "I cannot allow that."

"You cannot allow that," the man repeated. And he smiled. His canine teeth were long and sharp. He wasn't wearing plastic fangs. He leaned even closer, so that his cold lips brushed Godina's ear. "I will kill you and everyone on this train, *police man*. Your lives are nothing to me. Go home and forget you saw me."

The man stood up straight, and with a final dismissive glance at Godina, he turned and started back toward the connecting door. No one in the car moved or spoke. Godina watched the retreating form.

Godina shook his head, trying to clear it. All the legends and stories his grandmother had ever told him ran through his head. Strigoli. Nosferatu. Vampires. He didn't believe in any of them. Like that damned Dracula, they were fairy tales. Figments of imagination. He did not believe. He would not. This man was insane. That was all.

And yet Godina's legs were shaking as he forced himself to his feet. He could feel his heart beating in his chest and his breathing was too fast. He started down the aisle toward the tall man, who had almost reached the door.

The tall man turned and looked at him. He smiled again, wider this time, his teeth showing white and sharp in the artificial lights. He turned and looked to his right where a couple sat staring up at him. Slowly, almost languorously, he reached out and grasped the collar of the young man who was sitting closest to him.

The tall man pulled the young man to his feet and drew him close. The young man struggled weakly as the tall man grabbed a handful of his hair and pulled his head back, baring his throat.

"Stop," a voice said from behind Godina. He turned to see the American professor standing at the other end of the car.

"You're making a mistake," Carter Decamp said. "One on top of many."

"And who are you?" the tall man said.

"Someone who knows about things like you. Your kind only survives by living in the dark places of the world. You've already drawn too much attention to yourself with the recent murders. If you kill the passengers on this train, you'll be hunted down and destroyed."

"I am tired of hiding. I have hidden for decades. Let them come."

Decamp began to walk down the aisle. "You were careful enough to take the heads from your victims so they wouldn't become like you. You must still have some instinct for self-preservation."

"Habit," the tall man said. "The habit of long years."

Godina looked back at the tall man. He wasn't paying attention to his hostage, who was hanging there in his grasp with wide eyes. The tall man's nails were long and sharp. They rested on the young man's chin. If Godina was going to have a chance of helping the hostage, this was it.

As the inspector lunged forward, he heard Decamp say, "No!"

With an almost casual motion, the tall man drew his free hand across the young man's neck. The long nails cut through the man's throat, gouging out flesh. Blood spurted, splattering all over Godina.

The tall man let the lifeless body fall and caught a handful of Godina's overcoat and held the inspector at arm's length. "I told you what I would do, *police man*."

The passengers in the train car broke free of their trance as one. People began leaping from their seats, falling all over one another, trying to get to the doors. The vampire, yes he had to be a vampire, shoved Godina away and grabbed the nearest passenger and broke her neck. He began pushing his way down the center of the car toward Decamp, striking out with his claw-like hands, rending flesh and sending blood flying.

When he was almost to Decamp, the professor twisted the handle of his walking stick and Godina saw the flash of something metallic. The vampire leaped backwards and Godina could see a line of blood across his face.

The vampire said, "You cut me. How could you cut me?"

Decamp said nothing. From his position on the floor, Godina could see that Decamp held a slender sword. The blade had been concealed inside the walking stick.

The vampire took a step back, as if unwilling to face the sword again. Then, moving so fast that he was nothing but a dark blur, he surged at Decamp, snarling as he came. Godina expected to see Decamp torn apart, but he lunged into the attack, going low and thrusting upwards with the sword.

The tall figure of the vampire stood motionless for a moment, with the blade protruding from his back. The he toppled over backwards. He landed in the space between two seats and was still.

Any of the passengers who hadn't managed to get out of the car were flattened against the walls or cowering behind seats. At least half a dozen people were dead.

Godina said, "I didn't know. I didn't. . ."

Decamp gave a short nod. "Now you do. And there's still one more of them."

Even as Decamp finished speaking, Godina heard a terrible screaming and shrieking from the third car. "Good god. What is she doing?"

"Just what the other one said. She's killing everyone on the train. She must have seen what happened to her companion."

"Can you stop her? You killed the other one."

"I can try. I've lost the element of surprise."

"They are vampires. Real vampires."

"Yes, Inspector. Real vampires."

The screaming had stopped. Decamp started toward the door. Godina followed.

"You'd better wait here, Inspector," Decamp said. "There's nothing you can do."

"I set this in motion. I'll go with you."

Decamp said nothing. He reached out and opened the door. Beyond the portal was a nightmare. The overhead lights had been damaged and only one of them was still working. The dim interior of the car was like something out of Dante. Bodies were strewn everywhere. The walls and windows were splattered with blood, and more of the scarlet liquid dripped from the ceiling. There was no sign of the woman vampire.

"She must be in the next car," Godina said. He didn't know why he was stating the obvious. Or maybe he did. His mind was only half functioning. To think too deeply just now would be to risk running mad.

They threaded their way through the grim carnage, stepping over the bodies that blocked the aisle. Godina's heart was hammering. He hoped he didn't have a heart attack before he could see the end of this.

There were no lights in the last car. Beyond the window lay only blackness. Decamp opened the door. A rush of cold air blew over them, carrying the scent of fresh blood. Decamp pulled a small flashlight from his coat pocket and shone it into the car.

It was much the same as the third car. Bodies and blood everywhere. Now Godina could see where the cold air was coming from. A window near the back of the car had been smashed open. The vampire woman wasn't there.

"She has gone," Godina said. He hated himself for being relieved. The idea of facing another such thing turned his bowels to water.

Godina heard a loud crashing sound from behind him and then another chorus of screams rent the frigid air. Decamp spun and shoved his way past Godina.

"She's outflanked us," Decamp said, hurrying up the aisle.

Godina forced himself to follow. Beyond Decamp he could see people in the second car scrambling around. A man's face slammed into the door's window with terrible force. The glass cracked, but didn't break. The crushed, ruined face slid down the glass, leaving a smear of red.

Decamp threw the door open and stepped into the second car. Godina paused in the doorway. Over Decamp's shoulder he could see the vampire. She was standing near the other end of the car, holding the motionless body of a woman dressed as a princess. The woman's neck was torn open. The vampire's lips were smeared with blood.

The vampire threw the woman aside when she saw Godina and Decamp. Her eyes blazed red and she opened her mouth wide and shrieked at them. Then she came hurtling down the aisle toward the men, the other prey forgotten.

Decamp waited until what looked like the last possible moment, then lunged forward in a fencer's stance, sword extended. The vampire twisted away and the slender blade passed through her shoulder. Before Decamp could free his sword, the woman slapped him aside with such force that he went tumbling away.

Godina tried to back away, but he slammed into the door, which had closed automatically. The vampire stood in front of him, glaring with those red, red eyes. A trail of smoke rose from where the sword still pierced her shoulder. Apparently the blade was burning her.

The vampire grasped the sword's hand and slid the blade free. She dropped the weapon as soon as it cleared the wound, as if holding it hurt her. Her hands came up and she grasped the sides of Godina's head as if she wanted to kiss him.

"You should have let us go," the vampire said. Blood dribbled down the corners of her mouth. "He told you to let us go."

A distant part of Godina's brain wondered how this vampire knew what the other one had said. Perhaps he had told her before going to speak with Godina. Perhaps they were linked somehow.

One of the vampire's hands slid behind Godina's head, grabbing his hair. The other slid down to his chin in a motion that was almost a caress. He felt his head being pushed back so that his throat was exposed.

"Now you shall live as we lived," the vampire said. "Know what we know."

"No," Godina heard his voice breaking. "Please, no."

Godina began to flail, pushing at the vampire, grabbing her wrists, trying to keep her fangs away from his neck. His struggles meant nothing to her. She was far stronger than he was.

Godina felt the tips of the sharp teeth touch his throat and linger there for a moment. He tried to scream, but no sound would come. Then there was an explosion of fiery pain as the vampire bit into his neck and began to feed.

Godina saw something shiny out of his peripheral vision and then the vampire suddenly released him and staggered back. Carter Decamp stood their holding an ornate silver crucifix. He brandished it toward the vampire and she threw one arm across her face and continued to back away.

Without looking away from the vampire, Decamp bent down and picked up his sword. The vampire continued to move away. She stopped beside the shattered window where she had entered the car. Godina could feel the train beginning to slow as they approached the next stop. Had it really been so short a time since they left Timisu de Sus? It didn't seem so much could have happened.

"I am not done with you," the vampire said.

As Godina watched, the vampire's form began to blur, and then there was nothing but a cloud of mist that flowed through the broken window, into the night and the snow.

"Good God," Godina said. He felt a twinge of pain in his throat and his hand came away with blood when he touched the wounds there. He looked at Decamp. "Will I...?"

Decamp shook his head. "No, you won't become like them. If she had drained you until you died, then you would have turned. The wound will heal. But inspector, she has tasted your blood. She will be able to find you now."

"Oh God. What can I do?"

"I'll help you if I can. I'll be leaving the train here. I trust you won't object."

Godina shook his head. "Go. I will say nothing of your role in this."

Decamp said. "I'll see you soon."

The train stopped and the doors opened. Decamp moved quickly into the small crowd of people who were waiting to board the train. He pushed through them before anyone could see the red ruin within the train car. Then he was lost in the darkness.

PÉPÈRE'S HALLOWEEN TRAIN

Tony Tremblay

The fireplace in her grandfather's home barely kept the cabin warm. Evenings were cold this time of year, but he insisted the fireplace, a comforter, a good book, and a glass of scotch would keep his blood flowing. He refused to turn on the heat until daytime temperatures dipped into the forties. Shanna guessed by next week Pépère would be burning oil.

Gazing out the kitchen window, she could see that the double-pane windows he had installed a few years earlier were doing their job. While the inner pane was clear, the outer pane was spider-webbed with frost. Not all that long ago, the sight would stir a yearning to scratch at the gleaming white threads, disrupting their symmetrical patterns as ice crystals collected on the tips of her fingers. She would lick them off, delighted by the cold sensation on her tongue. Now the cold weather induced melancholy.

A New Hampshire fall had snuck up on Shanna. Soon, she would be standing in waist-high snow while waiting for her ride to work. Fresh from her senior year and five months employed at the supermarket, she had yet to save enough money for a car. Without her own transportation and her parent's unwillingness to let her borrow their only car, she had little chance to go out and meet others. She had yet to make any friends. The woman who agreed to bring her to and from work did so for twenty dollars a week, not from any sense of friendship. The ride to work was long, lonely, and cold in the mornings. At least she had Pépère to keep her company in the evenings.

Maxwell (always Maxwell, never Max) lived in a small cabin behind Shanna's home. He had given her parents an acre of land on his property to build their house. They were more than grateful to accept the offer—it seemed as if they couldn't get out of Haverhill, Massachusetts, fast enough. Though they now lived in the woods, a twenty-minute car ride to the center of town, Goffstown provided enough services to make living comfortable. With her adolescent troubles and non-existent social life in Haverhill behind her, Shanna was starting over, and her parents believed Goffstown a good place to do so.

"Pépère, you in the bedroom?" She called out.

The answer came in a low croak. "Yes, Shanna, you can come in."

Shanna was shocked by Pépère's appearance. His face, so yellow, stood in contrast to the white pillow he leaned against. The weariness in his eyes signaled defeat and the way he sucked his lips into his mouth only added to the feeling of hopelessness she was picking up. Two protrusions tented the far end of his blanket, reminding her how tall he was.

"Pépère, you don't look so good. Are you okay?"

The old man blinked, removed his hand from beneath the blanket and patted a spot. "Sit down, Shanna. I want to say goodbye to you."

Her spine went cold. She sat next to him.

"Pépère, what do you mean *goodbye*?"

The corners of his lips rose. "Well, I guess I should have said goodnight, but I'm an old man, and you never know." The croak in his voice was replaced by a smoother, lighter cadence.

Shanna placed her hand over his. "Don't talk like that," she scolded him. "Do you want me to get Mom and Dad?"

Her grandfather shook his head. "No, I'm fine. I'm just hoping the Halloween Train isn't coming for me tonight."

"The Halloween Train? What are you talking about?"

The old man chuckled, but there was little warmth to it. "When I was a kid growing up in Goffstown, that's what we called it—the Halloween Train. But it comes year-round. It circles the town, a slow train running, as it collects the souls of the dead at midnight to deliver them to their fate."

"A slow train running?"

"Yeah. You could easily catch up to it if you had a mind to. I'm not sure why it runs so slowly, but that's the way the conductor sees fit. It circles the town until all the fares are on-board, and then around the next bend, it's gone until the next evening."

Her grandfather was sick, talking funny. Did he think he was going to die? Was this his way of coming to terms with it? Shanna was torn between scolding him for the outlandish tale or placating him. Her curiosity decided for her.

"Pépère, when you say the Halloween Train delivers the souls to their fate, are you talking about bringing them to heaven?"

He nodded. "Yes, heaven, and in some cases, hell. Look, I know you think this is a foolish story I made up, but it's not. I've seen the train. When my father died, John Lemire and I biked out to Parker Station to see if the lore was real. We waited until midnight. Just when we decided to leave, we heard the whistle. It came, Shanna. The train was real. We watched it crawl past us and I saw my father in the first car. He was smiling, surrounded by his friends. He waved to me, and I knew he was going to be safe in God's hands."

Shanna took in a slow breath and then exhaled. She wasn't

sure what to make of the story. It didn't matter, really. If the tale made him feel good, who was she to challenge him on it? "Pépère, you said that it would deliver souls to heaven or hell. You also said you thought your father was going to heaven. Maybe you saw what you wanted to see." She smiled. "Maybe, everyone on that train goes to heaven."

Her grandfather lowered his head and sighed. "No, Shanna. Some go to hell. There were two cars on that train. My father was on the first. In the second car, I saw Old Man Holden. He was the meanest bastard in Goffstown. I won't say what took place in that car, but I'll tell you this, that man was on his way to hell." He paused for a moment. "In the end, we all get what's coming to us. When it's my turn to go, I know I'll be in that second car."

Unprepared for that last statement, Shanna released his hand, stood, and took a step back. "What are you talking about, Pépère? You are a good man. You've treated us so well."
He turned to his granddaughter. "Not always, Shanna. When I was younger, I was in the war. I did terrible things. I will have to pay for those things."

"Did—did you kill people?"

He averted her gaze. "Yes, and worse."

Shanna gently took his hand again. There were so many scenarios she imagined, so many questions. Now wasn't the time to ask him, though. He wasn't feeling well, and continuing to talk about that train didn't help. She decided to save them for another time. "That was war. Lots of things happen in war. You were trying to save people back in our country. Trying to save your family. I'm going back to the house now. Can we finish talking about this tomorrow? I want to hear about everything you did in the war."

Staring at his covered toes poking up at the end of the bed, he nodded.

"Thanks. I'm going to let Mom and Dad know you're not feeling well. They might call or check in on you." She left his side, but paused while holding the door to his bedroom. "Oh, and as for that train, it wouldn't dare come for my Pépère. I wouldn't let it."

He turned toward her with a bit more light in his eyes, and perhaps a smile. "Shanna, you're a good girl. I couldn't have asked for a better grandchild. Love you, kid."

"I love you, too, Pépère. Now, there's no Halloween Train coming for you. I'll see you in the morning."

Shanna exited the room. She couldn't wait to hear the stories her Pépère had in store for her. As she closed the door, a reply floated through the gap.

"I've already heard its whistle."

▬▬▬▬▬

Maxwell opened his eyes. Sunshine streamed through the room. Lying on his side, he took a moment to focus while gazing at the view through the windows. When his head cleared, he took stock of himself. The weariness that had overcome him the night before was replaced with an urge to rise and eat breakfast. He flexed his shoulders and stretched his legs. They were a bit sore, but that was normal upon waking. Whatever had ailed him was gone. It must have been a twenty-four-hour bug or something.

He sighed—all that worry for nothing. Still, he could swear he had heard that train whistle last night. It was not his time, he guessed.

Pushing the blankets off, Maxwell sat up and turned to see someone sitting in a chair at his bedside. He flinched and emitted a startled gasp.

"Dad, it's me, Peter! I didn't mean to scare you."

Once his fright wore off, Maxwell studied the man. His eyes were puffy and red, as were his cheeks. His chin was dropped and his shoulders were slumped.

"What's wrong? Why isn't Shanna here?" Maxwell asked. "Is she on her way to work? What time is it?" His eyes searched for the clock on his nightstand. He was confused when it read two p. m.

"Dad, Shanna told us last night you weren't feeling well. I checked in on you before I went to bed and you were sound asleep. I came back early, around six this morning. I couldn't wake you. Since you were sick, I thought you needed the sleep, so I left."

Maxwell exhaled slowly and ran his fingers through his hair. "Yeah, I was feeling off yesterday, but I'm much better now. All that sleep did wonders for me. I feel good. Thanks for checking in on me."

"I didn't come back to check on you, Dad. I—I have some awful news."

It was supposed to have been him that died.

Peter had checked on his daughter this morning when she didn't come downstairs for breakfast. When he entered her bedroom, she was still, her head covered in the blankets.

When he pulled them back, he froze. Shanna's eyes were open, blank, her face blue. He screamed for his wife to call 9-1-1 and he attempted CPR on her. When the paramedics arrived, they pulled him away and worked on his daughter. They asked Peter to leave the room. Shortly afterwards, they loaded

Shanna onto a stretcher and took her away. The lady EMT had said they restored Shanna's breathing, but all other information would have to come from the hospital.

Maxwell went numb, his head clouded with thoughts, questions. Shanna was just there. They talked merely hours ago. How could this have happened? He hadn't heard the commotion that morning. How could he have slept through it all?

I wasn't there for her when she needed me.

"Peter, how is she now? Do you know what happened?"

"She's breathing, but only because she is on a ventilator. Dad, Shanna is brain dead. There's no hope for recovery. We decided the best thing for her is to pull the plug. We will do it later, this evening. We waited so you would have a chance to say goodbye to her. As for why, they don't know. An autopsy is scheduled. We hope to know then. Dad, I searched her room for drugs or any other kind of clue. I found nothing. I thought you should know that."

As Peter relayed the information, Maxwell thought his son's tone was resigned, defeated. The more he listened though, he picked up something else—relief. Peter must have come to terms with the horrible decision he and his wife had to make.

When Peter finished, Maxwell nodded. "Thank you." He paused a moment. Wiping his eyes he said, "You know, there's been a mistake."

"A mistake?"

"Yes. *I* was the one who was supposed to die. I heard the train whistle. It was coming for me, not her. I should be the one on that train tonight, paying for my sins."

Peter reached and placed his arm around Maxwell. "Dad, you're upset, and I'm not sure I'm following you. I have no idea what this train is you're going on about, but when it comes down to it, we've all sinned, not just you. Something's bothering you, I can tell. When this is over, we'll sit and talk it out. Maybe confession will be good for both our souls."

Maxwell's love for his son grew stronger at that moment. It was tempered by the fact that he knew the talk would never happen. If things went his way, this would be Maxwell's last day alive.

"Could you do something for me, Peter? It's important."

"What's that, Dad?"

"Wait until midnight before you do anything. I know it sounds crazy, but I want you to wait until I have a chance to see her. I need to prepare, and I'll stop by her bed later this evening."

"Midnight? Dad, that sounds odd. Well, Sheila is there now and I'll let her know you've asked. I don't think it'll be a problem, though. Come on over to the house after it's done. You shouldn't be alone."

Maxwell nodded, but he had no intention of visiting the house. He had no intention of visiting Shanna in the hospital either.

▟▛▟▛▟▛

When Maxwell entered the living room, he paused for one last look. Pictures of Shanna, in gold and silver frames, sat atop the mantle. The room needed tidying, but it would cause him to be late. The wooden clock next to Shanna's pictures ticked, beating back the silence in the house, proclaiming it to be 10:13 p. m. Plenty of time before midnight arrived. At the back door, he bent low to a wicker basket and picked up a pair of warm gloves and a battery-powered lantern. He clicked it on.

The pickup truck cranked longer than usual because of the cold, but the engine caught and its headlights illuminated his front porch. Without waiting for the truck to warm up, he backed out of the gravel driveway, and then turned onto Route 114. An intermittent October wind whistled through the leaks in the windows as he drove, the sound intruding into his thoughts.

The drive to Parker Station wasn't long, but the walk into the woods behind it with its steep inclines would take some time. As a kid, he could make it from the parking area to the old rail line within ten to fifteen minutes, but he had no illusions he could match that now. He thought a half hour would be reasonable.

Arriving at Parker Station, he pulled into the last spot in the worn, hardpan parking lot. He grabbed the still-lit lantern and eased himself out of the truck. The keys tinkled when he tossed them onto the driver's seat before closing the door. Light from the orange colored half-moon assisted him as far as the tree line. Holding the lamp in front of him, he walked into the woods. There was no path to start this journey—it would show up around 100 yards in—so he relied on memory to guide him.

His memory served him well.

His legs swept the yellow, red, and brown crunchy leaf carpet as he dodged branches and slipped on the occasional rock. When he saw the opening to the path a few feet ahead, he sighed with relief. His breathing was heavy and his chest hurt from the exertion of walking up the steep grades. Stepping onto the path, he took note of the undisturbed leaves. He would be alone when he confronted the conductor.

Confronted the conductor.

That was his plan. He had no idea if it would work. In all his years, in all the stories he'd heard of the Halloween Train, no one had ever spoken of confronting the conductor. His heartbeat quickened. For a moment doubt weighed his shoulders down, but then he thought it through. If his plan worked, if he could convince the conductor to take him instead of Shanna, no one would see it happen. No one would be adding to the tale. He took solace in that if it *had* been done before, no one knew about it—so there was chance it had happened. This was enough to push him faster along the path.

Thirty minutes later, he came to a clearing, exhausted. Railroad tracks stretched and disappeared in both directions, bracketed by darkness. He stood on a tie, closed his eyes, and cocked an ear to the night. The breeze numbed his cheeks as he listened. There were no sounds. He bent at the waist, removed a glove, and placed his fingertips on the steel rail. Ignoring the cold bite, he pressed hard. There was no vibration.

I'm early is all.

Scolding himself for leaving his watch at home, Maxwell stepped off the tie and held the lantern high. He spied a boulder off to the side and made his way to it. He lowered himself against it and waited. When memories of Shanna threatened to crowd his mind, he shifted his thoughts. He had to steel himself for his confrontation with the conductor; this was no time for sentimentality. He closed his eyes and imagined various conversations the two men would have, and the points that he would need to argue for his granddaughter's freedom. If those failed, he envisioned a scenario where he would beg the conductor to let Shanna go. A picture of himself on his knees popped into Maxwell's mind. It dissolved quickly when in the distance, a shrill whistle carried itself on the breeze.

It's coming.

He rose to his feet. When his hips and knees protested, he

almost lost his balance. After straightening, he stood beside the tracks, his lantern held high. He faced south, where a small circle of light punctuated the darkness. It grew larger, but took its time. *A slow train running*. He lowered the lantern, and took a few steps toward the oncoming light. A good ten minutes passed before he had his first up-close look at the engine. A glance was the most he took in of the massive steam-belching machine as his eyes darted toward a movement in the lit window. Someone, the engineer he assumed, filled almost the entire opening. As the train pulled closer, his bladder let go.

The engineer was not human. Whatever it was, it had the head of a jack-o'-lantern—large, round, orange, with black triangles for eyes and a nose. Its smile was toothy, with the gap between them dark as coal. As the train inched forward, the Jack-o'-lantern's Man's gaze remained fixed on him. Maxwell shuddered. Did he have the courage to save Shanna? His doubt wavered when the front of the first car crawled into view.

The heights of the passenger cars were much shorter than that of the train's massive engine. The window was low enough for him to peer through easily.

There were at least a dozen people in the car. They were at ease, talking and smiling.

Closest to him was Claire Bisset, a woman he'd gone to high school with. Maxwell had heard she was ill. She must have passed away sometime last evening. Her appearance betrayed no sign of her sickness. She looked radiant, youthful. Surrounding her were her mother, father, and son, who died in a car accident when he was sixteen.

Dreading that Shanna had died, he stepped ahead, wondering if he was too late. He could see no sign of her. Instead, he saw a young boy he didn't recognize. The boy was with a much older couple, perhaps his grandparents. Out of nowhere, two other young boys appeared. All three of them got to talking and the original boy beamed with delight.

Shanna's not here.

Maxwell leaned close enough to the windows that his nose brushed the glass. Small steps enabled him to keep up with the train. He searched the car again, sidestepping to the front, but he couldn't see her.

Peter must not have pulled the plug. If he didn't, she's still breathing. She's alive.

Relief and trepidation tugged at him as he slowed. What if they *had* pulled the plug and she was breathing on her own, but brain dead? Lost in thought, Maxwell didn't notice the second car was upon him. Movement in the front window caught his eye. Before giving it his full attention, a chill traveled down his spine. The urge to look away was overwhelming.

He heard a voice. It was his own, demanding he close his eyes. But, he had to make sure. He needed to know his fear was unfounded. Maxwell stood his ground, looked forward, and waited for the car to advance.

When the second car pulled even with him, Maxwell screamed.

Shanna's face was pressed against the window. Her eyes were wide, unfocused, bloodshot, her mouth open, with lips pressed against the glass. Drool smudged the surface. Arms flailed at the window. One of them ended in a pulpy stump. Ripped flesh, cartilage, and muscle battered the glass, leaving thick streams of crimson. The nails on her uninjured hand raked the window, desperate for escape. Her face pulled away from the window, only to be smashed back against it. As the train inched past, Maxwell saw the rheumy eyes, cratered skin, thin cracked lips, and yellow teeth of someone behind Shanna. It was Old Man Holden, both his hands holding tightly to her hips.

No!

Maxwell pulled back from the car and vomited. As he heaved, an erratic beat hammered in his ears—it was the sound of her stump pounding against the window. This was wrong. Shanna was not supposed to be suffering. It should be him in that car. Without wiping his mouth, he made his way to the back end of the second car. He could see no stairs, no rail, no door. He faced the engine. He couldn't remember if it had steps, but the engineer had to have some way to get in there. He ran as fast as his legs would allow. When he passed the window, he yelled, "I'm going to get you out of there!"

Maxwell kept up his pace past the first car. He slowed once he was even with the engine. A padlocked gate prevented entry to a set of stairs. The engineer ignored his shouts to stop.

Panicked, he followed the train, waving his arms as he continued shouting. When that yielded the same results, he picked up some large rocks and hurled them at the windows of the engine.

The Jack-o'-lantern Man stared at Maxwell. After a few moments, it shook its head.

"You son of a bitch, stop this train! There's been a mistake!"

The engineer faced forward.

Maxwell had only one alternative. He ran ahead of the train. When he was thirty feet in front of it, he stopped and stepped onto the track. He lifted his right palm.

"Stop!" He cried.

The headlight of the train approached. It grew larger, brighter. He closed his eyes and waited for impact. He wondered how great the pain would be—if it would toss him aside with splintered bones perforating his flesh. Maybe, he would be killed outright and not feel a thing. The light was so close he saw white through his closed eyelids. He tensed and waited to die.

The sounds of squeaking brakes and rattling rails never reached his ears. His feet were grounded, and not so much as a breeze pushed him backward.

Maxwell opened his eyes.

At a standstill, the train was no more than a foot in front of him.

Maxwell blinked rapidly, then brought a hand up to shield his eyes from the intense light. Stepping off the rails, he made his way to the stairs at the side of the engine. He rubbed his eyelids in an attempt to wash away the bright circle imprinted on his vision. When he was able to focus, he lifted his gaze to the engine compartment. Jack-o'-lantern Man was at the top of the stairs. The engineer grabbed hold of the railings, turned his back, and descended. When his feet touched the ground, he faced Maxwell.

Maxwell shook. Words failed him. This was his moment— his chance to plead his case, and fear rendered him mute. His breathing increased, his shoulders heaved.

The engineer tilted its head and studied Maxwell. Its head straightened, and Maxwell thought he heard the words, "Oh yeah." The engineer placed its hands underneath his head and pushed. The jack-o'-lantern's head rose as high as the engineer's arms could reach.

It was a costume. A headdress. Maxwell came face to face with an older man with a neatly cropped beard, white handlebar mustache, and gray hair touching his shoulders. The man reached behind his back and withdrew a black cap, which he promptly placed on his head.

"I didn't mean to scare you, Maxwell, as you can see, it's a prop. I wear it only around Halloween. Keeps the kids scared and me amused."

His labored breathing slowed as Maxwell took a moment to gather his thoughts.

"Now," said the engineer, "in all my days, no one has ever so much as approached the train, never mind placing themselves onto its path. I had to stop and meet the man who had the balls to do so."

"I'm-"

The engineer didn't let him finish. "I know who you are, Maxwell. I should be asking the questions here, not you. So, let me ask, what in tarnation are you doing?"

"You know who I am?"

"Yes. Now go on."

Though more at ease knowing the engineer was an ordinary man, the fact that the man knew his name threw him off. "I—I need to speak to the conductor."

The engineer chuckled. "You're looking at him, Maxwell. I do all the jobs on this train. Now look, I'm on a schedule, and I can't be late. Nope, that won't happen. Since you want to be the one doing the talking, you better get to what you want to soon, or I'll be off."

"You-you've made a mistake. I'm the one who is supposed to be on this train, not my granddaughter!"

"Your granddaughter? Oh, you mean Shanna. Yes, she's supposed to be on this train. She passed last night, just after midnight."

Maxwell fell to his knees, his wail bouncing off the side of the engine and into the cool night. "No, no! You've got the wrong person in that car. It's supposed to be me. Shanna never did anything wrong. She's been a good girl as long as I've known her."

The engineer placed a hand on Maxwell's shoulder. "If it

makes you feel better, Maxwell, she was a good girl. Oh, she did a few things that would be considered naughty growing up, but that's normal for girls that age. You can be proud of her."

Maxwell stood, his face tight. "If she was such a good kid, why is she in the second car?"

Removing his hand from Maxwell's shoulder, the engineer shook his head. "You know when you were leaning against that boulder earlier? Well, you passed on, Maxwell, you had a heart attack just before midnight." The engineer pointed to the boulder. "Come on, let's take a quick look."

At the boulder, Maxwell gazed at his body. Instead of panic or fright, he acknowledged and accepted his fate with calm certainty. He didn't feel any different, anyway. However, his death did not change the situation he was in. "I don't understand. If my granddaughter and I are both dead, it should be me in that second car, and Shanna in the first."

The engineer smiled. "Maxwell, you will be in the second car. What you did in the war to those innocent people can't go unpunished. Take that woman you raped, and the men you mutilated—you need to suffer for those sins."

Maxwell closed his eyes. Revulsion for his actions turned his stomach. The engineer was telling the truth. Still, this didn't make sense. He glanced up to the engineer. "What's that got to do with Shanna?"

"That woman you raped? Her children witnessed it. Those men you slaughtered? Their mothers, fathers, sisters, and brothers cried out with every stab, every shot, every limb you lopped off. You put innocent people through trauma, through unimaginable grief. Should your punishment be any different?"

In a voice almost too low to hear, Maxwell said, "My God, she's paying for my sins."

The engineer heard him. His smile broadened. "No,

Maxwell, you don't understand. You're paying for your own sins."

For a moment there was dead silence. The engineer did an about-face and climbed the stairs. "All aboard!" he shouted.

Maxwell closed his eyes. When he opened them, everything before him had changed. He was inside the second car, standing straight against the wall. Shanna was there, pressed to the window, Old Man Holden behind her. Blood flowed down her backside and legs. Her amputated limb thumped at the window, the glass so smeared he couldn't see outside. Screams pierced his ears. He went to go to her, but couldn't move. An attempt to look away or close his eyes failed. His hands were above him, clasped together, an unseen pressure holding them against the car wall. There was no way to block out her screams, her pleas.

Thrust against the window, Shanna's face was turned sideways toward Maxwell. He could see the fright in her eyes, anguish in the way her lips parted and teeth gnashed. She made eye contact with him. Maxwell saw a glimmer of hope in the young girl's eyes.

"Pépère, help me!"

A shudder shook the compartment. Maxwell heard a hiss of steam and a shrill whistle. As the train inched its way forward, his granddaughter's pleas drowned any rumble of the wheels on the rails.

This was his penance. Only God knows for how long. He was on a slow train running.

DEVIL-POWERED DEATH TRAIN OF DOOM

Jeff Strand

Twelve-year-old Davy had been working on his train set all summer, and the day before school started he finally let his mom and dad come down into the basement to see it.

"Wow!" said Harold, his father. "This is incredible!"

"Is this a scale model of the entire town?" asked Patricia.

Davy nodded with pride. The setup was at least twenty feet long by ten feet wide, and the attention to detail was remarkable. Every single building on Main Street was there. The movie theater had actual tiny letters on the marquee, and the sandwich shop had a sign out front with its current lunch specials.

"And the train works?" Harold asked.

"Of course!" said Davy. "It goes around the whole town!"

Harold was flabbergasted by the accuracy of this replica. There were even miniature people all over. Harold recognized Bob and his hot dog cart, and the homeless guy who slept by a tree in the park.

"I had no idea you were so talented!" said Patricia.

"Good work, son," Harold said, patting him on the shoulder. "This is a very marketable skill. Your mother and I are proud of you."

Davy beamed.

Harold and Patricia went back upstairs and into the living

room.

"That really is amazing," said Patricia. "We may have a little genius on our hands. "

"Are you going to say it first, or should I?" asked Harold.

"Say what first?"

"You understand what's going on down there, right?"

"I guess not. "

"That train set will totally impact the real world. If his toy train hits one of the tiny people, they'll die for real. "

"What?"

"You didn't get that vibe?"

"No!" said Patricia. "How could you even think something like that?"

"Did you see the detail? Did you see the accuracy? Why would he put so much effort into a project like that if the train couldn't impact the real world?"

"Stop that. I won't have you accusing our son of working with Satan. "

"Who said anything about working with Satan? Why would your mind go straight there? We didn't raise him to be in league with the devil, but I'm telling you, if that toy train hits the tiny figure of Hot Dog Bob, somebody will find the real Hot Dog Bob splattered all over his cart. "

"You're being ridiculous," said Patricia. "Is this because of your failed dream to become an architect?"

"No. If anything, this would allow me to vicariously live my dream through our son. But that's not what's happening here. Don't believe me? Ask him. See what he says. "

"Well, if he's planning to murder people with his Satan-train, he won't admit to it. "

"But you'll be able to tell that he's lying. Davy is the worst liar ever. I'm always embarrassed for him. "

"Then let's settle this right now," said Patricia. They walked back down into the basement.

"Be honest with us," Harold told Davy. "If that toy train hits one of the miniature replicas of the people in town, will that person die in real life?"

Davy looked at the floor. "No. "

"Tell us the truth!"

"No, okay? I don't even like black magic!"

Harold sighed. "Son, we know that you're lying. Tell us why you want to murder the residents of our town. "

"I don't!" Davy insisted.

"Why can't you look me in the eyes when you say that?"

"Because you have creepy looking eyes!"

"I do not!"

"Davy, don't say things like that to your father," said Patricia. "His eyes are a little odd but they're not creepy. "

"They make me nervous," said Davy. "Whenever I read 'The Tell-Tale Heart' it reminds me of them. "

"How often do you read 'The Tell-Tale Heart'?" asked Harold.

"A lot. "

"Well, my eyes aren't going to cause Hot Dog Bob to explode into a bloody mess of bones and internal organs, so let's focus on what's important. "

"Let me ask him," said Patricia. She put her hands gently on Davy's shoulders. "Davy, sweetheart, we need to know if this train set is something where if you put one of those replicas of people we know on the track and run the train into it, it's like a real train hit them in real life. Be honest. "

Davy looked at the floor. "It's just a regular train set. "

"See?" said Harold. "He won't meet your gaze! He's evil!"

"Don't call our son evil when he's standing right there!"

"He's about to commit a supernatural murder. How is that not evil?"

"I didn't say it's not evil! I said not to call Davy evil when he's standing right there! That will make him *more* evil! This is why I have to do most of the parenting!"

"Yeah, you've done a swell job with that, considering that we have an evil kid. "

"I'm not evil," said Davy.

"I know you're not, sweetheart," said Patricia. "You're only using this train set to kill bad people, right?"

Davy looked at the floor. "Yes. "

"See?" Patricia asked Harold. "He's going to use it for something like getting revenge on the bullies who've tormented him for years. It's wrong and we'll stop him from doing it, of course, but it doesn't cross the line into evil. "

"It would depend on the severity of the bullying," said Harold. "If it's just kids calling him 'dork-face' or something like that, and he causes their gruesome deaths, yeah, that's pretty damn evil. "

"We don't even know if the train set works. "

"Right. We don't. Which takes us into philosophical territory. If he tries to use his supernatural train set to murder bullies who weren't really all that mean to him, but the train set doesn't actually work, is he still evil? Does his intention define his evil nature, even if his actions harm nobody? I just don't know. "

"And maybe he wasn't planning to use it," said Patricia. "Maybe just *knowing* that he could slaughter those who did him wrong was satisfying enough. "

"Were you planning to use it?" Harold asked Davy. "If you look at the floor I'll know you're lying. "

"I don't know. "

"What do you mean, you don't know? You wouldn't put that much work into this project without knowing if you planned to use it or not. You don't spend weeks designing the ultimate fishing lure and then not go fishing with it. Since we're not getting any answers out of you, I think we need a demonstration to resolve this question once and for all. "

Patricia frowned. "Are you saying that Davy should kill somebody with his train set?"

"No. I'm hoping he *won't* kill somebody with his train set, and that we'll find out it was all part of his overactive, delusional imagination. But since we can't drag an honest answer out of him, we need him to show us the train in action. Otherwise we'll spend the rest of our lives not knowing if he's in league with forces beyond our understanding. "

"Why are you saying it's my imagination?" asked Davy. "I told you it was a normal train set! You and Mom are the ones who said it might be magical! That's all on you! I just wanted to make a fun model!"

"He's right," said Patricia.

"Fine," said Harold. "I erred. But we still need to sort this out, and I'm afraid I see no other way to do it than to test out the train's powers. "

"And you're willing to kill an innocent person just to acquire the information?" Patricia asked.

Harold nodded. "Not one of our more important citizens, obviously. " He pointed to one of the miniature figures. "What about the homeless man? He's not contributing to the local economy. I'm not saying he deserves to die. It's not his fault he got laid off from his job and had pre-existing medical conditions that kept him from getting quality health insurance and had no family that could take him in and mental issues that led to him being expelled from the homeless shelter. But compared to, say, a waiter, he's not really doing much for anybody. "

"I don't like the idea of playing God," said Patricia.

"That's silly. If anything, we're playing Satan. "

"How does it work?" Patricia asked Davy.

"You flip this switch, and the train goes around the track. "

"But how do you use it to commit murder?"

Davy shrugged.

"I'd guess that we just put the figure on the track," said Harold, picking up the replica of the homeless man.

"Careful," said Patricia. "Don't crush his head. "

"I'm not going to crush his head. " Harold set the figure on the track. "All right, Davy, flip the switch. "

Davy turned on the train. It began to move around the track with a soft whirr. It had lights on the front and let out a "choo-choo" sound as it approached the figure.

It struck the figure, knocking it off the track, and kept going. Davy turned it off.

"All right, the dark deed is complete," said Harold. "Let's go see if there's a splattered vagrant near the park. "

"Oh, I don't want to look at any carnage," said Patricia. "That would be upsetting. "

"Then how did you think we were going to verify this?"

"I figured we'd see it on the news, with the gory parts blurred out. Maybe you could go check and report back. "

"If I have to look at scattered body parts, so do you," said Harold.

"We should have worked this out before we murdered him. I would've never have agreed to a deal where I had to gape at a dead body. I've gone my entire adult life without seeing a horribly mangled corpse up close and I don't plan to start now. "

"Fine. Davy and I will be right back. "

They got into the car and drove to the park. There were no train tracks to be seen, but Harold had to admit that it would be kind of ridiculous for his son's project to cause an actual railroad line to materialize around the town. If he had *that* level of power, by God, they could revolutionize the entire construction industry!

"Okay, the model train hit the figure right by that tree over there," said Harold. "Or was it a different tree? It was a tree in this general area. Maybe it's near all of that red grass. "

Harold realized to his horror that the grass was not naturally red. It was soaked with a red-colored substance. He parked the car and he and Davy hurried over to it.

"Blood," said Harold. "Appears to be about ten pints of it. And that's how much blood is in an average human being. "

"Look at all of those bones," said Davy.

"Yes, there are bones galore. I'm not going to take the time to count all of them, but I'd guess that there are about two hundred bones here, and if you round it up to two hundred and thirteen, that's how many I'd expect to have been part of the homeless man's skeleton. Obviously the broken pieces of a single bone only count as one. "

"I thought people only had two hundred and six bones," said Davy.

"Depends on your source. Either way, based on a rough estimate the math checks out. Plus, those are clearly human intestines over there, and the lungs are far too big to belong to a park squirrel, and if you squint, that chunk of face stuck to the tree looks very much like the homeless man's face. So though we can't rule out the coincidence of him being attacked by a wild animal or his body exploding on its own, I think we can say there's a very good chance that your train worked. "

"Okay," said Davy.

"How did it work?" asked Harold. "Did an invisible force drag him over to the spot where we moved his figure? Did his body just start moving on its own, as he desperately struggled to control his own legs? Did he walk over there unaware, thinking he was doing it of his own free will?"

"I don't know," said Davy.

"Did an actual train materialize out of thin air and smash into him? Was it a transparent ghost train? Was the train on fire? Did the ground split open and the train emerge from the depths of Hell?"

"I really don't know any of this," said Davy.

"So many unanswered questions," said Harold. "Let's go home to tell your mother. "

"Was he dead?" asked Patricia as soon as they walked into the house.

Harold nodded. "It was awful. It was like he was a giant Lego man, and they hadn't assembled him yet. You know that first stage where you open up the package and pour the Lego bricks out all over the floor, so that it looks nothing at all like the giant Lego man you're about to construct? That's what he looked like. "

"How ghastly. "

"Anyway, yes, our son's train set is capable of murdering people in real life. I guess it's good that we didn't waste an entire afternoon worrying about something that didn't pan out, but I'm still horrified. "

"So what are we going to do?" asked Patricia.

"We're going to get a pickaxe out of the garage and smash that thing to smithereens. "

"What if that angers Satan?"

"He'll get over it. "

"Shouldn't we think about this? Maybe there's a practical use for it that we haven't considered yet. "

Harold frowned. "You're sounding like a raging psychopath right now, and I don't like that one bit. "

"I'm not suggesting that we should go on a thrill-killing spree," said Patricia. "But what if, hypothetically, somebody had the power to use a toy train to kill Hitler, and, hypothetically, instead of killing Hitler they bashed it to smithereens with a pickaxe? They'd have felt pretty silly watching everything that went down during the Holocaust, don't you think?"

"We can't kill Hitler. This train isn't a time machine, to the best of our knowledge. "

"I mean the current equivalent of Hitler. "

"Yes, but who are we to judge that? One person's Adolph Hitler is another person's Mahatma Gandhi. "

"I feel pretty comfortable trusting my instincts," said Patricia. "We'd make sure that we researched our victim thoroughly before we started the train, just to make sure our opinions weren't unduly influenced by our social media echo chamber. "

"Are you actually talking about killing political leaders?"

"Not to start with. I mean, in the hypothetical scenario where a time-traveler went back to kill Hitler, they'd obviously want to practice by killing other people first. "

"I beg your pardon?" Harold asked.

"They'd want to—"

"I heard you. 'I beg your pardon?' was my reaction to being flabbergasted. And I don't even want you to explain the logic. It doesn't matter and your rationale will just upset me. Anyway, the model is only of our small town, so unless a deranged dictator shows up here for a visit, we can't really topple any governments. "

"Unless Davy can make models of any location he wants," said Patricia.

"Davy, can you make models of any location you want?" asked Harold.

Davy shook his head.

"See? So we either have to wait for a tyrant to visit our quaint little town, or we have to figure out some other way to make use of the train's nightmarish power. "

"What are you thinking?" asked Patricia.

"I don't know. I've never met a real life professional assassin, at least not that I'm aware of—I mean, I guess their whole thing is to blend in, so I could have met dozens of them without knowing it, but I know for certain that I've never had a one-on-one discussion about their career. Still, it seems only reasonable that they'd *kill* for a train set like this. Pun intended. "

"Was that actually a pun?"

Harold shrugged. "They'd *kill* for a train set like this. Joke intended. I assume the joke itself was self-explanatory. "

"Very much so. "

"You got it, right, Davy?"

"Yes," said Davy, without enthusiasm.

"I wouldn't take that material on the stand-up comedy circuit," said Harold, "but for something I composed in my head only a moment before I said it, it was reasonably effective. Anyway, let's move on with the discussion. "

"Are you suggesting that we rent the train out to professional assassins?" asked Patricia. "Or are you saying that we could generate revenue by starting our own pay-to-kill-by-train service?"

"Both ideas have merit. I assume that professional

assassins are unsavory people that we wouldn't want to welcome into our basement. On the other hand, people who would hire somebody to commit the act of murder aren't top-notch individuals themselves. So we'd have to abandon our current lifestyle of only socializing with high-quality people. "

"I like our social circle," said Patricia. "I don't really want to add reprobates to it. "

"Then what are we supposed to do? Squander the power of the devil-powered death train?"

"How did we even get to the point where we were talking about using it? I thought we started out being horrified by the whole concept. "

"I'm not sure how we got here," Harold admitted. "Conversations take on their own life sometimes, I guess. Part of the beauty of human interaction. If you'll recall, our first conversation was a lengthy discussion about *The Amazing Race* that ended with us having intercourse. That's certainly not where we thought it was headed, but there you go. "

"*It's not your train!*" Davy shouted, making both of his parents flinch.

"Please use your indoor voice," said Patricia.

"It's my train set, not yours. You didn't spend weeks in the basement putting it together. You didn't sell your soul to the Prince of Darkness. Why do *you* get to use it?"

Harold frowned. "Let's back up to the third of those four sentences. You sold your soul to the devil?"

"Yes. In exchange, Lucifer gave my model train the power to kill people in real life. Why should you get to use it? You still have your souls! I'm the one who's going to Hell, not you!"

"To be fair, I'm probably going to Hell for using your train to murder the homeless man, so don't pretend that your mother and I are headed for an afterlife of harps and cloud pillows. But why would you do this? Why is this train set worth eternal damnation?"

"Because on the last day of school Benjamin tripped me in the cafeteria and everybody laughed, and I told God that I'd go to church every single day for the rest of my life if He'd make Benjamin's head fall off, and God didn't do it like I asked, so I called upon Beelzebub, and he said that if I worked really hard and did a professional job with the train set and signed over my soul he'd grant me the power I craved. So it's *my* train set!"

"So, Davy," said Patricia, "as you spent your entire summer down in the basement assembling the model train set, did you have any moments of regret?"

"Yes. I regretted it as soon as I signed the contract in blood and it burst into flame. But then it was too late. "

"I have a problem with this," said Harold. "Benjamin is a minor. You can't go murdering minors without the police taking a very serious look at the circumstances. We still don't completely understand what happens when the train kills somebody. Did Satan explain it to you?"

"No," said Davy.

"Then we need to gather more information. What if a giant flaming train manifests itself in our plane of existence to run down the victim? What if Benjamin's parents are there when it happens? If Benjamin dies via Hell Train, and the police go door to door to investigate, and they find this eerily accurate model train set in our basement, you'll be headed straight to the poke. Now, if it's an *invisible* train, they'd have no way to connect you to the crime. So I hate to say it, but we'll have to commit another murder. "

"Or we could forbid him to kill Benjamin," said Patricia.

"Davy is going to spend eternity drowning in a pool of hellfire while fanged demons cackle at his misfortune. I'd hate for it to all be for nothing. "

"Then who do we kill?"

Harold let out a long sigh. "I like Hot Dog Bob. I do. He provides a quality product at a reasonable price, and he always has a smile and a witticism for his customers. But does this town *need* Hot Dog Bob? Will our economy collapse without him? Will our children's educations be affected? Will people be wandering the streets feeling lost and alone? So my vote is to kill Hot Dog Bob. "

"I'll bet he doesn't pay his taxes," said Patricia. "All of that cash exchanging hands. No way does he report it all. "

"What do you think, Davy?"

"I hope Hot Dog Bob suffers. I hope his final moments are filled with excruciating agony. "

"Okay, well, that's disturbing to hear, but to each his own. So here's how it's going to work. Davy and I are going to visit the hot dog cart and buy ourselves one final wiener. We owe him that much. Patricia, when you get a text message from me saying that we're on our last bites, you'll use the train. We'll take notes on what happens. Does everybody understand their role?"

"I want to turn on the train," said Davy.

"You can't. If you'd been paying attention while I outlined the plan, you'd know that you'll be with me near the hot dog cart. Unless Satan granted you the power to be in two places at once, it doesn't work. "

"It's my train. I want to do it. "

"Let the little rascal turn on his own train," said Patricia.

"Fine. I'll go alone. Make sure he doesn't, you know, grab dozens of figures and place them all on the tracks in an attempt to wipe out the entire population of this town. "

After driving into town and parking his automobile, Harold

walked over to the hot dog cart. Hot Dog Bob gave him a jolly smile.

"Lovely day for a hot dog, isn't it?" asked Harold. "I'll take one with mustard and onions. "

"Dijon mustard or yellow mustard. "

Dear God. Harold had forgotten that Hot Dog Bob offered two varieties of mustard. Were they making a terrible mistake?

"Dijon. "

"Coming right up! And would you like raw onions or grilled?"

Two varieties of onions as well! Hot Dog Bob didn't deserve this.

"Raw," said Harold.

"Absolutely, sir. " Hot Dog Bob went to work preparing the meal. Harold just stood there, wallowing in guilt.

The hot dog was delicious. The attention to detail on the placement of the Dijon mustard was exemplary. With two bites remaining, Harold wasn't sure he wanted to take another, because when he was down to his final bite, he'd have to text his family and ask them to commit an unspeakable atrocity.

Maybe he should call the whole thing off.

No. He wasn't going to be a damned liberal about this.

He took a bite of the hot dog, then texted Patricia: *Now.*

Hot Dog Bob stepped out from behind his cart, looking confused, and then terrified. "My legs!" he wailed. "I can't control my legs!"

He began to run, arms flapping as if he thought he could use them to offset the work being done by his legs.

Harold chased after him.

Finally Hot Dog Bob stopped. Harold recognized the spot. It was where part of the track of Davy's evil train set was located.

"What is happening?" Hot Dog Bob screamed. "Why did I run without my permission, and why can't I move now?"

The ground in front of him cracked open. Thick smoke billowed out, and trickles of lava spewed out. And then a train emerged—a black, flaming, skull-adorned train with horns.

"Tug me out of the way!" Hot Dog Bob shouted at Harold.

Harold just watched in horror as the train smashed into Hot Dog Bob. It was astounding how much gore was contained within a human body.

The train faded into nothingness. The ground closed up. Aside from the gruesome splattered remains of Hot Dog Bob, it was as if the train had never been there at all.

Harold glanced around to see if there'd been any witnesses. There were lots and lots of them.

"Rats," said Harold.

"This was all his fault!" said an onlooker, pointing at Harold. "I saw him purchasing a hot dog from our beloved Bob, and then I saw him tapping away at the screen of his cell phone, and that's when Bob ran to the very spot where the magical train struck him! It can't be a coincidence! Crucify him!"

"Crucify me? Seriously?"

"Well, that train was clearly driven by Satan, so it kind of got me thinking about religion and stuff, so the idea of crucifying you was the first thing that popped into my mind. Obviously, everybody else can veto it if they think it's going too far. "

The other onlookers agreed that crucifixion was the way to go.

Harold quickly sent Patricia a text: *In trouble. Kill the town.*

The onlookers grabbed Harold and dragged him to the center of the park. Fortunately for Harold, nobody had a giant cross immediately available upon which to nail him, so a couple of them hurried off to purchase some lumber and nails.

Suddenly, all of the onlookers began to walk away. Those who spoke said things like "What's happening?" and "Hey, I'm not doing this!" and "Why have I lost control of my appendages?"

But it wasn't just the onlookers. More and more people walked to the spot where Hot Dog Bob had perished. Harold began to fear that the entire population of town was gathering to be slaughtered. He kept thinking of people and searching for them in the crowd, and they were always here. Edith the Hairdresser. Gertrude the Cashier. Vincent the Sadistic Dentist. All of them were accounted for.

The ground split open.

"No!" Harold shouted. "That's too many people to kill at once! Satan, please stop! Show mercy! Find the kindness that I know is in your heart!"

The train emerged from the ground and rocketed forward.

So much death.

So much blood.

So many spleens.

A blood drenched Harold returned home, feeling sad. Patricia hurried out of the basement to greet him.

"Are you okay?" she asked. "I questioned your order to kill the whole town, but I knew you wouldn't ask me to do it without a good reason. What's that in your hand?"

"It's Benjamin's head," said Harold. "Since Davy will be forever haunted by the nightmare he unleashed, I figured he should at least get this bit of satisfaction before he's consumed by madness. We'll have to move to a new town since there's nobody left here to keep the infrastructure going. I expect to lose at least one of us to suicide. I thought this adventure would have a happy ending, but I see now that I was fooling myself."

Davy walked into the living room. "I know you're all worried about me. At least Mom is, because she heard me laughing the whole time. But I just want you to know that I made figures of each of you, and I had the presence of mind not to include them when I was shoving everybody else on the track. So you should be worried about my mental state but not *too* worried. "

"Glad to hear it, though I don't think we'll be turning our backs on you anytime soon. Pack your things. We have to move at least one town over. Oh, and I brought you Benjamin's head, just so you don't feel like all this ghastly carnage was a waste of time. "

Davy frowned. "That's not Benjamin's head. "

"Well, shit. "

TUNNEL VISION

Elizabeth Massie

Buckroe's Surf Park had been in business for nearly eighty years. It stood on an 11-acre stretch along the shore of the Atlantic, a combination of updated games and super-sleek new rides as well as sand-blasted old standards like the Whip, Tilt-a-Whirl, Bullet, merry-go-round, wooden roller coaster named "The Hurricane," and the Buckroe Express mini-train. One of the few classic amusement parks on the East Coast, it drew decent crowds in from April until October and had recently been declared an historic site. Tourists and locals alike kept it alive. Former residents came home whenever possible to relive better, simpler times.

Rick Via, however, came home because he was flat out of money and needed to lay low for a few days.

Things had spun out of control in Philadelphia. A legal tornado ripped through the biz thanks to some fucking, death-wish mole. Churned it up, spit it out. Several of the biggies – including Dr. Thompson himself – had been arrested, but at least Rick, a minor player, had been thrown clear, beyond the scope of the authorities, able to slip away.

Another job down the tubes.

For the last twenty-two years, after leaving the North Carolina town of Buckroe, which included his bitchy wife June and pre-teen daughter, Robin, Rick had survived by taking on temporary gigs in big cities here and there across the country. Some of the work was legit, much of it not. Most recently he'd been a lowest-level, off-the-books "employee" of Dr. Thomas Thompson, a cosmetic surgeon and wheeler-dealer who made money through a variety of secretive but blatantly illegitimate ventures. Rick, himself, never did anything all that bad; he wasn't that kind of guy. He delivered cash around the city. He acted as scout along streets and in the parks. He bought and disposed of cell phones for Thompson's higher-ups and, since he was terrified of guns, carried a small camp hatchet under his shirt for protection in case he was ever attacked. The other guys? They were the brutes, the thugs. They did the dirty, bloody work when it was called for.

But now, with Dr. Thompson and his closest cohorts in custody, Rick had to skip town. He caught a 5:00 a. m. Amtrak south, fairly certain no one would be looking for him. By the time the detectives sifted through the tangled web of Dr. Thompson's dealings, Rick would have gotten his hands on enough money to fly to Mexico to start over. He knew a little Spanish and was sure he could find someone there who could use a good run man.

Rick's now-grown, now-wealthy banker daughter, Robin, who had a massive 5-bedroom beachfront house in Buckroe, could certainly spare a few thousand bucks. He'd asked for money from her before, seven years earlier when he'd quit his job guarding customers in an illegal gambling parlor in Atlanta and needed a financial stopgap. Robin had agreed to fork it over, but only after he played what he came to think of as the Daddy Game. He'd left her so long ago and he had to make up for it, even if just for a few days. He'd had to pretend to be glad to see her, to pretend to like her. He had to do exactly what she'd told him to do, including listening to her practice her karaoke (several agonizing hours of ear-splitting, off-key yowling), mowing her lawn, walking her four nippy-snippy dogs, and cooking her breakfast. It was hard, but he got through it and it paid off. But now, he'd have to do it all over again. Robin had long since grown into a bitch like the two women he'd known best during his life – his ex-wife and his own mother. They were women who always complained, always blamed others, always took advantage. But Rick knew he could stomach a weekend with Robin. Hell, he'd stomached much worse. Like watching what had happened to Pinto Longo last Christmas Eve.

And so, as he parked his rental car in Robin's driveway and climbed out, he was ready to offer his apologetic Daddy smile and his "Sure, Honeys" and "Thank you, Honeys," and "Love you, Honeys." What Rick wasn't ready for was the fact that Robin now had a kid. A red-haired five-year-old boy named Mark.

Shit on all this, Rick had thought as Robin ushered him into her marble-floored foyer and Mark – all freckles and bright blue eyes – had stood beside his mother, holding a remote control car and staring at Rick. Now, Ricky would not only have to play the Daddy Game, but the Granddaddy Game, as well.

If I had any other option, he thought as Robin introduced Mark, and the boy, surprisingly, dove in to give Rick a hug around the knees, *I would never have come back here.*

▆▆▆▆▆▆

Rick was born on the wrong side of the tracks of Buckroe. He was a dirt road kid from a backroad family. Number three of five kids. His father was a handyman. His mother had died when Rick was eight. Rick spent a good share of his childhood and teen years in Surf Park with his friends, keeping watch while they stole food from concession stands, searching for quarters in the dirt so they could play the water balloon game or ride the rides. Rick's favorite ride had been the Bullet, which threw its passengers up and around and down at, well, bullet speed. Rick's best friend, Pete, extorted free Bullet tickets from Bobby, the mottled-faced man who was in charge of the ride by threatening to tell the park manager that Bobby was fondling the manager's daughter during his break. The other park amusements, Rick could take or leave. Not much fun. Easy to ignore.

But then there was the mini-train, the Buckroe Express. Fuck that steel-and-rails piece of trash. And fuck the goddamn tunnel through which it drove. Oh, sure, the kiddie ride tried to be endearing with its smiley-faced engine and cartoon characters painted on the sides of its open cars. The oval track was lined with human-sized animatronic animals that bobbed and waved as the train went past. The tunnel was on the far side of the oval. Eighty feet long, it smelled like mildew and dread, and it was dark as midnight inside except for the grinning faces on the walls and ceiling that would flash on as your car passed by. Rick's friends thought the faces were funny. Other kids and parents seemed to think they were cute.

Not Rick. They were anything but funny. Anything but cute.

People had disappeared in the train tunnel. Georgie Miller's mom vanished the year Rick was eight. She was an abuser; beat the shit out of Georgie, one of Rick's third-grade classmates. She'd been riding the Buckroe Express with little Georgie while she was drunk as a skunk and then *poof.* When the train exited the tunnel the last go-around, Georgie was alone. Martha Arnold's uncle had disappeared in the tunnel the year Rick was thirteen. Mr. Arnold was a suspected rapist and sexual abuser though had never been arrested. *Poof.* No more Mr. Rapist. Over the years several other adults had gone missing in the tunnel, too. Buckroe citizens believed these men and women, scumbags all, had hopped out in the darkness, hidden, and then sneaked away. Bye-bye. Good riddance.

But Rick wasn't so sure about that. There was something darker in the tunnel than the darkness itself; something conscious, something creepily aware. Yet to keep from being called a pussy, he rode the Buckroe Express whenever his friends insisted. He closed his eyes while in the tunnel as everyone else screamed with delight. Even then, he could sense that the grinning faces knew who he was and were watching him closely.

Even though he was not a bad kid.

Even now, he had nightmares about the faces in the tunnel.

Even though he was not a bad man.

▓▓▓▓▓

Saturday, July 5th in all its sweltering glory; Buckroe's Surf Park was packed with post Fourth of July revelers.

Rick stood in line for the Buckroe Express. One hand was in the pocket of his jeans, tearing at the stray threads. Gnats taunted Rick's face; nervous sweat soaked his tee-shirt. Kids and parents in front and behind him shuffled back and forth, talking, giggling, looking forward to their turn. Little Mark held Rick's free hand and bounced on his toes. Robin stood with them, her arms crossed and a punitive smile on her face.

The train was running, rumbling around its acre-and-a-half track. The engineer, an over-sized woman in an over-sized bright blue conductor's cap, pulled the whistle – *Whoo whoo!* – to the delight of the passengers in the open cars. Richard noticed that one of the animatronic figures beside the track, a big, pink furry cat with a faded red bow, had lost one of its hands and was waving at the passengers with a stump.

Made Rick think of Pinto Longo.

"I don't wanna wait," said Mark. "I wanna go now!" His hand was sticky from the remnants of an earlier ice cream cone.

"Patience," said Robin, her voice a snide purr. "Your Granddad wants to ride, too, but see how nicely he's waiting his turn?" Robin pulled her sunglasses down and gave Richard her snotty, arrogant look. She knew he detested the train. He'd told her that many times when she was young, though never said exactly why. It was always, "What if the tunnel caves in?" Or "What if bats live in the tunnel? Bats can have rabies." Or "What if the train jumps the track and we're all killed?" Of course, that last excuse never worked, as the train seemed to be a great deal safer on the ground than the Hurricane, Tilt-a-Whirl, or Bullet. But still, he made excuses and never went on the train with Robin. So, she went alone or with her mother.

Today, Robin was savoring the Daddy Game she was making him play. Forcing him to ride the Buckroe Express was just one of the ways she would manipulate him for her own entertainment.

Just ride the goddamn train, thought Rick. Get it over with. Ask her for the money tonight, after she's had a few drinks. She'll say yes. Not because she cares about me but because making me obey her orders is worth the three thousand dollars I'll be asking for.

I need a drink.

The concession stand on the other side of the Hurricane sold cold cups of cheap beer. But of course, Rick couldn't go for any until this goddamned ride was over. To please and appease his daughter, he'd have to do what she said and get on the Buckroe Express. He'd have to pretend to like the train. He'd have to pretend to like Mark, the kid he'd never met until yesterday.

Whoo whoo!

The mini-train, sending up jets of smoke from the engine, came around the oval and slowed with a loud, metallic rattle to a stop beside the gate.

"Line's too long," said Mark. "I don't wanna wait." He kicked his heel against the sandy soil and squeezed Rick's hand more tightly.

"Now, Mark," said Robin, "see all the other kids in front of us? They want their turn, too, and they got here before we did."

"Not fair!"

"Life's not always fair, Sweetie. But in a minute, you'll be riding the train. Granddad loves that train. Don't you, Granddad?" Robin looked at Rick, pursed her lips, and tipped her head the bitchy way her mother used to. The way his mother used to.

The train emptied its riders, who scurried away to the exit gate. The ponytailed ticket girl stepped up to the gate. Her bubble gum made a brief, sparkling appearance at the front of her mouth.

"Don't you, Granddad?" pressed Robin.

"Sure. Right." *Fuck this shit!*

"No running to the cars," said the ponytailed girl. "Once you choose your car, remain seated during the ride." She opened the gate and began collecting tickets. Passengers exploded through the gate, spreading out from front to back, claiming cars and sliding in.

"Mom, c'mon!" said Mark.

Robin shook her head. "I'll wait here. You and Granddad have fun."

"Mom! C'mon!"

"Go on, you two. Have fun," Robin said and stepped out of line. She winked.

Mark pushed through the gate along with the tumbling crowd of children and adults, and made it to the last car just ahead of three other young boys. He plopped down and gave the thumbs up. Rick stopped short and shook his head. "No, Mark. we're going to sit in the middle. There's an empty car right here."

Mark scowled. "No! I want to be in back!"

Fuck it. "Mark, here. Come on, now. Middle is better." Middle is better. In the back, those tunnel faces show up longer. In the middle, they flash on and off more quickly.

Mark bagged his fist on the side of the car and shouted, "No!"

"Mark!"

"Mom!" squealed Mark. "I wanna sit in the back! Granddad said we can't sit here!"

Robin was at the fence, her arms draped over. Rick couldn't see her eyes behind the sunglasses, but knew she was smirking. "Of course, you can sit there," she called. "That's the most fun place to sit."

Rick went to the last car and squeezed in beside Mark, his knees folding nearly to his chest. "This is the best car," said Mark. "We can see stuff better in the back!"

I don't want to see stuff. I want my three thousand dollars. I want to fly to Mexico. I want to start over.

"Stay seated, keep your hands inside the car, and let's have a fun ride!" called the engineer up front. She pulled rang the bell and pulled the whistle.

Whooo-whoo!

Some of the kids on the train cheered. Mark cheered. Rick bit the inside of his lip and looked across the grassy stretch at the tunnel. The train jerked, shuddered, and began to move.

Robin waved from across the fence.

Cool it, Rick. It's a fucking kiddie ride. The faces might not even be in the tunnel anymore. It's been years. They've probably gotten rid of them and put in images from some damned Disney movie or something. Bambi, Mickey, or one of those stupid princesses.

The train picked up speed. Mark laughed and pointed at the giant, pink, animatronic cat as they passed by. The cat waved its stump and bared its fangs. Rick shuddered and looked away. Onward toward the first curve where a huge, yellow teddy bear grinned, bowed, and held out a rusted honey jar. Its head turned toward Rick; the eyes glowed white, then flashed red.

They weren't red when I was a kid. Were they?

Around the curve, rattling, rumbling.

Whooo-whoo!

Mark tried to stand on his seat. Rick jerked him back down again.

"Don't do that!" shouted Mark. "I wanna stand up!"

Rick began to say, "They'll kick us off the train if you do" but then realized that's exactly how to end this fucking ride.

"Okay, go ahead!" said Rick. "Stand up!"

Mark stood and waved his arms.

The woman in front of them turned. "Boy," she said, "you best stay seated or they'll never let you ride again."

Mark slumped back down.

"Mind your own business, lady," said Rick, but she didn't hear him over the squeals of delight from her own little girl.

The train passed an animatronic kangaroo with a baby in its pouch. The baby was sleeping and the mother was rocking back and forth on her tail. The mother opened her hinged mouth and what came out sounded like a guttural growl.

On the straight-away now, the back stretch, with the tunnel up ahead. It's huge, midnight-black maw gaped. The blackness grew larger, larger, as if ready to swallow the train.

And then they were inside it. Rumbling, clacking.

The faces began to appear on the damp ceiling and walls of the tunnel. Flashing off and on like someone playing with a switch inside a wickedly dark cellar.

A toothy rabbit.

A smiling wolf.

A bug-eyed pig.

A drooling elf.

Flash-flash-flash.

Mark pointed and laughed.

Rick glanced at them and then away, though they still appeared in his peripheral vision. His heart pounded. He could feel them training their critical gazes on him.

A hydrocephalic crow.

A mutant fairy.

Don't look at me like that! I'm not a bad man!

A distorted skunk.

A mangy unicorn with a crooked horn who said, "Shame on you, Rick"

A misshapen wizard, who hissed, "Shame. Shame!"

I didn't hear that! That wasn't real!

I'm not a bad man!

With a rattle-rumble-clack the train rushed out of the tunnel.

"This is fun!" shouted Mark.

Rick's breaths came in short gasps.

Just two more times around. Two more trips through the tunnel. And I'll never have to ride this nightmare again!

Along the stretch, into the curve, past a frowning hyena holding out a plastic tulip, past a cinderblock castle with a snarling princess staring out from the tower, then along the fence-line and past the entrance gate where parents and grandparents cheered and snapped photos and Robin stood nodding with her arms crossed.

Whooo-whooo!

Forward, onward, heading for the big pink cat again. Rick gripped the side of the car. *I can do two more trips around. I can do this!*

They passed the cat. It leaned over Rick, waved its stub, and said, "So easy to forget certain things, huh, Ricky?"

Mark laughed. "The cat said, 'howdy-doody, toody-roody!'"

No, it didn't!

Around the curve, past the other animatronic creatures who glared at him, and then charging the back stretch to the tunnel.

To the faces.

Racing into the tunnel. The darkness.

The first face flashed on – the toothy rabbit, much larger and brighter than before. Its lip hitched and it said, "Did you love her scream?"

The second face flashed – the smiling wolf. It seemed to be hanging down from the ceiling directly over Rick's head. It said, "Did you love his scream?"

The bug-eyed pig, the drooling elf, the hydrocephalic crow – flash, flash, flash, bright as shocks of lightning, each much larger, sharper, closer this time – the mutant fairy, distorted skunk, crooked-horned unicorn. Each angrier. Each accusing him, "Bad boy."

"Bad man."

"Bad boy."

"Bad man."

Just as the car carrying Mark and Rick reached the tunnel opening, the wizard's bright finger reached down and touched Rick's hair – *close, goddamn, much too close!* – and it whispered in his ear, "They never had a chance, did they?"

Who? What? I didn't do anything! I'm not a bad man!

Out of the tunnel, the sunlight blinding Rick. Mark squealed with delight. The engineer blew the horn – *whooo whooo!* "Yay!" shouted Mark.

I gotta get off! I gotta get out!

The animatronic animals along the track were now a blur. Around the curve, heading for the gate where parents and grandparents cheered on the little train. Rick grabbed the sides of the car and tried to hoist himself up and out. It didn't matter if he and Mark were banned for life. It didn't matter if he fell and broke an arm or leg. He would not go through that tunnel the third time.

Rick wriggled and tugged, trying to un-wedge himself from the car. It felt as if he'd swollen, as if he were a cork pushed too deeply inside a bottle, never to be dislodged.

"Goddamn it!"

"Mama said don't cuss," said Mark.

The train headed for the stub-armed cat. Rick kicked, pushed, twisted. The cat waved the stump, said, "Bad man."

"I'm not!" Rick continued to twist and squirm.

"Not what?" said Mark.

Around the curve, past the life-sized teddy bear that wasn't holding out a jar of honey anymore, it was holding out a woman's head.

Mom?!

Past the kangaroo, who was no longer rocking a baby in her pouch but was rocking a ragged, bloody human arm.

Pinto!?

Barreling toward the tunnel, Mark giggling manically, Rick clawing at the side of the car, kicking, struggling. *Get out get OUT!*

Heading for the tunnel.

No!

Rumble rumble rumble.

Whoooo whooo!

And he remembered.

Remembered what he'd promised himself not to remember.

His mother, bitching, oh, god, bitching nonstop. And while crossing the tracks with her on the way to the grocery store early one morning, he pushed her down in front of the approaching freight train and her head was severed. An accident, it was determined. And Rick, not a bad boy, forgot what he'd done.

Closer to the tunnel. *Whooooo whoooo!* The opening seemed to have teeth now, shark's teeth.

He remembered.

Pinto Longo, standing with Rick in a trash-laden alley, having a smoke on a cold, sleet-covered Christmas Eve. Pinto had told Dr. Thompson that Rick had been stealing some of the cash he was supposed to deliver across town, even though it was Pinto who'd pilfered. Pinto was laughing, smoking, making fun of Rick for being a big, fat nothing. And so, Rick knocked Pinto to the ground, pinned him, and used his hatchet to chop off Pinto's arm and crack open his skull. Then Rick, not a bad man, forgot what he'd done.

Into the tunnel they rumbled, and there the faces waited. They were now enormous, with necks and torsos and tentacled arms. They were on both sides of the train track, glowing, wavering, waiting for Rick to pass.

"I wanna go again after this ride!" said Mark. "Okay, Granddad?"

Luminescent arms reached out for Rick.

I'm not a bad man!

Two arms coiled around Rick's neck and yanked him up and out of the car. The faces drew close to his and jabbered celebratory nonsense.

Then they began to feed.

The train continued on without Rick, through the tunnel and out into the bright July daylight.

The Buckroe Express held off for the next ride, giving the engineer time to search the tunnel for the missing man. But, of course, he wasn't there. Robin, who was pissed at her father but tried not to show it, told Mark that Granddad had probably gotten out in the tunnel because he forgot he was late for a meeting and, when no one was looking, had left the park. And she believed it, for there was nothing else for her to believe. Mark was upset and stomped the ground until Robin promised him another ice cream cone and a ride on the Hurricane before they went home.

PLAGUE TRAIN

Scott T. Goudsward

Mason milled about by the side of the road where the others were gathered. Loads of people crowded the street. The morning had started off wrong. His car wouldn't start; he stole a bike to get to a bus stop and hitched a ride from there. His old car sat dead in a strip mall parking lot, where he'd been living out of it. By now, the thing would be stripped by scavengers.

The crowd looked friendly enough: chatting, sharing stories, coffee, and photographs. Everything Mason had to remember *family* by was back in his dead car. Maybe someone here would drive him back to it after the train came through.

The train tracks gleamed in the morning sun. Mason wondered for a moment how far he'd get if he jacked a car from one of the assembled people. He was a mourner, too, technically, even if it had been a few years. It would be a super shitty thing to do, though, steal a car at a funeral gathering. At the intersection of two state roads, the crowd waited for the railroad crossing gates to lower and warning lights to flash.

Mason walked through the people, nodded to a few, and looked down the rails in both directions. Nothing. No plume of smoke, screaming hiss of brakes, or air horn piercing the day. The white arms of the gate were up, and no alarms rang. Mason didn't know if this was even the right date. He'd found a flyer on the ground with his last name, Dixon, on it.

His first name was a cruel trick from his father, who thought it was the funniest thing in the world. His father would sit in his chair, reading prepper magazines, shouting, *"Come on, boy, cross that line!"*

Mason watched mourners pass around tissues. He didn't make contact with their failed handshakes or attempted hugs, ignoring their snotty upper lips and red rimmed eyes. What caught his attention was the shine of metal flasks passing back and forth. People didn't care about the drinking age after the plague covered the planet and the dead started to walk.

Mason didn't ignore the flasks though he should. What was anyone going to say? It wasn't like the crowd was full of badges. He listened to tales of loved ones, accepted and drank the free liquor. He thanked strangers and moved closer to the tracks.

At the crossing, he looked up and down the route again. Nothing. He pulled the balled-up flyer from his pocket. It was how they notified people; some poor fool running mimeographed, hand-printed lists of names and then chucking the papers out of the side of a plane. All he had to go by was the name *Dixon* about a third of the way down. No first name, no address, nothing. Was it *his* Dixon? It'd been so long. After a few minutes of staring at the ties and the rocks between them, he stuffed the paper back in his pocket and turned.

The asphalt was littered with flyers. He compared one from the street to the one in his pocket. The dates were the same. The train was coming.

The tracks were flush with the road. Even if he had an unobstructed view, he'd never be able to see. The flat transport cars were a good two or three feet off the track, with plastic storm fencing to keep the cargo in place. Mason took off at a slow jog, looking for a bridge or an overpass. He followed the tracks and was aware of the people staring as he left. Mason kept an eye open for movement. The dead weren't sneaky, but you never knew when you'd stumble into a pack. Being eaten alive by the undead wasn't on the day's agenda.

"What do you mean the fuel's gone?" his father roared. Mason nodded and stepped back, afraid his father's fist would fly. His father reached for his belt and the big metal buckle that kept his pants up. Mason pushed dark hair from his eyes. He needed a trim, but his father was against leaving DNA behind on the floor in a strip mall.

"I went out to check it, just like you said. The genny's still there, but the barrels are gone." His father calmed, the red tint of his face fading.

"Oh, I moved them," he said. "I thought you meant from their new spot. We can't keep them in the same place, you know." He walked to his recliner and fell into it. The footrest popped up when his weight hit it. Mason sighed and went back outside.

The backyard was all dead grass and brown leaves. Typical for October. Foliage season was over, and now it all lay dead on the lawn. Off in the woods, he saw the shed that hid the door leading down to the cargo containers where they'd live.

The bridge was an old two-lane thing that desperately needed repair. A faint, shrill whistle echoed, and Mason quickened his pace. He heard hurried footfalls, a bunch of looky-loos had decided to follow. The tracks ran close at the very least.

Mason looked back to see at least six people pursuing at a slower, suspicious pace. Perhaps they thought he was luring them away to murder them, then toss their bodies on the tracks. Mason slowed, waiting to hear the louder footfalls. *Most fucked up game of cat and mouse.* When the steps got louder, he took off at a sprint. One thing he'd gotten from his father was he'd learned to run fast.

"Pump those legs, boy!"

Mason didn't need to be told a second time. A third time would mean a strapping. He bolted through the yard, hopping over cinder blocks and leaping over the fire pit, then ran into the woods, his father yelling something behind him. In the trees, he stopped and put an arm around a pine to catch a breath. When he heard his father again, he ran faster, deeper into the woods.

Mason saw the shed, partially concealed beneath a cluster of pines, his father having moved it from the backyard to someplace more remote. Roy had paid their neighbor to come over with his fork truck to move it. Once the holes and tunnels had been dug out, he'd built two more in the yard as decoys. Then the freight containers were delivered.

The forest floor was covered in pine needles and cones. Mason looked over his shoulder and pushed sweaty hair from his forehead. No one was coming. Out here, he couldn't hear his father's yells or him lumbering up the trail. On the front of the shed was a number pad. He punched in the five-digit code which unlocked the hidden door inside and took out the keys, one from a string around his neck, the second out of his pocket. He opened the door and slipped in.

The shed was dark, but Mason knew where the camp lanterns were. He closed and locked the door; he'd get beat harshly if he made that mistake again. Be smart, be living. *Mason moved the pallets covering the secret door, opened it, and climbed down the metal rungs set into the wall.*

█▌█▌█▌█▌█▌█

Mason slowed when he heard the train chugging. He whispered "Choo-choo" and stopped to catch his breath. The bridge was ahead—two lanes with Jersey barriers blocking the way on and off. The bridge had holes in it—big enough to swallow a tire or cause a bad accident if a driver wasn't paying attention. Weather and time faded "Danger" signs were bolted to the barriers. No movement on the other side, the road was clear.

He hopped the barricade and thought he felt the bridge sway a little. Mason was lightheaded from exertion. He hadn't eaten or had any water to speak of, only swallows from flasks. The people following him were coming into earshot. And beneath the approaching people, there was a growl, something guttural and hungry. The dead were near.

The support girders needed help. Paint chips lay on the road beneath, pockmarks of rust dotted the metal. The railing was tarnished and corroded. The tracks had a shine to them, and the wooden ties underneath were in good shape. Trains, after all, were the government's last best plan for transporting the infected corpses. Shipping bodies via jets or across the oceans on freighters simply weren't options. The consequences would be horrific if something happened.

"Why'd you run like that?"

Mason screamed, turned, wind-milling his arms to not go over the rail. A young lady stood there, watching, minor amusement on her freckled face. "People back there think you're mocking them, the way you ran off. We're all here to grieve, you know."

"Yeah, sorry. Been a morning. My car died." Mason cringed as the word slipped from his mouth. "No food or water yet, but I did have some class-A moonshine."

She smiled. Her teeth were a little crooked, but the smile lit up her face. "I'm Elaine," she said, holding out her hand.

"Mason," he replied. Elaine reached into her sweatshirt pocket and pulled out a water bottle. She drank deep and handed the rest to Mason, who drained it.

"Where'd you learn to run like that?"

"Running from bullies. From my father. You know, all the usual stuff. What about you? You kept good time."

"I ran track. If you had any control, you would have outpaced me. Never would have found you."

"Why'd you follow me? You're not going to shank me and leave me for dead, are you?"

"Following seemed like the right thing. If you're nice, I'll drive you back to your car." She smiled and brushed brown hair behind her ears.

Six people gathered by the Jersey barriers. "They followed me because I was following you," Elaine said. "Lemmings. Pack mentality—I have no idea who they are. I'm hoping they're going to watch for the dead." She shrugged. Mason took hold of the railing. He reached into his pocket, pulled out the crumpled flyer, and showed it to Elaine.

"My last name is on here. I didn't know if it was my father, thinking better, I have no way to identify it unless I jump down to the car, hope I get the right one, and investigate." Back at the intersection, the train cars would be too high to see anything, so I went for the bridge here."

"Not the safest bridge in the world," Elaine said. "Some of those bigger holes go all the way through. Get all cut up on broken concrete and rusty rebar on the way down."

"Hoped I'd be able to see from up here. Frankly, hanging over the side and dropping down seems more terrifying than what the train is carrying. And then I have to get off the train without maiming myself," Mason said. He looked down the tracks the dead were coming, two or three from what was visible. He could tell from their gait and staggered moves they weren't alive.

"Sick as this sounds," Elaine said. "I have no idea who's on the train. I follow the flyers. My parents followed jam bands when I was a kid. I guess it's hereditary." She looked at the other people near the concrete barriers and shook her head. They started back to the intersection. "I wait in my car until I hear a plane, and then I follow it until I see the flyers pouring out of the back, then I go to the next stop. There's a few of us who do that." She shrugged. "Not like we have jobs to go to."

Mason nodded and pointed down the tracks. The train had come into view, a massive machine with a cattle catcher on the front. He grimaced a little as it plowed through the dead stumbling along the tracks. The air horn blasted. Thick smoke plumed from the engine, and the train left a trail of gore in its wake.

"There's people who follow the train. They're like professional mourners. It's an addiction to them," Elaine said

Mason walked to the rail. He kicked a loose piece of stone off the bridge and watched it fall. It was at least two and a half Mississippis to the tracks. When he touched the railing, he felt the vibration from the oncoming train. He took a deep breath.

"What are you thinking?" Elaine placed a hand on his arm. "There's more dead down there."

"I'm going to hop the rail, hope I hit a car, and see how it's all labeled. If I'm lucky, jump car to car. If I'm not lucky, fall under the train and get run over or get devoured screaming in agony." He inched closer and grabbed the railing with both hands.

Mason saw the engineer lean out of the compartment and wave. Was he warning him off the bridge or acknowledging him? The driver wore a hazmat suit. It was a warning. Using cables for support, Mason climbed up on the railing. The engineer was waving frantically now.

No guts, no glory. When Mason looked down at the train, it seemed to stretch on forever. It wasn't just a twelve-car train like he imagined. Each car held hundreds of bodies, all of them stacked and wrapped, held in place by bright orange storm netting. Mason stepped down. Instead of jumping, he leaned over. There were markings on the white plastic wrapping the bodies. Beneath him, the engine trundled on under the bridge.

▟▛▟▛▟▛

Mason waited until he heard the slam of the metal door. Getting down the rung ladder was tricky enough in the light, never mind carrying the camp lantern. Hiding the door and locking it sometimes seemed impossible, no matter how many times they practiced. Start down the rungs, lean out, push the bar away that held up the pallet that covered the door, don't get hit in the head, climb the rungs and spin the lock, don't fall.

If you fell in the dark, you were fucked.

His father had always said that one of them would likely be alone in the shelter, and since Mason was a runner . . .

There was enough water to last a few years, maybe more if rationed, enough MREs and canned foods to last longer. If the air filtration system broke, there were enough vents to keep fresh air coming. The water system would supply enough for a moderately warm shower once a week. Not clean enough to drink, but clean enough to wash in using anti-bacterial soap. Clean enough to flush refuse into the holding tanks. When those filled, there was a switch to purge them into the connected sewer line.

"Get the generators rolling!" his father bellowed. Mason grabbed a flashlight and found the panel in the wall. A big gray metal switch. He grunted and pulled it down. The lights in the top container blinked to life. Mason reached under a table loaded with weapons and ammo and turned on the space heaters.

There were five different caches of fifty-gallon drums full of fuel on the property. Once one ran out, the survivor would have a hell of a time getting the fuel lines attached to the new cache.

His father came into the room, limping. He must have missed at least one rung and fell to the floor. He held on to the door frame for support, and he was bleeding from his arm and leg. Mason stood transfixed at the crimson droplets coming off his father's pinky ring.

"I can't do it," Mason whispered. He watched the cars passing beneath the bridge. He listened to the roar of the engine pulling the cars. Felt the vibration. "I hope this bridge doesn't collapse before the train is gone. Elaine, if I miss, take care of me."

Elaine grabbed his arm. "Let's walk off the bridge. Go back to the barriers and find an embankment to climb down."

Mason nodded as she started to lead him away.

Elaine looked at him, worry filling her brown eyes. "Are you ok?"

Mason stopped, and her grip slipped free from his arm.

"No," Mason said. He closed his eyes, took a deep breath, and ran. He pumped his arms and moved his legs as fast they would go. He jumped, pushing off the railing and sailing off the bridge into the air.

When Mason's momentum took a turn downward, he flailed his arms and kicked his legs. He was going to land *safely* on one of the cars. Was it the one with his father on it? Or was he going to land on top of a cargo car piled with the corpses of strangers?

They both screamed; Mason a wordless shriek and Elaine something that sounded a lot like *incinerator*.

Mason landed with a sick *whump*. Something had broken, and he was sure it wasn't him. The first thing he noticed was the smell—it explained why the conductor had the hazmat suit. Only God knew how long the bodies had lain around before being loaded on the train, baking in the sun.

He lay there for a moment, trying not to breathe too deep just in case whatever had killed them was still active and puffing through microscopic holes in the plastic. He also didn't want to take in the stink of the bodies.

Or worse.

Something moved.

The plastic crinkled.

He stared down at a plastic-wrapped body. There was a hazmat label on the tarp. Then another of a flame. Written in blue marker on the head was *5-18-23*. Mason guessed that was the date of death. Whatever was inside twitched. A large letter B. He counted the cars from the engine. He was in the second one. Which meant he had to jump out, not fall to his death under the train, and keep jumping until he found the D car.

"You're bleeding," Mason said and jumped from the table. His father stood in the doorway, drops of blood spattering the floor. "I'll get the med kit."

"You'll do no such thing. Get those generators going first. I ain't bleeding out. Nothing bit me." Roy looked away from Mason. "The damn door slammed on my hand, then I fell the last three rungs." Mason hot-stepped it over to the fuse panel, flipped the large switch, and everything hummed to life. His father took a deep breath of recirculated air. Mason knew his father was lying about his wounds.

"You want some water?" His father shook his head, and Mason sat at the table again. He turned on the radio, spinning the dials looking for something besides static. They'd rigged an antenna from the radio through the ceiling to come out right near the first shed.

"This is real, Mason." His father smiled a little. "The real deal." He took a nearby chair. The walls were corrugated steel, painted gray. At the end of the top container – the action room as his father liked to call it – a ladder led down to the second container, where the living quarters were: beds, chairs, and a makeshift bathroom with a shower.

Mason turned on the bank of monitors that was hung on the walls. There were security cameras in the trees so they could see what was going on.

"I heard the news through my phone when I was running, before I dropped it. It's a pandemic. We're down here for the long haul, Mason. You and me."

Mason closed his eyes and pushed hair from his face. "I should have brought the damn clippers with me."

"Daddy." Mason felt odd using that word. It was always Pop, *or sometimes when he was pissed, it was* Roy. *He nodded at the hand. Blood was trickling now more than spattering. His pinky ring mostly invisible from the blood flow. There was a widening puddle on the floor. Roy nodded at the monitors. A crowd of people ran past the shed. They were followed by a voluminous gray and black cloud.*

They sat in silence under the ground and waited for the cameras to clear. Then the cloud was gone, revealing a blanket of bodies on the forest floor. Mason looked at his father and started to cry.

"I don't go for that normally, but this seems like the right time." A tear slipped down Roy's weathered face. "Best get me that medical kit. I think this is getting worse." Mason got up and was heading toward the supplies when his father fell off the chair.

█████

Mason walked as gently as he could, hoping his steps landed in the mid-thigh region on the bodies. He was too afraid to cut open one of the tarps and see dead eyes staring up at him—or worse, yellowed teeth biting at his hands. He took a handkerchief from his pocket and tied a makeshift mask over his nose and mouth. Every footfall brought the snap of a bone. Each step he imagined walking on offal under plastic, pictured it flowing from the plastic and oozing up over his shoes. He tried not to think of the moving corpses groaning in some after-death agony. The train chugged on.

Mason reached the end of the car. A high metal wall separated Mason from the tracks. He climbed up and sat on the edge, watching the ties pass by under his feet. His shoes and cuffs were clean. He hadn't torn anything open. He let the breeze wash over him and lifted the mask for some fresh air—as fresh as one can get riding on a train stacked high with pandemic corpses.

He saw the C car, not so far away he couldn't jump—but far enough that if he missed, he'd likely cripple himself, or the train would roll over his legs, and he'd bleed out in the dust. If he *didn't* jump, then this whole thing was a big waste of time. Not like he had a job or a home to go back to. The underground shelter was empty. No food, no fuel, no people, dead or otherwise. "This is my life," he whispered. He looked back at the tarp-wrapped bodies and cringed. He swore he saw his footprints on some of them. "I can't get a running start." Mason stood, holding his arms out for balance, forming a shadow T on the ties below. He took a deep breath, held it, and leaped.

██████

Mason took a tentative step back. "Dad?"

Roy lay in a pool of blood on the floor. The wound on his arm looked like it had spread as if someone had taken a cheese grater to him. It seemed the entire limb was oozing blood. One of his legs was bleeding bad—he'd been cut by something. Maybe an old trap he'd set or someone running behind him. The belt buckle that had struck his back and legs so many times reflected the overhead lights. Mason grabbed the medical kit—an old tackle box—set it on the floor, and sat next to it.

He stared at his father's lifeless eyes, centered on a spot on the ceiling. Something dripped from one of the vents. Not a clear something, either. Mason stood and walked to where a small, vaguely sulfurous-smelling puddle had formed. He heard his father's voice. "Boy, get that patched up and quick!" Mason took a step back, tripped over his father's corpse, and landed ass-first in Roy's blood.

"Shit." He stripped out of his pants, tried to cover his father's face best he could, and went for the ladder. After taping a plastic sheet over that vent, he climbed down, put the ladder and med kit away, and went to the living area for some more pants. None of the other vents had leaks.

"What do I do?" He tried to make plans—maybe pushing Roy down the ladder to the living area. The stink would be overpowering, and things would get worse when the body started to decompose. A tear slipped down his cheek. He wiped it away angrily. "No time for that shit." Mason sealed the bag of crackers and left them on the chair. Now it was his chair, alone and underground until everything was right again. With only one person, he figured the rations could last four or five years if he didn't go crazy first. "First trip back to the house for whatever reason, pack up the DVDs, puzzles, and comics." Mason stood up, getting his head back in the game.

"Only one thing I can do." Mason got the pistol from under the table and stuffed it in his back pocket. He climbed to the first level and sat in front of the monitors. Nothing was moving outside. He looked at the corpse. The plastic over the vent was doing its job. "God bless duct tape," his father always said. There was some fluid accumulation, and it would have to be sealed properly or reinforced, but growing up a son to a redneck handyman wannabe had benefits.

Mason saw the plan in his head, realized how much work it was going to be, and how disrespectful. But Roy Dixon's body had to go outside. Mason thought he saw movement on the monitor. He stared closely at it until he had to blink. Was that an arm twitch? Did someone's foot move? A squirrel bounded across the bodies and disappeared off screen. Mason rose, shaking his head, and went for the tools for the task.

▮▮▮▮▮▮

Mason looked back at the B car, which now seemed a mile away, and walked carefully across the bagged cadavers until the other car loomed closer. *I bet the guy in the hazmat suit wasn't expecting this today.* Mason looked over his shoulder, half expecting to see the conductor charging him with a pipe or shotgun or some other kind of weapon.

"All right, I can do this." Mason walked to the end of the car, the wind whipping his hair. "No pain, no gain. Or whatever." He stepped on the rear barrier and leaped. This time, eyes open, he watched the D car coming. Saw the ties passing below his feet. Realization set in, then panic. He flailed his arms, but nothing slowed him. If he *had* slowed, it would have been face-meet-railroad-ties.

"Now what?" Standing, he pulled a small box cutter from his pocket. It was the only defense he had. Once he'd left the shelter, he'd never gone back, which in hindsight was pretty fucking stupid. The firepower. The protection. There were always supplies to be found or stolen. The shelter was safe.

▮▮▮▮▮▮

Trying to keep his eyes mostly closed, Mason wrapped his father's body in plastic tarps. He spied the wound on Roy's leg.

He had been lying. There was a bite taken out of his thigh and it looked more human than animal.

Mason looped the nylon climbing rope over his shoulder. If nothing else, Roy had been prepared for almost anything. Neither one knew what the carrier might have been, air, water, or the pizza delivery guy. They had been ready for almost anything. Maybe the big artery in his leg had been nicked. How else could Roy have bled out so fast?

Or was that common for the bites? Would Roy turn? And if he did, how long would it take? Mason tried to move a bit faster. He remembered from TV how to kill something that had been bit. Destroy the brain. Sever the connection to the spine. Fire cures all.

Mason climbed the rung ladder to the surface. With a grunt, he got the door unlocked; with another, he got the debris-strewn portal open. Sunlight beamed in through the wide doorframe. There were bits of board and shards of wood all over the shed floor. Someone had kicked the door in, probably chasing Roy or looking for shelter.

The weight of the . 38 police special tucked in his belt was comforting. He dropped the rope on the shed floor and went to the doorframe. A blanket of bodies covered the ground, most of them swathed in dirt and other debris the cloud dragged with it.

He recognized one of his neighbors and a girl he'd had a crush on in school last year who turned him down when he asked her to go to the dance. This was no time to reminisce, he thought. He turned and found the spare pulley for the well. After climbing a tree and securing it, he looped the rope through it.

"This is going to suck." Mason got the gloves from his back pocket, put his feet against the tree, and pulled the rope tied around his father's plastic-wrapped body. He'd dragged him far

as he could and now hoped he was strong enough to get him to the outside.

🛤️

Hand raised, not-terribly-sharp box cutter positioned, Mason stopped. Was whatever killed these people also dead? The moment that blade sliced through the plastic, would he be releasing another wave of the virus? His father hadn't shared much about how it all started. Meteor strikes worldwide. With the meteors came the virus that decimated the population.

Was he actually going to cut open each one of the *packages* and see whose face was looming behind the plastic? Would some living corpse reach for him? His father had been gone for years—would Mason even recognize the decomposed body? It was more than a face, though. If he saw that awful pinky ring and belt buckle, he'd know he had found Roy Dixon. Maybe his father would take care of him.

And then what? He didn't have a gun to shoot his father in the head or fire to light it up. Nothing but a boot-clad foot to stomp on its head. The thought of revealing and moving hundreds of corpses nauseated Mason. He gagged and fought the moonshine down.

Hop off the train? Run to Elaine for a ride back to what was left of his car and maybe a quickie in the back seat? Hop off the train, break an ankle, and drag himself to the street? Too many questions.

You can't be on this car, Roy. You should have been burned up long ago. Mason's shoulders hitched as he stifled a cry. He stood and looked hard at the rolled up *packages*, gave a sigh, and stepped gingerly toward the orange storm fencing that held the bodies. The landscape seemed to move by a bit faster.

He looked three cars down. The conductor was still waving his arms. Mason shook his head and waved back.

The only thing separating him from possible broken bones, gravel burn, and—if he was lucky—a concussion, was some thin plastic fencing meant to hold back snow on parade routes, back when there *were* parades. It also blocked people from them too.

"Is this worth it? Do I need to know this bad?"

Mason closed his eyes and took a deep breath. "One, two, three . . ."

"Come on, you son of a bitch!" Mason screamed and pulled in the rope again. Inside the gloves, his hands were bleeding, the blisters ripped and running. He felt the skin flaps on his palms and fingers. He'd grabbed the wrong gloves. Each pull of the rope brought his father a little farther up the tunnel to the shed. He played a game, trying to imagine what it was like reeling in a swordfish on a deep-sea fishing boat—something Roy had always promised, but like so many other things, failed to deliver.

Mason screamed, loud and feral, as the tears streamed down his cheeks. It was more emotion the old man deserved, but Roy had been the only family there was. And family takes care of family. When Mason saw the top of the tarp-wrapped corpse, he pulled harder, gritting his teeth so tight he thought they'd chip and break. And then Roy was free of the tunnel, dangling from the makeshift pulley system in the tree.

The corpse swung and twirled on the ropes. Mason carefully tied off his end and fell back on the pine needles and grass, his chest heaving. His arms and legs burned, and he didn't know if he'd be able to stand, never mind get Roy down and in the shade of the tree.

He didn't know how long the body would keep or if anyone would come looking for them. He cried out, taking the gloves off. His palms were a wreck of ripped skin and blood.

"You're home, Roy." Mason steadied the body and gingerly untied the knots until the package landed on the ground. Pain lanced through his hands and wrists. "See ya around, I guess. If you see Mum wherever you end up, tell her I said Hey." Mason walked back to the shed, pulling the good rope with him, and disappeared down the tunnel. The sound of locks sliding into place echoed.

Mason crashed on the floor of the control room. Roy's blood had been soaked up with sawdust. Can't waste water! With bandaged hands and dirty face, Mason got up and rubbed at his neck. He stared at the pile of blood-soaked sawdust and moved to the bench where all the monitors were. Outside it was light. He must've been knocked out from the crash to the floor, though he had no idea for how long. His father's body was still under the tree, wrapped tight. Though some of the others who'd been overtaken by the cloud were gone.

Mason didn't jump. He screamed to the passing landscape. He took a step back, sat, put his hands on his knees, and tried to compose himself, ready himself again for a pretty certain injury. Something crinkled to his right. He expected a bird or a fallen stick from a tree. He saw nothing. Mason squinted at one of the bodies. It had a large "D" written on it in blue marker. Around him plastic moved and rustled. Mason tossed the box cutter off the train, watched it bounce and disappear beneath the "E" car.

He looked over his shoulder, there were dead staggering near the "A" car. Six of them weatherworn, with bite marks and solid eyes. Hair hung like dead grass from what was left of the skin on their heads. Mason was hypnotized, watching them advance slowly and the train leading him right to them. One bite, and he'd be wrapped in plastic on the train. Many bites, he'd be a pile of gore on the embankment.

Mason slid the mask off his face and took a deep breath. Where there were a few dead, there were more.

"Fuck it," Mason said. He edged to the fencing. He spied a bush that should cushion the landing. "Jump, roll, and run." Run for the road, find Elaine and ask for a ride back to the shelter.

"You can do this, Dixon." Mason looked back at the dead getting alarmingly close and jumped for the bushes.

THE MIDNIGHT TRAIN

James A. Moore

The road was clear. The tracks were clear. Everything was silence, which was exactly as Dane Henderson preferred it. He lived in the country for a simple reason: he wanted to be left alone.

Oh, it wouldn't last. It never did. Sooner or later somebody would come down the road and bother him, but what can you do? The world apparently believed that people should be around each other. Dane did not agree.

Just to prove his point the dog from across the street started up again. Dane glared out his window in the dog's direction. It was a nice enough dog, really, but it barked if so much as a butterfly went drifting past.

"Shut your damned mutt's mouth, Baker." He said the words without venom. Carl Baker wasn't around, and no one was there to hear him other than Hercules, the dog. Hercules was a joke of a name. The basset hound looked like a puddle of fur on the best days.

Retired, and with no particular agenda to keep him busy, Dane lay back on the couch and contemplated reaching for the TV remote. Too much effort. Instead he closed his eyes and drifted.

"What?" The nap ended when he heard the shrill scream of a train whistle amid the clatter of wheels thumping rhythmically over the tracks. The sounds were not expected.

Dane's heart hammered in his chest and he sat up quickly,

aware that he was sweating heavily. He licked the perspiration from his upper lip and looked around, trying to find the source of the noise.

The sun was in a different position. He'd fallen into a proper sleep until the train's whistle damned near blew out his eardrums.

It took three tries to crawl from the couch and then head for the windows on the backside of the house, closest to the railroad tracks. Tracks that had not been used in over eighteen years. The old east-west line had been abandoned a long time back and all the better. Dane had always hated that damned train coming through the area. The noise was enough to deafen, and more than one cake had collapsed from the vibrations over the years. Back when his folks were alive, and he'd been a child in the same house, it was almost impossible to have a birthday cake that wasn't flattened on one end. If bread had suffered the same problem his mother would have lost her mind.

Dane pulled on his light coat and baseball cap. It wasn't very cold out, but it wasn't quite warm either. October did that every damned year. He walked out the back door and made his way down to the gully where the train tracks still lay. In the distance the mountains still shimmered, the trees still stood, and the clouds scudded through on their trek to God alone knew where.

No one had come by to survey the land that he knew of. Not a single person had come down to examine the tracks. Why the hell were they sending trains down the way without a proper inspection first? That was how accidents happened. Wouldn't take too much to derail a train. He'd seen the results once, back in the seventies. They'd been weeks cleaning up the debris from that particular accident.

"Lost their damned minds is what's going on." Dane squinted against the autumn sunlight and looked at the weed-strewn pathway the train had to take. None of the underbrush that hid the old tracks had been disturbed. The parts of the tracks that he could see were as damaged as he'd expect after eighteen years of neglect. Metal was rusted and old wood was faded and splintered. Impossible, of course. The train moving through would have cut away the greenery resting on the actual rails at the very least, but nothing was out of place. None of the sawgrass was so much as knocked aside by the weight of the engine or the cars that followed.

Dane lit a cigarette and sucked the smoke into his lungs, resisting the urge to cough. He took his time examining the tracks, walking along the same path, and looking for signs of a train passing by. He found none. He knew the sound of a train. Had grown up with the damned things only forty feet from the back door of the house. It was a sound he knew as intimately as he had known his Eleanor's kiss before she'd been taken away from him, and he'd known the noise for much longer.

Hercules started barking again and Dane listened to the old hound, grateful for a racket he was used to. The dog made sense in his world. The train did not.

With one last lingering examination of the tracks, Dane turned toward Carl Baker's house. Baker was a pain in his ass, but he wasn't all that horrible as neighbors went. At least he had given up on trying to invite Dane over for every holiday. He took the good where he could find it.

Hercules ran along the length of the property, wagging his pudgy tail and panting away like an asthmatic running a marathon. He never barked at Dane, just at everything else in the known universe. Despite himself, Dane smiled. He supposed as dogs went, the neighbor's old hound was tolerable enough.

His neighbor had already put up a few cheap Halloween decorations, and Dane made a note to buy a pumpkin and a few paper cutouts to replace last year's models, as he rang the man's doorbell. He didn't like people, but he was okay with kids in small doses.

Baker answered after only thirty seconds. He could say what he wanted about the man, but his neighbor was quick to respond to a doorbell. "How are you, Dane?" Carl's smile seemed genuine enough but was diluted by his puzzled expression. In the twenty years they'd lived next to each other Dane had never found a reason to knock at Carl's door.

"Oh, I'm all right, I guess. I was just wondering if anyone sent you a letter about the train line starting back up."

Carl looked over his shoulder as if he could see right through the walls of his house to the old train tracks. His brow was cloudy with thoughts, no doubt, of how unholy loud the train had been and would be when it came through.

"The Wickham line?" Carl frowned. "Nothing I've heard about. When is it supposed to start running again?"

"It just did. Not fifteen minutes ago." Not for the first time he wondered if the younger man was hitting the sauce when no one was looking.

Standing in his doorway, Carl crossed his arms and shook his head. His lower lip protruded in a pout. "I'd have heard that, Dane."

"I *did* hear it. Woke me from a perfectly fine nap."

Carl shook his head again. "You must have been dreaming, Dane. Nothing's come by here. I'd have noticed."

Dane made an excuse and headed back for his house, frowning the entire time. No way he could have dreamed it. Not a chance in hell.

The neighborhood wasn't much to look at. Ten houses on either side of a street that ended in a cul-de-sac. Most of the small homes were occupied by retirees. There had been a time when that was a different set up, of course, but Dane had lived in the same place for all of his seventy-seven years and had seen the demographics change a few times.

The subdivision had never been trendy as far as he knew, and he was fine with that. He preferred it that way. The closest thing to a young neighbor was Baker and that man was only young in years. He lived alone and seemed to prefer it. If he even dated, he had the good sense to do it away from the prying eyes of Mitzy Holloway and Dinah Cooke.

Those two watched the neighborhood like hawks in the hopes of finding juicy gossip. They were harmless, but annoying. Neither of them had any knowledge about the train coming back around and they hadn't actually seen or heard anything either, which meant the only logical answer was that Dane had indeed dreamed the whole incident.

Damned vivid dream. He'd have sworn on a bible or twenty that he'd felt the vibration of the train hitting each bump on the tracks, that he had heard the whistle tear up the day, but there wasn't a hint of proof, was there? No sir. Not so much as a single blade of grass clipped from the tracks.

Delighted with the idea of never having to hear a train come through while he was trying to nap, Dane settled back into his routine, pushing aside the half-composed letter of complaint that he'd been contemplating sending to every newspaper and government office he could imagine.

The quiet was back and that was a lovely thing.

Dane was just sitting down to dinner when the train came

again. He heard the rumble, felt the rhythmic *thud-thump* of train meeting tracks, and climbed out of his seat at the dining room table, moving with speed because he needed to see the damned thing this time, to make sure he wasn't losing his cotton-picking mind.

Hercules was barking up a fit in the next yard, but Dane didn't have time for that. He wanted to see the train. Needed to see it, really, because if some damned fool had reopened the line, he'd have that somebody's head on a platter.

The back door opened easily enough, and he stepped out onto the porch. The train tracks were hidden by overgrowth, but he could see the vegetation shaking as the train came close. The noise was a wall of sound, closing in and crushing against his body. It was made worse when the whistle blew, a shrill scream that utterly shattered the concept of silence.

There was nothing to see. No train came up the tracks. No engine riding high enough that spotting it was inevitable, no cars hauled along in the mighty engine's wake. Nothing. Still the grass shook and the ground carried vibrations. Dane could feel the breeze generated by the train passing by, but there was no train.

He stayed in place until the noises faded down to memories, unaware of the open-mouthed gape he offered the world around him. No train, just the noises and those vanished as the sun set.

"Well, what the blue hell was that?" In counterpoint to his question he heard the sound of the train's whistle cutting a distant, haunted note as it passed the mile marker on Sullivan Street. That, too, was an impossibility. The train couldn't pass Sullivan Street if it never passed his house.

Hercules answered his question with a loud bark and an enthusiastic wag of his tail. No one else responded. Slowly the crickets started to sing again, and the birds let out their evening songs, just as they always had when the train came by toward sunset.

Dane thought long and hard about his options and then went back inside, uncertain of himself.

"Damn it, I can *smell* the train, I know it passed by." He spoke softly, not trusting himself to speak too loudly lest someone else hear him. He was talking crazy and he knew it. It was possible he was losing his senses wasn't it?

It was six hours later when the train came again. This time he had warning. Just as the train's whistle blew after it had come through, it also blew beforehand this time, over at Miller's Pond Road. Just as it had when he was a child.

This time, damn everything, he would be outside before the train came around the bend. This time he'd see it with his eyes, and he'd film it, too. He had no particular love of his smartphone, but he knew how the camera function worked.

Dane was outside and waiting. He heard the sounds, felt the vibrations as the train came closer, and the displaced air brushed past his body as the sounds grew louder still. Midnight and the damned thing was coming around like it had when he was just a kid, back before anyone ever worried about how loud it was or what sort of damage a train could cause if it left the tracks and hit one of the houses in the area.

Dane looked at his phone's face and saw that it was exactly twelve-oh-two. Right on time.

He hit the record function and began filming the area where the train would be if it came through. The massive light at the front of the train cut the night open and bled away darkness as the engine rumbled closer. A sickly yellow glow covered every item the shadows had hidden away, stealing any secrets that might be lost to midnight. The rattle-clack of wheels moving over track was impossible to ignore and Dane held his position, continued filming as the train finally broke into view.

It was all shadows in the cloudy night, silhouettes and darkness that was somehow blacker than the night.

Lord, but he forgot how damned BIG those engines were. This one was no exception. Twelve to fifteen feet in height if it was an inch, and wider than he was tall. The thing lurched forward, hauling its burden as if it might stumble and fall, but it came forward just the same. Fifteen feet from the tracks and it barely seemed far enough. Dane felt a momentary fear that the wind from the train might drag him to the tracks and crush him under the heavy wheels, but he braced himself and kept his phone aimed at the sight of the locomotive pulling, straining with its burden. One car, passed, then two, three...twenty...fifty and then suddenly the thing was past him, the *clack, thunk, clack* of the wheels fading away as it continued to blunder down the tracks.

And then it was gone, the silence a tomb around him as he lowered his phone and stopped filming.

Dane listened for another ten minutes until the distant whistle cut loose with a low, mournful cry and faded into nothingness.

A sad fact of life: It didn't matter how much sleep Dane got, he woke up at six-thirty in the morning. He'd finally managed to wander back to his bed just after two in the bloody A. M. and come the morning he woke up at the usual time, groggy and foggy.

Coffee helped, but not as much as he'd have liked.

The night had been filled with half dreams and recollections. Mostly he dreamed of the train wreck that happened when he was a younger man. He remembered walking the tracks and climbing up to where he could see the wreckage. Just thinking about the devastation made his guts twist around themselves. Seventeen people died in that wreck. He never saw a one of the bodies, but he'd counted the derailed cars and seen the debris scattered from here to perdition.

It'd taken weeks to clean up the mess. Even when the crews were done, old man McPherson found odd bits and pieces for months afterward.

One rail was twisted over itself in the impact. He remembered that, too. He remembered looking at the ruined metal and being stunned by how much force had to hit steel to do that sort of damage. The damned thing was magnetized by the force of the train hitting it. Nails and paperclips that had somehow found their way to the tracks stood out clearly against what was left of the rail.

He couldn't get the wreck out of his mind.

Was that the cause of the ghost train? As he recalled the wreck had happened in October, near the end of the month. There had been discussions about canceling Halloween that year, but nothing had come of it.

Ghost train. When had he decided that was what he was dealing with?

He looked at his phone and the pictures he'd taken. Seen together they showed a cloud sliding along the tracks. Not a storm cloud or anything that clear, more like a shadow passing by. A shadow, moving along the rails in the middle of the night. There was a noise, but it was weak and lifeless, not at all the sounds of a train coming through.

Still, he knew what he'd seen. What he had felt, and smelled, and experienced. It was a train. No doubt of it in his mind. Just not one that everybody could see or hear.

Seventeen dead. The number was there, locked into his mind. Sometimes that thought haunted him. Seventeen lives taken away because of a foolish error. Seventeen lives stolen away because one of the rails was crooked. That had been back when the train came through every day like clockwork. You could set your watch by it.

You could hear it, and feel it, and hate it as much as you wanted, but it was a fact of life in the area. Three times a day, every damned day, the Wickham screamed past the house and offered a *merry get screwed* to anyone who cared to be upset by the notion. Back then the letters to the local papers didn't matter in the least. Like as not, the mayor tossed any complaints into *File Thirteen*, because the railroads provided work and had been running before the neighborhoods got settled. The company paid for the privilege of coming through the area.

The wreck changed that, of course, but it took years for the ripples to be felt. Eighteen years. Seventeen lives. Sometimes he wondered about the peace and sometimes he worried over the dead. It changed from day to day.

Dane spent the day listening for the train. It did not show at two in the afternoon or at six in the evening. Still, as midnight came closer, he knew the damned Wickham Line would be coming through. He felt it in his guts, the same way he could see certain cloud patterns and know there was going to be a helluva storm coming through.

Late October.

How many years had it been, exactly, since the train wreck came along and killed seventeen people? Did anyone remember the disaster? Used to be he could count on an article in the *Post* about it but not the last few years. It was barely a footnote in town. The dead were all just passengers passing through, after all. Hardly like they were locals.

"Why now? Why not years ago?" He climbed out of his recliner and sighed to himself. Did it take time for the dead to manifest? Did they have to make some sort of deal with the devil to even show up in the first place? Was it the devil? Was it God seeking vengeance? He didn't know.

All that mattered was he knew the train was coming again, that the whistle would blow, and the wind would pick up as the weight of the train shoved air aside. The great lamp at the front would put out its leprous light and cover the old, worn down tracks with sickly illumination. The whistle would scream, oh yes, with the voices of seventeen dead people.

He knew it in his heart.

Just like he knew this time things would be different.

It wouldn't matter that he left the rails alone. The damage had been done, oh, so long ago now. Almost long enough ago for him to forget his sins.

Oh, he'd known that the Wickham Line carried people in the evening and in the afternoon, but it was rare for the midnight train to carry live passengers. At least that was what he'd heard. He probably should have checked.

Off in the distance the first wail of the whistle blew. It wouldn't be long now.

Dane stared at the point where the train would show itself, the first cast of pale light was hitting the long grass and the overgrowth now. The ground was shaking with the weight of the engine and the cars that followed along, clacking and thumping their way over rails long since rusted and rotted away. Eighteen years of disuse had certainly taken their toll on wood and metal alike. Hell, just a few months back he'd taken a walk and seen railroad spikes thrusting from the ground where the wood had completely disintegrated. Nothing left in those spots but the powdery remains of wood rot.

Dane liked to think he was a good man, but the reality was he'd planned out the train disaster all those years back. Young and cocky and so sure that the only damage would be to whatever freight was being hauled. He hadn't even considered the conductor when he plotted out the derailment. That should have been enough to stop him. Would have been if he was half as smart as he'd liked to think.

The *clackety-clack* of the train came closer, and Dane felt his hair pushed up by the breeze. The light came around the slight bend and Dane squinted against it.

The great shape of the train was visible even behind that light, a massive thing, bigger than life. Hell, bigger than death for that matter.

Dane stood his ground as the midnight train came around the bend and cut across his lawn, shoving grass and dirt out of its way in heavy waves. The ground shook and the engine thundered, chugging furiously through the forty feet of turf that separated him from the spectral locomotive. He knew that in the morning there would be no sign of the earth being violated by the engine, just as the grass was unbroken on the tracks.

In the distance he could hear Hercules the dog barking and calling out a warning that he did not heed.

All his life he'd never once climbed aboard a train, not even a subway car.

Dane stood his ground and felt his knees shaking. This time, the one time, he would wait patiently.

Seventeen souls demanded no less of him.

LUST FOR LIFE

Errick A. Nunnally

The clothes they gave him felt like paper. Rough, crinkled. They'd taken everything he was wearing, even his underwear. He shifted in his seat, hating the way the material rubbed against his balls, and ran a finger along the inside of the cuff that held him chained to the table.

"You thirsty, Mr. Feldman, can I get you some more water, a cup o' coffee?" Detective Marshfield asked him.

Jack shook his head 'no' while staring into his own eyes in the giant mirror behind the detective. He wondered how many people were watching, plotting how to further ruin his life. Thus far, a long chain of uniformed police officers, technicians, and paramedics had worked hard to build a file on his situation. The detectives were the last stop, if television were any true indicator of how the criminal justice system worked. Managing a national group of regional sales managers wasn't the best way to learn the law. He wasn't guilty, though, hadn't committed any crimes—except adultery—and what the fuck, were people even prosecuted for that anymore? The point was, he figured he was better off without a lawyer, for now.

Because he was innocent and cooperating. That had to matter, right?

"You comfortable, then? We're sorry about the cuffs. Procedure, you know? Just while we set the record straight."

Jack nodded. The fat cop had been treating him well. His

partner, however, was a cold slap to the face, and always to the point.

"Great, good. Ah, here comes my colleague now and we can continue." Marshfield inclined his head, wearing a warm smile.

The other detective, Burrs, came back into the dull room. He was a dark-skinned man with close-cropped hair and round shoulders. He handed Marshfield a folder and traded a look with his partner before sitting down and exhaling deeply. Marshfield opened the folder, flipped through its contents and placed it on the table and shrugged. Burrs' thick cheeks puffed out, turning the Van Dyke he wore from a trimmed oval into a circle.

"Okay, Mr. Feldman, you said you were on the train with a companion, a Miss..." He checked his notes in a small pad. "Valeria Thomarsson?"

"Yeah, that's right, that's what I said. I spelled it, people misspell it all the time, I spelled it for you. I thought you wrote it down?"

The second detective—Burrs was his name—wore a cold look on his face as he showed Jack his notepad and tapped where he'd written the name down. "Amtrak has no record of that passenger on the train."

"But... She bought the tickets."

Burrs asked, "Was that her blood all over your clothes?"

"Some of it, at first." Jack swallowed hard again and felt woozy.

Marshfield smiled and said, "Well, I'm sure that'll all sort itself out as we go down the list and identify everyone who all was on the train."

"In the meantime," Burrs said, "we have *your* name on two tickets. This Ms. Thomarsson of yours is nowhere to be found."

"I—"

Burrs asked, "She your wife, you said?"

"No, we—"

"Then what's your wife think about Ms. Thomarsson?"

"I never said I was—"

"I bet she don't like it," Marshfield said, "I know how that goes."

"She doesn't—"

"You're married, Mr. Feldman. You didn't mention that earlier." Burrs checked his notes again, jabbing his finger in the spot he was reviewing.

Jack's jaw clenched.

Burrs said, "Social media's a hell of a thing, your whole life laid bare. Hell, you don't even have to have an active account."

"Your twins are beautiful, by the way," Marshfield said, "Just gorgeous. How old?"

Jack sucked in a breath to answer.

"Okay, never mind that," Burrs cut him off. "How about you tell us why you were on that train, where were you headed? All that, from the top."

"But, I already—"

Marshfield smiled again and said, "You want to sort this all out, right Mr. Feldman, so we can all go home and the families of those people can put their loved ones to rest? Right? Closure. This is how we do it, we need all the details you can give us. We go over it multiple times to make sure we have all the details right."

Burrs added, "We're still interviewing the other passengers, but none of them were in the sleeper cars with you. The only other survivor from your section, the porter, is still unconscious. What did you do to him?"

Jack swallowed a dry lump in his throat, reminded of the blood, the bodies, and said, "Nothing. I didn't do anything to him, he did that to himself." He sighed raggedly. Everything was coming apart and it had been *so good*. He needed to be clear, to make them understand that he couldn't have done this, that they understood what had happened on the train. He still had time before anyone outside of this room needed to know.

He had to give them more, as unbelievable as *more* was going to be.

⚏⚏⚏

She'd bought the tickets as a surprise. A gift, a bit of fun because she knew Jack was going to have the weekend for a meeting of regional managers in New Orleans. The meetings wouldn't run long and Jack could spend the balance of the time with Valeria. *In New Orleans*. His skin had tingled with the thought for over a week.

Valeria was the best thing that had happened to him in the past year. A chance meeting, in a coffee shop. An invite to lunch. It had been like a dream the first time they had sex. Downtown, a fancy hotel, her treat. She had all sorts of travel points and perks, worked some kind of promotional gig with travel companies, she told him. He didn't pry, it fit the fantasy he was living, this was everything he desired. He'd even dropped fifteen pounds during their time together, the pounds just melted away. A beautiful woman wanted to spend time with him, no strings attached, and he allowed it. Encouraged it. Valeria didn't even require birth control, since she couldn't have children. She made him feel like a king.

Unlike Karen. Supremely fertile and dull Karen. And the twins. Good God, they made him feel like he was suffocating every minute he shared space with them. Marriage was the worst decision he'd ever made, followed by having children. Karen's hips seemed to get wider every year and the kids whinier. He needed a break and damn sure brought home enough cash to have earned it. They'd be fine, they had a grand home, spending money, and whatever else they needed. His time with Valeria was sacred, a welcome respite from the grind.

The train ride would be an overnight. Meaning they had a sleeper car and time to get dinner and a few drinks to prime the pump. Trying not to appear like the stereotypical lunkhead, Jack passed on the steak and ordered skillet chicken with pan sauce. Valeria ordered the prime rib. They'd already had a couple of scotches and she teased him over the meal when it arrived.

She asked, "See something you like?" There was a predatory twinkle in her eye that drove Jack mad and tightened his pants.

"Red meat is the last thing I want that's in my line of sight." He smiled, testing the crispiness of his chicken's skin. Her toes tickled the inside of his calf and it shocked Jack how much she got his engine going. Slim figure, long blond curls, incredible hips, crystal blue eyes, sensuous lips. He couldn't have dreamed for more.

"Have you been to New Orleans before?" she asked.

"Only once. A college trip I barely remember."

Valeria made a distasteful face. "There's so much more to that city." She grinned. "I'll show you a few things. By Sunday, you won't have a care in the world."

From that moment on, Jack's memory got fuzzy. He was so intent on fucking Valeria that not much else mattered. They paid the tab, made their way to the station and onto the train. Escorted by the porter, it was uneventful, routine. He remembered asking after the whereabouts of her bag, but she was coy with the answer, something about being a goddess of travel. Jack dropped it, same as any other question about Valeria's background. Whenever he was with her, it was about the moment. The cabin was relatively small and everything folded or slid against the wall. Jack grinned as he spotted the bucket of iced champagne on a side table. As soon the door to their cabin slid shut and locked, the nightmare began.

No, that wasn't right.

It was intense, sure, passionate even, but the nightmare wasn't immediate. As the train picked up speed, they dove into each other. Jack tried to swallow her tongue before he made his way down her neck, running hands along her taut body, clutching her flesh. She wore skin-tight jeans, the kind with a little Spandex in them. He undid the button and zipper, peeling them down to just below her knees as he knelt, burying his face in her crotch. The train lurched hard and *that's* when the nightmare began.

█▌▌▌▌▌▌█

Marshfield asked, "Do you recall the porter's name, Mr. Feldman?"

"I... Ron, I think?"

"What'd he look like?"

Jack twitched, trying to think past the ugliness of death. "Uh, light-brown skin—not dark like you—"

Burrs pinned Jack with a hard stare.

Jack stuttered. "I—"

"Now, now," Marshfield said, looking from Jack to Burrs. "Let's remain calm. Please, continue, Mr. Feldman."

Jack looked from one detective to the other before

continuing, "Uh, balding, a little thick around the middle, mustache...."

"Anything else?"

"No, I don't think so. The uniform, I guess."

"Did you see anyone else on the way into the train?"

"Uhm... No—yes! There was that other guy who took my bag, a white guy, thin, clean-shaven. He had the, uh, the vest? He was wearing just the uniform vest, shirtsleeves, no jacket."

"Okay," Marshfield said. "Good, that's good. So, the porter escorts you to your car, shows you the room. Anyone else around?"

"Not really. I mean, there was someone in the room diagonal to us, a family. We didn't talk." An insistent sorrow pulled at Jack's face as he tried to bury the memory when he did meet what was left of them.

Both Marshfield and Burrs nodded, taking notes.

Burrs said, "So, you're getting heavy with Ms. Thomarsson—who does not seem to exist—"

"She *exists* and you need to *find* her!"

"Okay, easy, Mr. Feldman," Marshfield put his meaty hands up: one towards Jack, the other to restrain his partner. "Go on, tell us the rest."

Jack toppled toward Valeria, throwing his weight into her pelvis. Off balance, she went backward. Her arms flailed and found no purchase in the tight space. The back of her head caught the corner of the table bolted to the floor, knocking her unconscious.

The sound shocked Jack. Her body went limp and her head slid between the table and door. The next sound was like breaking off a turkey leg as her neck broke. Jack felt a stab in his heart.

His guts demanded to be emptied, but he choked the vomit back. She lay at a disturbing, unnatural angle. Jack lurched to his feet and stifled a scream, knowing he'd throw up if he put his diaphragm to work like that. He heaved once and regurgitated everything anyway. Turning his head, he choked on the stream, and struggled to regain control.

Valeria was dead, no question. He could see that, didn't need to feel her pulse or hold a hand in front of her mouth to check for breathing. There was a patch of blood on the edge of the table and a pool spreading beneath her head. Jack rinsed his mouth in the small sink and clutched at his hair.

A jumble of thoughts bounced around inside his skull. This would ruin his life. He had to keep it quiet, no one else *needed* to know. It was an accident, he hadn't meant to knock Valeria over, it just happened. He'd need help, though, someone to move Valeria's body, at least, and clean up. *The porter.* Jack thought maybe he could pay him a little something to keep the matter quiet. Sweat ran down his neck and the smell in the small room overwhelmed him. He yanked the door open.

Quiet and empty in the passageway.

Valeria's blood spread farther. Jack stepped out of the room, his head swimming with alcohol vapors. The dining car was closed, so he went the opposite direction, through the next sleeper car, toward baggage.

As Jack neared the end of the car, the porter appeared, took one look at Jack and asked, "Are you all right, sir?"

Jack, desperate to sober up, ran one hand roughly over his face and into his hair. "I'm okay, but I need your help. My girlfriend. She fell and..."

"Okay, okay, let's go. Let me by and follow me."

"Yeah, listen, this situation, it doesn't need to be a big deal."

The porter glanced over his shoulder, a skeptical look on his face. "Okay, sir. Let's just take a look."

Together, they headed back to Jack's cabin. The porter came up short several feet before their destination and muttered, "Jesus Christ."

A half circle of puddled blood had leaked across the passage, drag marks marred the flow. They led from the cabin towards the darkened dining car.

Jack could see smears of blood on the walls and floor and his mind scrambled. *What the hell?*

The porter eased over to the door, tiptoeing around the marks on the floor and carefully slid it open. He covered his nose at the stink of vomit and blood before he straightened to face Jack. "This isn't some kind of prank, is it? I ain't got no patience for that sort of thing."

Jack peered over the porter's shoulder. The room was empty. No body. He looked into the porter's eyes. "No, no, not a prank! She was... She was on the floor, her head, her neck... It was fucking awful. Now—now it...looks like...someone *took her body*." Movement caught Jack's eye through the glass of the door to the dining car. "There! Holy shit, I saw someone."

The porter glanced over his shoulder. "Stay here, I'm going to call this in, then we'll sort it out."

"Is that necessary?"

The porter stared ice into Jack's soul before turning to walk towards the other end of the car, straddling the drag marks on the floor. "Stay *there*, sir."

As the porter duck-walked, he kept glancing back at Jack who did his best to assure the man he'd stay put. At the end of the hall, the porter peeked around the corner before stepping into the alcove. He picked up the phone and punched a few numbers, eyeing Jack the entire time.

Behind the porter, the door opened with a bang. The man disappeared into the darkness of the dining car and the door slammed shut, severing the wire to the phone. It happened fast and clean.

Jack's pulse ramped up and his muscles tensed. There'd been no time to call out a warning or react. He heard a muffled scream and a scrabble. Jack ran to the door, forgetting about the blood on the floor. The porter's ruined face smashed into the glass. Jack made terrified eye contact with the man before he disappeared, leaving a slick of dripping blood.

Jack recoiled and squirmed in place, standing a foot from the door, unable to think. He waved his hands, feckless and impotent, before gurgling out a rough syllable of shock. Something killed the porter. It killed the porter and it took Valeria's body and he was certain that he was next.

▦▦▦

"So you saw the killer?" Burrs asked.

"No, just a shadow." Jack held his palms up on the table.

"And there was no one else in the hall?" Marshfield asked, "No one peeking out their door at all this commotion?"

"No, I... It wasn't noisy, just a little thumping. I doubt anyone inside a cabin could hear any of it. But, this thing—"

"The killer," Marshfield said.

"Right. Yeah. They—"

"'They'? The killer was—what—nonbinary, trans, gender fluid? You know that, but you didn't *see* them?" Burrs asked.

"Hang on, partner, let him tell his story. I'm sure he'll get to that part. Right, Mr. Feldman?"

Jack nodded a little too vigorously and continued.

Jack couldn't breathe. He felt vulnerable in the hallway, like someone was about to stab him between the shoulder blades. His entire body itched and he stared at the bloodied glass in the door.

A face, tinted red, peered at him then disappeared.

Jack yelped and jumped into his room, sliding on blood and vomit. He spun, pinwheeling his arms, and slammed the door shut. He locked it and it felt right, he felt safer. All that could be heard was the roar of the train and nothing else. He stood there, listening for the longest minutes of his life before he eased into the remaining, clean seat.

The door thumped and rattled. Jack jumped like a startled cat. It went quiet again for a few seconds before he heard metal screech and glass shatter. There were screams, high pitched and ragged. What sounded like sandbags being tossed against the walls came to his ears. Then nothing. He curled into himself and covered his head, trying to bring calm back into his world by sheer will.

The train roared on and Jack remained still.

Water had condensed around the bucket of ice and pooled on the small table. A tiny rivulet slid down the side, through the blood. He found it hypnotic to watch. Each small drop spattered in the pool of ichor spreading into the cabin from under the door.

Blood was coming *in*.

"Hang on," Burrs said. "Are you saying that you were inside your cabin the entire time the murders were committed?

That's your story?"

Jack blew out a ragged breath and sat back. He shrugged as much as he could while chained to the table. "It's the truth."

"The blood was coming in but you didn't stay in the cabin, did you?" Marshfield asked.

Jack clenched his teeth and said, "No. I didn't."

┅┅┅┅┅

The red pool of someone's life crept farther into the cabin. Jack raised his feet and cringed. The scent in the cabin clung to his skin and hair. His nerves jangled and Jack squirmed in place. *Get out,* the only thought he could have. *Get. Out.*

The train eased into a turn and the puddle rippled towards him. Jack's jaw chattered and he braced both of his palms against his face to stifle the involuntary action. He took a deep breath, regretted it, and stood up on the seat to brace his hand against the overhead bunk. Then he placed one foot on the sink and reached for the door frame. When he shifted his weight forward, his foot slipped off the sink.

Both of his feet splashed in blood. Gagging, Jack froze, struggling with himself. For several long seconds, he worked to unclench his body and slow his breathing. In a slow, delicate motion, he put one of his hands on the door's latch and gently unlocked it. The clack came loud to his ears. Sweat dripped into his eyes. Stillness. Nothing. He looked down at the blood swirling around his feet and released a shuddering breath he didn't know he was holding.

Jack eased the door open. The smell of viscera overwhelmed him and he gagged. The porter lay like an emptied rag doll across the doorway, his remaining three limbs at unnatural angles. His face was a mangle of gouges, a large chunk missing from the back of his head. Jack stepped gingerly over the dead man, desperate to not walk through any gore. The walls were spattered and smeared with bits and pieces of chum, unrecognizable as human. The cabin diagonal to his was open, the aluminum door bent inward. He glanced in the other direction, toward the dining car. Its door was closed, the window still bloody.

The train rocked, a gentle sway along the tracks. Jack eased his way towards the next sleeper car, peeking through the glass in the sliding door. He saw more carnage down the passage. A few broken doors leaned into the aisle and glass littered the floor along with the bodies. Every cabin hadn't been occupied, so there wasn't as much death as there could have been. The realization didn't comfort Jack. He looked back toward the dining car, where the porter had been killed and discarded.

Which way should I go?

He minced back to the dining car door and peeked through the bloody window. The car was dark and empty, no movement. Looking down, he could see a woman's shoe, speckled with dark bits.

Valeria's body was likely on the other side of the door.

"All that blood… This all started when I killed Valeria. What if this is my fault?" he whispered to himself. "No, I didn't kill her, it was an accident."

He had to get out. There'd be more people in coach and other classes, on the other side of the dining and lounge cars. Jack eased one hand into the latch and pulled. The door didn't budge. He tried again, harder. No motion. It wasn't locked, it was jammed. He looked more closely and saw the dent, how it was wedged in place. He couldn't get out.

"Oh, shit, no one can get in." A wave of despair pushed him

into a squat. Jack held his breath and groaned, holding the sides of his head.

Maybe the monster was nesting in the dining car. Maybe it was sleeping, waiting to come back and finish the job. He had to go the other direction, toward baggage.

Jack clenched his teeth and started toward the front of the train, picking his steps carefully, desperate to minimize any noise. The lights flickered and the squeal of wheels on rail startled him to a halt. He took a deep breath and continued, willing himself not to look at the mess in the adjacent cabin. A glance confirmed that he shouldn't have looked. He eased the door to the next car open and slipped through. In between cars, the air was fresher, if tainted with the scents of heavy machinery. He slipped through the next door. The coppery stink floating in the atmosphere motivated him and he moved more quickly, avoiding anything but a glance into the torn open cabins. His feet crunched through glass and he stepped as carefully as he could over the bodies protruding into the tight passageway. Ten feet ahead, baggage awaited.

Someone coughed.

"So someone was still alive when you tried to leave?" Burrs wore a derisive look on his face as he stared at Feldman.

Feldman gulped and opened his mouth twice before any words came out. "Yes. She, uh…"

Marshfield asked, "The mother, you mean, and her child?"

Jack nodded, looking over Marshfield's shoulder, into the two-way mirror.

"Can you describe them?" Burrs asked.

"I can." Jack broke. He'd held it together this long, fearing for his future, his fortunes. But his future had been foretold and he wasn't sure he could hold back the fear anymore. He choked off the sobs, but hot tears overflowed his eyes. The memory was something he wanted buried. It would mean living it again. He knew that it was going to look bad, the decisions he'd made. These detectives were hard men, however, they *should* understand.

"C'mon, Mr. Feldman," Marshfield said, "you can do this."

Jack kept both eyes on his own ugly face in the mirror and nodded.

The woman at Jack's feet had been crippled. She coughed again, struggling to form words. Air came in tiny gasps as she stared at Jack with one good eye. Her other eye was half out of the socket in the center of a bruise covering half her face. Cuts and disarray dotted her body and clothes. She had a mother's outline, red-brown hair, and eyes to match.

She reminded him of Karen.

Jack squatted and tried to shush her, not wanting to draw attention. He leaned into the cabin and put his ear as close to her as he could without settling in blood and glass.

She ground out two words, "My daughter," before breathing out her last word, "Please." After that effort, she went still, all of the tension of life gone from her ruined face.

Jack let out a long, wavering breath, not wanting to follow his ears, refusing to look. He pressed his fingers into his closed eyes, trying to convince himself not to look, to not hear the tiny, panting breaths. He did anyway, his gaze tracking along the floor, into the cabin from which the mother sprawled.

The girl was on the floor, staring up at the ceiling. Like her mother, she struggled to breathe and, like her mother, had the same auburn hair and eyes. The same as his wife and his children. Jack watched her chest rise and fall like a rabbit's. Young life was relentless, stubborn. The little girl lay broken, though, punctured and pale and broken.

"I can't help her," he whispered to himself, "there's nothing I can do." He nodded, speaking more to himself than the woman, agreeing with his assessment. He eased out of the cabin and hauled himself to his full height.

"What the fuck have you done!?"

The panicked shout startled Jack bad enough that he jumped into the wall. The baggage porter—pale, reedy, wearing a red vest and shirtsleeves—stood several feet inside the car, his entire body reflecting a turmoil of emotions.

█▌▐█▐█▌▐█

Burrs asked, "The porter saw you?"

"I mean, yeah, he scared the shit out of me," Jack said.

"Because he'd seen what you did?" Marshfield's eyebrows crept up.

"No! I meant: he saw me, but I hadn't done anything. He just...startled me."

Burrs leaned forward. "So why'd you coldcock him?"

"What?"

Burrs started ticking points off on his fingers. "You were covered in several victims' blood, you massacred eight people—including children—then you invented a woman no one can identify in order to cover your ass, and finally you attempted to murder the only witness to your crimes."

Jack recoiled in his seat. Locked to the table, he couldn't pull much further back. He looked to Detective Marshfield who slouched, arms folded, one hand on his chin. The detective shrugged and raised his eyebrows in a 'what can I say?' gesture.

"I didn't do this!" Jack slammed his palms on the table and kicked his chair into the wall.

Burrs stood.

Marshfield came to his feet too. Unconcerned, he rounded the other side of the table, collected Jack's chair and reset it. "Let's all have a seat and finish sorting this all out. Okay?"

Everyone sat down.

Jack rocked in his seat, the detectives sat like stone gargoyles. Jack looked at the mirror, once again wondering who was watching, what they might be thinking. Knowing he was innocent, he finished his story.

▦▦▦▦▦

"Jesus Christ, you scared the crap out of me, man! I am so glad to see you," Jack said to the younger man. He exhaled in relief. If this kid was alive, then he himself could make it out alive. Jack took a step toward the porter.

The porter tensed. "Hey, you stay away from me, motherfucker!" His wild eyes kept tracking to the carnage around and behind Jack.

Jack tried to reason with the young man. "Hey, hang on, I didn't do this. I know what it looks like, it's awful back there. Listen, we need to find somewhere safe—"

The baggage handler muttered a string of curses as he hopped from foot to foot. He ended with a final curse, turning and running at the same time. He crashed headfirst into the jamb of the door. His limp body rebounded off the opposite wall and crumpled to the floor where his head made a sound like ripe fruit hitting the floor. Blood seeped from a wound on his forehead.

Jack stared, an incredulous look on his face. "Holy. Shit."

The door to baggage slammed open and the thing stepped out of the shadows towards him. It was tall enough that it had to stoop. It was all long spindly limbs and pale skin drawn taught over lean muscle and sharp bones. Everything about it appeared elongated. Its jaw barely held a mouthful of long, sharp teeth and hung down to a bony crest of a chest. Dead eyes like dull, black plums pinned Jack to the floor.

In a motion too quick for Jack to follow, it surged forward and snagged him by the throat. Fingers of long bone compressed his trachea, choking off any screams. Its mouth bore the hot garbage stench of its victims. It pulled him close, teeth tickling the side of his face. Inhaling deeply, it uttered one word: "Jack." The fingers loosened as they shrunk. Its skin gained color as the bones receded back to a form Jack had lusted after for a year. She released him and he dropped to his knees, too distraught to notice the pain.

Jack coughed hard a few times before he could take in enough air to say her name, "Valeria?"

"You do not disappoint, Jack, you really know how to fuck shit up." She cupped his chin and raised his face to look her in the eye.

Jack sobbed, confused, and placed his hands on her hips, caressing her smooth flesh and familiar curves.

With her other hand, she slapped him hard across his face. "This was going to be a lovely weekend ending with your life and a trail of bodies pointing at you, but instead it's all this." She indicated the death all around them.

Jack shook himself. "What...What is this, what's happening?"

"You killed the part of me that's rational, you asshole, my human skin. As a result, I had to massacre all of these people. I was *hungry*." Valeria waved at the train, a sweeping gesture. "What a fucking mess."

Jack trembled and shook his head and wailed, "What the fuck are you?"

Valeria snorted. "Your uneducated ass wouldn't know." She waggled one hand. "You *might* know my mother, she was biblical."

Jack sagged and Valeria snapped her fingers twice in Jack's face. "Focus, Jack. I thought you were a poor excuse for a man before this. Did you really think I was interested in a man like *you* as a companion? I took exactly what I needed from you. Your half of the species is well and truly delusional. Makes it easier for me, though. It would have been simpler to end you and move on once I had everything in place. But now? I think it's more fitting to let you twist on the hook." Valeria shrugged and said, "Good luck with all this."

She moved backward with sickening speed, through the door and into the night. Jack caught a glimpse of her tanned skin disappearing into the darkness as the train hurtled onward.

▓▓▓▓▓▓

"That's it, that's your story," Marshfield said. "To be clear: you had a year-long affair with a supernatural monster-woman that we can't find any record of, accidentally kill her, which somehow kicks off a massacre. Then she decides to stick you with the bill, 'cause you're an asshole, she says."

"*Yes!* That's why you've got to find her." Jack said, dripping with sincerity. He looked back and forth from each detective.

Marshfield and Burrs glanced at each other. Burrs shook his head.

Marshfield said, "Welp, if that's the story, that's the story."

"Exactly," Jack said, "that's what happened." He felt good. It felt right to tell the whole story, to tell it in a way that would make it clear he wasn't at fault.

The detectives stood up and approached Jack from both sides of the table. Marshfield produced a key for the handcuffs and unlocked Jack from the table.

Jack said, "Am I free to go?"

Burrs twisted Jack's arm behind his back and Marshfield answered, "Nope."

The other cuff pinched Jack's previously free wrist. Burrs tightened the manacles to the point that Jack gasped with pain.

Marshfield picked a folder off the table, the same one Burrs had brought in earlier, and flipped it open. Inside, there were several photographs and medical reports. He spread them out. Each one contained a homicide, all men. Each one was messy, just like the train. "We can place you at every one of these crime scenes, Mr. Feldman. Maybe you shouldn't have jacked off after every kill."

Jack twisted feebly in the cuffs, a detective at each elbow. "I don't understand, I didn't--"

"Your sperm," Burrs said, "Mr. Feldman, is present at every scene. Can you explain that?"

Jack sputtered, in response, his memories of Valeria ping-ponging around his skull: I took exactly what I needed from you. Well and truly delusional. I think it's more fitting to let you twist on the hook. Biblical.

"Your killing spree ends here." Marshfield recited Jack's Miranda rights again, for good measure.

Jack went blank, unblinking, not hearing the detective's

drone. From the other side of the glass, he could hear the muffled screams of his wife's wretched voice and the pounding of her fists. She cursed his name.

"You really are an asshole," Burrs said.

COUNTRY OF THE SNAKE

Stephen Mark Rainey

"BEWARE THE DOOM THAT CAME TO EDEN,
THE COUNTRY OF THE SNAKE."

—Engraved on a stone tablet found in the
Chihuahuan Desert, Western Texas, 1896

A faint, distant rumble told the Switchman the train was coming. He plucked his old pocket watch from his tattered vest, noted the hour, and slipped it back.

3:30 p. m.

Right on time.

With a groan, he drew himself up from the wooden bench inside his makeshift shanty. The desert sun pummeled his face like a hot iron fist as he peered around the door and down the tracks. There it was: the faraway plume of smoke in the east, gradually moving closer.

There was never any whistle. No signal of its approach. But it was never a minute early, never a minute late.

Mr. Lancaster's private train.

The Switchman shuffled across twenty feet of sand and gravel to the switch lever. With tough, callused hands, he grasped the hot metal handle, and tugged. With a scrape and a clank, the switch rails slid and locked into position to send the train onto the diverging track. He released the lever and stepped back. The approaching wave of sound swelled and crashed over him.

The huge, black locomotive roared past and veered to the right, onto the northwest track. Apart from the engine and coal tender, there were only three cars. Most times, curtains in the windows blocked any view of the inside. On occasion, though, the Switchman might glimpse a random figure or pair of eyes peering through a murky pane. He never knew anyone on the train. He didn't know Mr. Lancaster or anything about his business. He didn't care.

The Switchman had only one job. To put the train on the right track, and then return the switch to its original position. This was what he did. This was what he lived for.

As the train thundered away into the endless northwestern desert, he took hold of the switch lever and dragged it back to its original position. With what sounded like a sigh of relief, the steel points swung into place.

For a moment, the Switchman peered after the train, as he always did. Only Mr. Lancaster's train ever went that way. Once it diverged onto the northwest track, it might as well no longer exist. He had no idea where it was going. He had never known.

He did not want to know.

The Switchman ambled back to his shanty and sat down on his bench to hide from the blazing day star. In exactly twelve hours, when the desert sun was long asleep, the train would roar through on its way back to Sweetwater. And tomorrow at this time, he would hear the rumbling on the rails, step outside, and throw the switch again.

He leaned back, closed his eyes, and was gone.

The train car had been converted to an opulent office. Looking across the huge mahogany desk, Matthew McBane met Mr. Lancaster's eye and took a sip of the whiskey his new boss had given him. Very smooth, very rich. When he set the glass down, he glanced out the window to his left and noticed a pair of glinting steel rails curling away through the desert. The train had switched to a different track. Curious that there should be a switch out here, in the middle of nowhere.

"Mr. McBane, you are to be one of my personal bodyguards. When I get off the train at Eden, I will need protection."

Lancaster's voice sounded like the deep groan of his train engine starting up. His icy blue eyes didn't blink. Smoke from his thick cigar curled like groping, ghostly hands around either side of his broad, tanned face.

"I thought Eden was back east of here. Not much to it."

"Not Eden, Texas."

"New Mexico, then?"

Lancaster ignored the question. "You have impressive credentials, Mr. McBane. Your references are known to me. I expect you will do a fine job."

"You may count on that, Mr. Lancaster."

"Count, count, count!" The little bald man behind him had a shrill, maddening voice and he rarely shut up. He wasn't exactly little. He just had no legs. "Mr. L. Call him Mr. L."

McBane raised an eyebrow. Lancaster gave a humorless chuckle. "You may call me 'Mr. L,' if you wish. Now. Here on the train, you are free to do as you wish. Once we disembark, you will be at my disposal at all times. You will do exactly what I say, when I say it. You will use those sharp eyes of yours to detect any threat to my being. Should you be instructed to shoot, you will shoot to kill. I trust you have no reservations about the terms of your employment?"

"No, sir."

"Then we may look forward to a long and mutually beneficial business relationship."

McBane smelled the woman's lavender perfume before he felt her hand fall on his shoulder. "It's a long trip," she whispered in his ear. "We have time."

He didn't turn to face her. She glided, snakelike, around his left side and touched his hand with cool fingers. Raven-haired, emerald-eyed, fine-featured, slim. Physically lovely. As appealing to the eye as Lancaster's other subordinate was repellent. She wore a long dress of pale gray satin. He detected amusement in his employer's gaze.

"Mr. McBane, meet Miss Rosa Starling." When Lancaster smiled, his bright, perfect teeth glistened like ivory. "For now, you are dismissed. Feel free to enjoy Miss Starling's company until I call for you."

McBane nodded, rose from his chair, and turned to the woman. "So, Miss Starling. Something tells me you'd be interested in a drink."

"A drink?" She appeared to ponder the idea. "Oh, very well."

"I'd like a drink!" came the legless man's shrill voice. "Will you buy me a drink?"

McBane glanced down at the poor creature. His cloudy eyes, droopy jowls, and gray beard made him somewhere around fifty. Most likely, he'd lost his legs in the War Between the States, some thirty years back. His hips rested on a metal contraption with wheels, the whole business apparently strapped to his lower torso. His upper body arched forward, propped on two muscular arms. His disproportionately large hands grasped a pair of short wooden crutches, which he used to propel himself forward and backward. McBane couldn't imagine what use Mr. Lancaster might have for him.

"What's your name, soldier?"

A broad smile turned the man's ugly face even uglier. "William Winkler. That's *Sergeant* Winkler, to you. Remember that, Mr. Man."

"At ease, Sergeant." McBane stepped past him with Rosa Starling in tow. The train car swayed ever so slightly as it sped into the west, the wheels rumbling and ringing in a mechanical symphony. He tugged open the connecting door between cars and stepped onto the narrow metal plate above the coupling. Here, the clatter of wheels and angry *chuff-chuffing* of the steam engine assaulted his ears. Deafened, he led Miss Starling into the next car, which contained the staff quarters. When he slammed the door behind him, the harsh clamor softened to a mellow, rhythmic chugging.

The narrow corridor led to four closed doors in succession. The first of them opened to his cozy berth, which contained a cot, an armoire just large enough to hold a change of clothes, a few shelves for his personal items, and a small desk and chair. Outside the window, the endless sands of the Chihuahuan Desert rolled past like a vast, golden sea. Countless miles distant, a huge mesa dominated the skyline, a titanic castle of the dead. The desert played host to a great many dead.

Miss Starling followed him inside and scanned the compartment. "Yours is larger than mine. But mine is happier."

On the desk, a bottle of expensive whiskey, compliments of Mr. Lancaster, waited for him. McBane grabbed two tumblers from the shelf above the desk, half-filled both of them, and handed one to the young woman. "So, Miss Starling, what is it you do for the man behind the big desk?"

She took a small sip, touched the tip of her tongue to her lips, and smiled. "I don't kill people."

"Are you sure?"

"Very." She gazed at him with eyes of green fire. "How many men have you killed?"

"A dozen or so." He gave a wry chuckle. "I don't keep a close count. Could be a few more. Or a few less."

"Only for money?"

"Not always."

She stepped close to him. "What, besides money, would drive you to kill someone?"

He answered honestly. "Being a worse monster than I am."

"Are you a monster?"

"Some say."

McBane went to the armoire and took out his small travel bag, which he had yet to unpack. From it, he drew a large, folded paper, gingerly opened it, and laid it on the desk. It displayed a photographic image of a man with a thin, chiseled face, narrow eyes under sharply angled brows, and a dark, ragged beard. The text read, "WANTED—DEAD OR ALIVE—JAMES "STINGER" COREY." The reward for his capture or killing was a generous $2,000.

"Have you seen this man?"

Miss Starling's eyes turned wary. "You know that Mr. Lancaster demands total loyalty. He does not look kindly on—shall we say—side ventures. You'd best not let him see that."

"Noted. But have you seen him?"

She didn't look at the poster. "No."

"Are you sure?"

"Very." She sighed and glanced out the window. "Wouldn't you like to know something about where we're going?"

"Eden." He shrugged. "What is there to know?"

"It's not like anyplace you've ever been before."

He killed his drink. Then he reached into his vest pocket, pulled out a cheroot, and lit it. "I've been to a lot of places."

"Not like Eden." She tossed back the rest of her whiskey and gazed at him. He intentionally took no notice, so she poured herself another glass.

He regarded the image of Stinger Corey for a moment before refolding the poster and putting it away.

His brother.

Miss Starling had either not noticed or simply ignored the obvious resemblance between the two men. He guessed the latter. McBane was no more his real name than Lancaster was the train man's. He had used the alias for so long he sometimes forgot he had stolen the name from a dead man.

"How far is it to Eden?"

"We'll be there at sundown."

He chewed on his cheroot. "So, our Mr. Lancaster needs protection. Frankly, he looks like a man who can take care of himself. Must be a dangerous town."

"You could call it that."

"Well. You wanted to tell me about it. Go ahead."

"In Eden, Mr. Lancaster is, you might say, the boss. Your job is to make sure he stays boss. But there are many who would like to have that title. You will meet some of them."

"Is that why you asked how many men I've killed?" He touched the handle of his custom Army Colt . 44 and smiled at her. "Are you concerned for my welfare?"

Her eyes went to the window again. He followed her gaze and saw the sky had darkened. It was still a couple of hours till sundown.

Curious.

"The only welfare I'm concerned about is mine," she said in a flat voice.

"A woman after my own heart," he said. He unbuckled his holster and draped it over the desk chair. Then he reached out and touched the collar of her dress. "I'm going to make myself comfortable. Are you?"

She smiled at him. "I thought you'd never ask."

He glanced out the window one more time, shrugged at the darkening sky, and snuffed his cheroot in his empty whiskey glass. He drew the heavy shade over the window, and an almost opaque shroud fell over his berth. In the new darkness, his hand reached out and touched Miss Starling's.

She had fallen asleep and lay with her back to him. It was close quarters in the cot, but her body felt good.

The rhythmic clatter of the wheels on the rails lulled him, and he felt physically comfortable for the first time in a long time. Only murky, copper-colored light oozed around the edges of the window shade. It couldn't be long before Mr. Lancaster summoned him. Best to get moving.

Taking care not to rouse Miss Starling, he pulled himself upright, retrieved his clothes, and got dressed.

With his .44 in hand, he knelt by the cot and considered the shadow-draped figure. Had she known his brother? Slept with him? Of course she had claimed not to know him. He touched the cold steel barrel to her cheek. She stirred but didn't awaken.

Perhaps he would kill her. And Lancaster—or whatever his real name was—if McBane should determine his brother was dead and they had anything to do with it.

He knew James had boarded this train three months earlier. A hired gun, same as he. Probably recruited by the same mysterious character: a one-eyed gambler who had slipped a gold piece into his hand in an Abilene saloon. His brother accepted it because he needed work. McBane because he had *allowed* himself to be found, so he might discover what had become of James.

Good with a knife, his brother was. Hence "Stinger." But he did love his pistols; perhaps too much. Once he drew, James cared little for who ended up in his line of fire, even when his purpose was righteous. So he ended up with a price on his head.

James's trail had ended at this train. McBane had nothing more to go on than his gut, but he trusted his gut implicitly. That was how he had survived so long in this business. His gut told him that his brother no longer dwelled among the living.

He reached across Miss Starling's sleeping figure and lifted the window shade.

His blood froze.

The sky had become a dome of liquid fire, the desert sands an expanse of pure, black tar. Towering stone mountains, tinted crimson and violet, protruded like jagged teeth from the nightmarish landscape. Far away, among the dark crevices between the huge peaks, an array of flickering golden lights suggested the presence of a town. The train track, unseen amid the inscrutable shadows, was apparently curving toward the lights in the valley.

Eden?

McBane perceived a presence close at hand, and he swung around with his Colt ready to greet any trespasser. To his shock, darkness swelled like a thick, living substance in the small compartment. He didn't see anything or anyone—until a tendril of reddish light crept through the window and fell on a homely pink face, which floated in midair a few feet away. The once-murky gray eyes glowed like turquoise-tinted lanterns in the uncanny black space. "Mr. L. will see you now," came the shrill, strident voice.

The dull light expanded to reveal the legless man's figure hovering several feet above the floor. A grotesque grin split his face; a deep gash drawn with a knife across a rotten cantaloupe.

This had to be a dream or a vision. Not reality.

"Waste no time!"

The grinning lips had not moved.

His hand *wanted* to lift the gun, point it at the grinning horror, and pull the trigger. But some tingling sense warned him that, if he did, something far worse than this would happen.

The door to his berth opened inward. The floating horror turned in the air, drifted into the corridor, and vanished. The door drew itself closed.

"I told you Eden is like no other place."

He turned to see Miss Starling propped on one elbow, her lovely features brightened by an amused smile.

"This can't be real," he said, looking past her at the warped, black-and-blood-colored landscape. "*Is* this real?"

"You don't want to keep Mr. Lancaster waiting. He detests tardiness."

He glared into her mocking eyes. "Who *is* Mr. Lancaster?"

"Your employer," she said in a sharp, severe voice. "And you have a job to do. "

His instincts goaded him to shoot everyone on the train, including the woman, hop off, and take his chances with the desert. Except that, outside, the desert no longer existed. He holstered his Colt, turned his back on Rosa Starling, and went out to the corridor, leaving her in the chamber of swirling, unnatural darkness.

He started to open the door to Lancaster's car but stopped

short. If only for a moment, he would have to go *out there*, and the prospect chilled him. How many guns had he faced in his lifetime, only to be stricken with dread by the prospect of reality gone totally insane?

He drew himself up, pulled open the door, and stepped onto the iron plate above the coupling. He lowered his eyes, focused on the sandblasted metal surface. The familiar roar and clatter of the wheels on the rails offered a moment of reassurance. Of resolve. He turned to gaze at the landscape speeding past the train.

Black, tar-colored sand. Gleaming, purple towers whose apexes pierced angry red clouds roiling with flame. Now he could make out vague, black-winged shapes whirling around the spires like ravenous birds of prey. That he could see them from such a distance meant they had to be gigantic.

Monstrous.

It was enough. He turned away, opened the door to Lancaster's train car, and stepped inside.

"Ah, there you are," came his employer's grating voice. "You are forty-two seconds late, Mr. McBane. Or shall I call you Mr. Corey?"

Lancaster's presence brought back clarity. Whatever was happening out there no longer mattered. Only what happened in here.

"So you know my name."

"I know everyone's name."

He shrugged. "Then I'm sure you know my brother, as well. Or knew him."

The icy blue eyes and gleaming white teeth shone in the gloom surrounding Lancaster's huge desk. "He came into my employ as willingly as you did—though your motive was less honest."

"Is he still alive?"

"If you wanted to see him, all you had to do was ask."

"So, I assume that means he is in Eden." He motioned to the windows. "Tell me, Lancaster. What is this place?"

From the case on his desk, Lancaster took one of his big cigars, clipped its end, and spent a long, leisurely time lighting it. After blowing a billow of smoke huge enough to have come from the train's smokestack, he made an expansive gesture. "It is mine, Mr. McBane. I have overseen this land, shaped it, for far longer than your mind could grasp."

McBane felt a shift in the train's momentum. It was slowing down. From the engine, the sharp scream of the whistle slashed his eardrums.

"We'll soon arrive at our destination. Mr. McBane, for as long as I have been administrator of this territory, I have been forced to defend my position. Perhaps this surprises you. But thanks to the efforts of men such as yourself, I have always prevailed, and I intend to continue to do so."

"Forget it, Lancaster. You can tear up our contract. Whatever this is, I'll have no part of it."

Lancaster offered him a sympathetic frown. "I understand your trepidation. But I am afraid that is impossible. Once you have signed on, the contract is unbreakable."

"The hell with that." McBane's right hand went for his . 44. But rather than the solid handle of his gun, his fingers fell on cold, scaly flesh. He spun around and found himself regarding the gray-eyed, scowling face of Sergeant William Winkler, the legless man, again hovering above the floor as if suspended by invisible cords. Winkler drew his hand away from the gun and waggled his finger before McBane's eyes.

"No way out for you!" the thin voice screeched. "No way out. Not ever!"

McBane took a shocked step backward. His eyes shifted to the horrid landscape, now creeping past the windows as the train slowed. He took a moment to regain his composure. Then he turned to face Lancaster once more.

"I must be mad. Or dead. Am I dead, Lancaster?"

"Whether or not you are mad, it is not for me to say. But you are most assuredly not dead."

A gust of fetid breath brushed McBane's ear as the floating man leaned close to him. "Not yet."

"Then this can't be Earth."

"Oh, it is Earth. But not the one you know." Lancaster's brilliant blue eyes turned frigid. "Have you read your Bible, Mr. McBane? Yes? Then you are surely familiar with the story of a great war in the kingdom of heaven. It's a very old tale, and not a very good one. But, like all such stories, it contains an element of truth. Perhaps you'll recall that, at the end of this war, the earth became the province of 'the fallen. ' But even as it happened in heaven, discord has always festered in this province. You see reflections of this chaos in your own world."

"Then I will ask again. What *is* this place?"

"Did you think that, after man lost the Garden of Eden, it would remain empty? To wither, perhaps? No, it became ours. Here, in the reality just *beneath* yours." Lancaster paused and clicked his tongue. "The reality that *was* yours. Once you have left it, you do not return."

Outside, creeping black shadows obscured the fiery sky. The train jerked to a stop.

McBane gazed at the blackness—so like the organic blackness that had earlier filled his compartment. "If I weren't seeing *that*, I would say it's you who is mad."

"But you are seeing it." Lancaster jammed his cigar into the ashtray on his desk. "And now, Mr. McBane, it is time for us to depart."

"Wait." His throat had become sandpaper, and he suddenly craved a drink of water. "My brother. James. You said—"

"You would like to see him?"

He nodded.

"Then see him you will."

He smelled lavender perfume, and he swiveled to find Miss Starling standing before him. She once again wore her gray satin dress. For a second, she glanced past him, at Lancaster. Her face remained impassive. But then she smiled at him.

"I will escort you from the train. I'm sure a familiar presence will help put you at ease."

She leaned forward to kiss him. Their lips touched, and he felt her tongue probing for his. Then, with a gurgling cough, he pulled away from her—or tried. Her embrace had become a steel vise.

Her cool, smooth tongue delved deeper. Its tip was forked.

"Matt!"

He barely made out the voice above a strange, warbling, roaring sound. The voice sounded familiar.

"Matthew!"

James.

"For God's sake, wake up!"

Consciousness flickered in and out, like the sun beyond a wall of trees as viewed from the windows of a speeding train. As his eyelids creaked apart, he discerned only a vague, shifting chiaroscuro, as if he were seeing moving images through a cracked, murky lens. His lips felt dry, his throat arid.

At first, he couldn't feel his arms and legs.

"Matt. You have to shoot."

The swirling panorama crystalized, became so sharp and clear he wanted to clench his eyelids shut again. But he could not.

Against the fiery sky, he saw distant purple and black towers standing out like jagged, broken teeth from inflamed, bloody gums. As he had from the train, he made out formations of huge, bat-like shapes whirling around their daggerlike apexes, and from across that vast distance came faint but sharp, keening cries, like the screams of whores trapped inside a burning brothel. Closer at hand, a thick brown cloud blanketed the tar-black sands, and within its depths, a row of tall, spindly shadows whirled and lurched like insane dancers to the strains of a mad, thunderous ballet. One by one, the shadows emerged from the whirling dust cloud and assumed solid shapes.

"Ready yourselves and prepare to fire!" came a familiar, screeching voice.

McBane twisted his head to his right and saw his brother—or what had once been his brother—encased in some hellish steel construct, his outstretched arms ending not in hands but long, glittering metal tubes.

The barrels of some unfathomable—*unthinkable*—guns.

As did his own.

"Oh, my God."

He also stood sheathed in some kind of suit that vaguely resembled an armor-plated human skeleton. His legs disappeared into form-fitting steel pipes, each ringed with sharp metal spikes. His brother James wore a tight crown of protruding silver spikes, and sharp pressure against his forehead and temples told him such a crown encircled his head as well.

James's red-rimmed eyes rolled toward his. "We can't let them through," came his low, gravelly voice. "We have to shoot them."

A floating, legless silhouette rose into view just beyond his brother. "Ready!"

The things emerging from the dark cloud might have once been human. But they stood at least twenty feet tall, their naked bodies weirdly elongated, their flesh black and scorched. A dozen of them, all tramping toward James and him. Beyond his brother, he made out of number of other figures, all encased in similar metal exoskeletons.

He had gone insane. Utterly, screaming, horribly insane.

"Aim!"

The monstrous shapes marching toward him froze his blood—or whatever hot fluid now raged in his veins. He saw tiny but blazing red eyes gleaming beneath heavy, arched brows. Arrays of short, spiky horns sprouted from their domelike skulls, which swung back and forth on spindly necks, as if they were maces preparing to clear a path before them.

"Just relax," came James's voice. "The shock will pass. You'll be all right—as long as you stop them."

The legless figure of Sergeant William Winkler came drifting up the line. His gleaming turquoise eyes focused on McBane.

"Fire!"

A *roar-hiss-BOOM* shattered his eardrums. Twin streams of blinding white gold burst from the barrels of his brother's arms. The streams blasted through the advancing giants and shattered their ranks. Those directly in the beams became writhing, roiling towers of flame, which quickly transformed into masses of hot red cinders and then whirls of dissipating black dust. Fire washed over several of the others like a wave of molten lava.

But one of the tall, demonic things was barreling toward him, its fiery eyes drilling like cutting torches straight through to his brain.

"It *will* kill you," came James's voice. "Shoot it. Shoot it now. Just think it. *Will* it!"

McBane *wanted* to destroy the demon. To see it burn, wither, and vanish as the others had.

FIRE.

Some impulse flashed from his brain to his arms. Raw power jolted his entire body, and he felt both his arms recoil. Another white-gold flash erupted before his eyes, and the streams from both barrels engulfed the approaching horror. When the flames died, the demon had vaporized.

Vanished.

"My God, the power," he whispered.

The legless man hovered next to him. He smiled an ugly, encouraging smile. "For the first time in your life, you truly have power."

McBane still stood like a statue. He decided to try moving his legs.

He had barely, consciously willed it before the *armor* lifted his right leg. He took a full step. Another. And then another.

Effortless.

He raised one deadly arm, pointed it toward the distant, swirling dust cloud. More shadows danced in its depths.

Power.

Twin streams of fire ripped into the cloud. The shadows retreated.

"Mr. L. has chosen wisely." Sergeant Winkler's sharp voice sounded proud.

"You'll get used to this," came James's reassuring voice.

"Maybe even embrace it."

With a quick, simple thought, McBane swiveled his armored body 180 degrees. Some distance away, atop a high, stone dais lit by white-flamed torches, Mr. Lancaster sat behind his huge desk. The sapphire eyes gazed approvingly at McBane as he lit one of his big cigars.

His coarse voice drifted across the distance. "And so, Mr. McBane. In the twinkling of an eye, you have been changed."

From somewhere beyond his range of vision, the train whistle blared like a mighty trumpet. He heard a hiss of steam and the grating groan of the engine starting up.

"I think you will enjoy your role as bodyguard," Mr. L. said. "And I think I will be sitting behind this desk for a long, long time to come."

McBane raised one rifle-tipped arm in acknowledgement. He knew nothing of this land, or of his future, but he knew his old life had forever passed into oblivion. And his brother was here.

He could foresee a day when *he* might be smoking a cigar behind that big desk.

He apparently had all the time in the world to reflect on the prospect.

At precisely 3:33 a. m., the train roared through the switch on its way back to Sweetwater. The Switchman poked his head out the door and watched the train lights cut through the desert darkness until they vanished in the distance. The ringing in the rails dwindled and soon fell silent.

The Switchman heard a faint rustle, and his eyes turned toward the tracks, whose rails gleamed faintly under a silver crescent moon.

There they were—the trio of huge black snakes he sometimes saw before or after the train came through. The sound of the locomotive's passing seemed to draw them out from some unknown lair. He had never sought it, much less found it, but he viewed the serpents almost as old friends. Quiet, unobtrusive, benign.

As they often did, the three creatures seemed to peer at him for a time, regarding him as if they were sentient. The eyes of the largest one shone blood red. Another had bright turquoise eyes that seemed to glow from within. The creatures gave him the impression they somehow recognized him.

Perhaps they did.

With a tired groan, the Switchman ducked back into the cool darkness of his shanty. Morning would come early, and with it, the desert heat.

Far away—many miles by now—the train whistle screamed faintly in the night.

A TRAVELER BETWEEN ETERNITIES

Amanda DeWees

She knew from the look on the doctor's face that the news was bad. He straightened, removing the wooden listening tube from her belly, and drew her husband aside.

While she watched anxiously, the two men conferred in whispers. Her husband was so eager for this baby. Indeed, when they had married just a year ago in May 1864, he had joked that one of the best qualities of a wife from a bucolic background was that she would be much healthier and better able to carry children than her London counterparts.

Ruth had thought the remark in poor taste, but she had been so flattered that this financier from the city wanted to marry her that she had dismissed it, as she had done with so many other remarks of his that she told herself were not meant to offend or injure her. Like her brother Frank, who had gone to Canada the year before to work for the Hudson's Bay Company, she was impatient to leave what at the time felt like the stultifying boredom of the farm...but she had not fully understood all that she was agreeing to in giving up her old life.

"You're certain?" came her husband's sharp query, and her breath quickened as she waited for the doctor's reply.

The doctor glanced back at her, drew her husband still further away, and spoke in a low voice. She longed to protest that she deserved to know what he was saying, but she knew that both men would tell her not to worry.

Well, that was futile. She had done nothing but worry for two days, ever since the baby in her womb had ceased moving. At this stage of her pregnancy, she was accustomed to feeling activity from the baby. But then it had suddenly gone still, and when she had summoned the courage to voice concern to her husband, he had brought in the doctor at once.

Now the doctor ended his whispered discussion with Alfred and returned to the bed where Ruth lay, an artificial smile on his face. "Not to worry, Mrs. Whitlock," he said heartily. "I'm sure your baby is perfectly healthy. You must simply rest more and exert yourself less."

Somehow his cheerful manner was less reassuring than if he had shown some concern. It made her suspect he was trying to hide something. "You can tell me the truth, Dr. Price," she said. "I can bear it. I just want to know."

"For goodness' sake, Ruth," her husband snapped. His brows were drawn together, and when he looked at her she saw the anger in his pale blue eyes. "Why would you doubt the doctor's word? He is the one best situated to know all about your condition. But then, perhaps after growing up immersed in animal husbandry you feel you are an expert."

Dropping her eyes, she said, "No, Alfred."

"Very well, then. If I cannot rely on you to listen to Dr. Price, he may have to administer a dose of laudanum. Do you want that?"

She did not need to answer; he did not truly expect her to rebel. The doctor closed his bag and gave her another one of his false smiles. "Be easy in your mind, Mrs. Whitlock. That is the best thing for you and the baby—not to give way to hysteria and irrational fears. I shall look in on you again in a week."

Her husband thanked him, while Ruth struggled not to

speak her thoughts. When the door had closed behind the doctor, Alfred came to stand over her as she pushed herself into a sitting position in the bed.

"Rest," he said curtly. "You heard the doctor." In moods like this his face took on a thin, pinched look, and he looked every one of his five-and-forty years. When they had married, the twenty years' difference between them had hardly been evident at all; increasingly, though, Alfred seemed to look his age.

"What did he really say?" she asked, trying to keep her voice as gentle as possible so that he would not accuse her of being recalcitrant.

Her effort went for naught, though. He glared at her. "Who are you to challenge the word of a doctor?"

"I merely thought that he might have told me what he did to keep me from fretting. If he believes there is something truly wrong, I wish to prepare myself."

"Prepare *your*self! Can't you think of me, Ruth? Everything I have worked to achieve in life means nothing if I have no children to inherit it. That is what makes a man's work worthwhile—the legacy he leaves behind him, the sons to carry on his name." He strode to the door and jerked it open. "What good are you if you cannot bear live children?"

The door banged behind him. Ruth bit her lip to fight back tears. Alfred had such a horror of them that even in his absence she was afraid to give way.

His words, though they might have been motivated by pessimism, seemed to indicate that the doctor had given him bad news. *If you cannot bear live children. . .* Her greatest fear was that the child inside her had already died. She placed her hands protectively over her rounded belly and stared at the portrait of Alfred's first wife, which held a prominent place on the wall. The first Mrs. Whitlock had died during a miscarriage, she knew, after a string of such calamities. For the first time she wondered if her death had happened of its own accord or if her husband might have encouraged the doctor to help it along.

She shivered. If only she could be at home once again with her mother—to hear some words of comfort and practical good sense, escape the foul London weather and see the blue skies of Surrey once again, hear only cowbells and the whistling of stable hands instead of the raucous clatter of city traffic. The wild hope came to her that perhaps Alfred would agree their marriage had been a mistake, that the two years could be wiped away, and she could return to live with her family once more.

It was a foolish thought, but it conquered the urge to cry. Perhaps she could arrange for her mother to visit, at least. Did other wives not have their mothers present during their confinement?

"Out of the question," Alfred said when she tentatively voiced this thought that evening. She was taking her meal in bed on a tray at his insistence.

"Why?" she asked.

His pale blue eyes regarded her without tenderness. "The last thing you need is another person underfoot when you should be resting."

"Mother would help me feel more tranquil," she ventured, but he shook his head and checked the time on his pocket watch.

"There is no point in discussing it further, Ruth. I'm off to my club." Dropping a perfunctory kiss on her brow, he departed.

The long minutes alone in her bed gave her a great deal of

time to think, and the idea of going home, at first little more than a whim, set fire to her imagination. Could she make the journey on her own? The next day Alfred would surely be at his office, giving her a certain amount of freedom. Granted, upon his return in the evening he would probably question the servants about her movements—but what if she had already managed to flee the city by then? She had a feeling that if she could reach Surrey before he knew, he would find it beneath his dignity to drag her back to his house.

If he caught her before then, though...

She shivered. It must not come to that.

▓▓▓▓▓▓▓

In the morning she made her preparations with care. After breakfast she told the housekeeper she would be resting and wished not to be disturbed, so she moved about her room as quietly as possible to foster the pretense and prevent any interruption.

She selected her plainest, most ordinary dress, a black merino wool, and a mantle and hat of the same dark hue. Alfred liked her to wear dark colors since they did not show wear as easily and thus could be worn longer. He was wealthy enough to dress her in satin and velvet, but his money was stored up carefully for the children he was determined to have.

Her pocket money, for that reason, was paltry, but she had no expensive pastimes on which to spend it. She counted what she had tucked away, and found a guinea given to her for luck on the occasion of her wedding. It would be more than enough for train fare—particularly since she was not going to purchase a return ticket.

Her gaze swept the room as she stood by the door, poised

to leave. There were few objects of sentimental value here; it occurred to her that her bedchamber might as well have been that of a stranger, so little did it speak of her character or tastes.

Just as well: it meant that she did not have to carry much, and would thus be more inconspicuous. Had her arms been filled with parcels a cabbie might remember her later if Alfred made inquiries. As it was, there would be nothing to distinguish her from other women.

She made her way down the front stair, careful not to make a noise. From the back of the house she could hear chattering and laughter—the servants speaking more freely in the absence of the master. With her heart thudding against her bodice she stole down the corridor to the front door and—with one more glance around to ensure that the house was empty— slipped through it.

Her jubilation lent speed to her steps as she left Alfred's house behind her and waved at a hansom cab. "Waterloo Bridge Station," she told the driver as she climbed in, wondering belatedly if she should have waited for a closed carriage to appear. She felt vulnerable, exposed to view as she was, and drew the veil of her hat down as far as she could.

In part because of the fog, the going was slow, and she fought down alarm as they made their halting way forward. It was already midmorning, and she did not want to spend any more time than necessary on the journey to the train station. "Can we go any faster?" she called up to the driver, and received an unintelligible response.

Then, disaster. While they were halted as another carriage passed in front of them, men's voices came from the sidewalk, and a group emerged from the fog. Dressed in office attire, all strikingly similar except for one pinched, peevish face. Alfred.

Any hope of going unobserved died when his eyes passed over her and then halted. He came to a stop, staring, as two patches of red began to burn in his cheeks.

"Driver, *please!*" she cried, and the cab lurched forward into an empty stretch of road. Alfred's outraged face was swallowed up in the fog.

But he knew now that she had escaped, and no doubt guessed where she was going. Her thoughts darted about frantically. Were it not for the fog and its paralyzing effect on traffic, she could go to another train station, but as it was the journey might take hours. She needed to be on a train, speeding far away from the city.

"Is there a faster way to the Waterloo Station?" she called up to the driver, and received what sounded like "Waterloo, yes, ma'am."

Blessedly, the new route took them out of the worst of the traffic, and soon they were passing through an ornate set of gates into a secluded tunnel entrance that she had never seen before. She disembarked and paid the driver and, greatly relieved, hurried to purchase her ticket.

It was not until this chore was accomplished and she took a seat in the second-class waiting room that she took the time to truly look about her.

She did not have a great deal of experience with London train stations, but this one was still peculiar. A hush hung over the waiting room, and there were a great many people wearing black, clustered together. She ventured out into the corridor and peeped into another waiting room, and to her astonishment it was fitted out with all the accoutrements of a chapel. Surely this was not the Waterloo Bridge station.

She returned to the ticket window. "Are you certain this is the right train?" she asked. "It will take me to Surrey, you said."

The man in spectacles gave her a reassuring smile. "Yes, madam, all the way to Brookwood Cemetery, and then back again this afternoon."

"Cemetery!" she exclaimed.

"Yes, madam. This is the Necropolis Railroad." When she stared at him, baffled, he said with the air of a man who had learned to have infinite patience, "This train carries the departed from the London terminus here, near Waterloo, to the largest cemetery outside the city—and, of course, it carries their loved ones to see them interred."

At first she could only think of how morbid it was for a train to be devoted to only funereal activities. But then she thought of the waiting room and chapel. It was definitely a more soothing environment for the bereaved to await a train than the bustle of ordinary stations.

Of greater immediate importance was that Alfred would surely never guess that she was taking this train. "How many stops does it make?" she asked.

"Just three, madam. The Brookwood station less than a mile from the cemetery, the Anglican cemetery station, and the Nonconformist cemetery station. And of course we only make one journey per day."

So even if Alfred made some wild intuitive leap that led him to suspect what train she had taken, it would be in Surrey before he could board it.

All of her questions must have puzzled the clerk. "Is something amiss, madam?"

"Not at all," she said. Thank heaven the cabbie had either misheard her or mistaken the station in the fog. It felt as though Providence had intended for her to be on this train.

Before returning to the waiting room she took a quick inventory of her appearance. The only bit of color she wore was a cluster of red velvet roses on her black hat. She pulled this off and tucked it into the pocket of her mantle. Now she looked like any other mourner. For the first time since Alfred had sighted her in her cab, she began to relax.

Once the train boarded, however, her brief confidence ebbed and depression crept into its place.

The train car was shabby and worn, clearly past its best days. The clumps of black-clad mourners conversed in whispers, prayed softly, or wept. The sight of so much misery made Ruth feel guilty and aware that she was one of their number under false pretenses.

Eeriest of all, the fog had found its way into the car, and it lay over the floor like a thick mist, so that people appeared to be dissolving at the ankles. A little girl in white drifted from person to person, tugging at a sleeve here, a skirt there, fruitlessly seeking attention. It was a forlorn sight.

Ruth sank into a seat near a window and tried not to let herself be discouraged or disquieted. Out of habit she rested one hand on the curve of her belly and then froze as belated realization struck her.

She had not felt the baby move at all that day. As busy and agitated and active as she had been, if all had been well with the pregnancy she surely would have felt some kicking or the pressure of a small hand or foot, even fleetingly.

Until now she had been clinging to hope that the stillness was temporary, was harmless. But now she was certain. Her baby, without ever having lived in the world, had died.

She squeezed her eyes shut to force back the tears. Then she realized she did not need to hold them at bay.

Surrounded by strangers mourning their own dead, she dropped her face into her hands and let herself weep for her child.

There was a bittersweet comfort in letting the tears flow. She did not have to worry about being conspicuous or unseemly. It was a relief to let the sobs wrack her body until finally they exhausted themselves and, depleted, she sat back against the worn upholstery of the seat and sighed, letting her hands fall to her lap.

Then she started as a small, cold hand slipped into one of hers. She saw that the little girl in white had come to sit next to her, regarding her with a sweetly serious expression that seemed too old for one who could surely be no older than six.

With her unoccupied hand Ruth fumbled for a handkerchief and blotted her eyes. She found a smile for the little girl. "Thank you," she said, in a low voice so as not to disturb the other passengers. "You must have seen that I needed company."

The little girl just gave her a timid smile. Ruth looked at the other passengers, all absorbed in their own grief, and suspected the little girl had felt lonely and left out; the idea of death was probably not yet real to one so young, so she had no reason to weep like the others. Perhaps she found some comfort with Ruth, just as Ruth found some in regarding the elfin little face with its wide eyes and the trusting way she held her hand.

Then, with a little frown of concentration, the little girl reached out with her other hand and touched Ruth's belly. She whispered, so softly that the words were nearly inaudible,

"You had a little girl. But she is gone."

Ruth had hoped for her baby to be a girl, and fresh tears rushed to her eyes. Before she could compose herself to reply, the child whispered, "I could be your little girl."

Ruth gave a shaky laugh and put her arm around the child, who snuggled readily against her. "You may be my little girl for the journey, if you wish," she said. "But I cannot take you away from your real mama and papa."

The child made no response to this, though a forlorn expression flitted across her face. She neither spoke nor moved for the rest of the journey.

Ruth stayed alert for anyone looking for their little girl, but no one seemed to be missing her. Perhaps there was a kind of benign fate in Ruth's being on this train, so that she was able to offer some companionship to the poor child while her family was absorbed in their grief, just as the child's company was bringing her comfort. She thought briefly that perhaps the child, like herself, had boarded the train mistakenly; her attire suggested otherwise, though, since many parents liked to dress their children entirely in white for mourning.

There was a brief stop at the Brookwood Station, where no one disembarked or came aboard, to Ruth's great relief. She could still picture an enraged Alfred storming into the railway car to browbeat her and force her to return home. After that, passengers began to collect themselves for the next stop, gathering overcoats and umbrellas and the like, but still no one seemed to be searching for a little girl, and if a glance happened to fall upon Ruth and her small companion, no one's face lit up with relief or pleasure.

She looked down at the girl, who returned her look with so trusting a face that Ruth's heart gave a pang. "Are you with someone here?" she asked. "Your parents, or relations?"

Without so much as looking around, the child shook her head.

Something was wrong. "Do you know nobody on the train? Perhaps your people are in the first-class compartment, or…?"

Another shake of the head. Ruth looked around in vain for a ticket taker or someone in a position of responsibility. "Do you mean to say that you ride this train by yourself?" she asked.

"Every day." The words were no less certain for being spoken so softly.

"But surely you are missed—are wanted—" She trailed off. It did not seem possible that a child would make this grim journey each day of her own accord. There was the expense, apart from anything else. And surely none of the railroad staff would permit so young a child to travel by herself.

Unless they were unable to see her.

A growing uneasiness tightened the hair at the back of her neck. Was something unnatural at work here? No child dressed all in white would be able to disappear into a crowd of people dressed in black and board the train each day. Once, perhaps, but not as a regular thing. A wild idea came to her of sympathetic clerks and ticket takers deliberately looking the other way, but why would they do such a thing? And how lax or apathetic could her guardians be, to let her spend the greater part of each day in a graveyard?

Growing up in the country, Ruth had learned that there were matters that could not be explained in rational ways. Living very nearly the same way that her ancestors had for centuries, she and her family knew it was impossible to reason away certain things. Like ensuring a good harvest by consulting the phase of the moon before sowing. Like nailing an iron horseshoe to the barn door for luck. Like placating the family ghost when it was noisy and restless by leaving a fresh bundle of rowan and holly in the loft.

The little girl seemed like a mortal child, it was true. She had substance; Ruth felt the weight of her as she leaned against her side, being jarred by the rattling, shaking motion of the train just as Ruth herself was. She did not speak much, and that barely audible, but that could be shyness.

And yet.

Ruth looked again at the child, at her innocent face. "How long have you been riding this train?" she asked, as dread gathered in a pit in her stomach.

The cold hand squeezed hers more tightly. "Come and see," the child whispered.

The train was slowing, and passengers were getting to their feet. Misgivings warred with an instinct that the child meant no harm. Would it be safer not to answer the summons? Then Ruth's glance fell on the slight swell that marked the presence of the too-still child she had wanted so much. If that desire had been thwarted, she had little enough to risk. . . or to wish for. Her future was already a blank.

"Very well," she said, and the child's face brightened with a pleasure Ruth told herself contained no ulterior motive.

No one seemed to notice the child at her side as they descended to the station platform. The station was small, though there was what appeared to be a tea shop, and under other circumstances she would have offered the child something to eat and drink. But the girl was tugging her hand urgently, and they followed the stream of passengers toward the cemetery.

Its vastness filled Ruth with awe. The grassy meadow, as it must once have been, spread as far as she could see. There were monuments scattered about, all looking new, as they must have been less than half a century old, and free of the soot and filth that seemed to begrime every surface in London. It was a peaceful sight. There was little sound as the murmurs of the other passengers receded behind them.

The girl passed between the gravestones without even glancing at them, so certain was she of her objective. The hem of Ruth's skirt was soon damp with dew as she followed her guide, and she was nearly out of breath when the child's footsteps slowed and came to a stop before a simple monument whose inscription was still crisp.

Oliver James Fenton Matilda Jones Fenton
d. November 2, 1855 d. November 2, 1855

Maude Charity Fenton
d. November 12, 1855

Ruth looked at her guide, who gazed at her with solemn eyes. "Maude?" she whispered.

The little girl nodded. Now knowledge unfolded in Ruth's mind of a small family, with only one daughter, who were all stricken with smallpox. The images that came to her unbidden made her heart constrict with pity. Maude's father had gone first, then her mother, and then, after an agonizingly lonely interval, Maude herself. There had been no one left to watch over her. The gravestone must have been the gift of a distant relative—someone, at least, who had not come to keep Maude company in her final illness.

"You had no one to mourn you?" Ruth asked, but she hardly needed the child's answering nod. That was why the girl did not lie quiet in the earth, why she haunted the funeral train. For the past ten years she must have tried to find a passenger who could see her and find room in the midst of their own grief to feel compassion for a strange child.

The cluster of red velvet roses was still in Ruth's pocket, and she knelt to place them at the base of the monument. Closing her eyes, she thought a wish that Maude and her parents would know peace.

When she opened her eyes, there was no sign that the little girl had ever been there. She felt a bittersweet mingling of relief and sorrow. There had been something so sweet and winning about the girl. At least Ruth had been able to help her, and now her spirit had been appeased.

Then, as she started to get to her feet again, there came a strange rush of warmth through her, a kind of tangible glow like sun-warmed honey, which flowed through her limbs and came at last to settle in her womb. She stared down at herself, the sound of her heartbeat loud in her ears—and then she realized it was not one heartbeat, but two.

Holding her breath, fearful to move lest she jar this loveliness away, she kept perfectly still. In time the golden warmth and the double heartbeat subsided. Then, carefully, she got to her feet. When she put a hand to her belly, she felt a kick, strong enough to make her laugh in delight. She looked again at the inscription in the granite.

"Maude," she said softly, and the child in her belly wriggled as if it could hear her.

She shut her eyes, raised her face to the sun, and laughed in joy and gratitude. Then, when she was finally ready to leave this peaceful spot, she walked back toward the station with unhurried steps. No doubt there was an errand boy who could summon her mother to come fetch her home.

From there she knew her family could help her find passage to Canada. Ruth was unafraid of the future now. Far away from her husband she could keep house for her brother and bring her daughter into the world out of Alfred's knowledge—and in complete freedom.

THE LOST SPECIAL

Sir Arthur Conan Doyle

The confession of Herbert de Lernac, now lying under sentence of death at Marseilles, has thrown a light upon one of the most inexplicable crimes of the century—an incident which is, I believe, absolutely unprecedented in the criminal annals of any country: Although there is a reluctance to discuss the matter in official circles, and little information has been given to the Press, there are still indications that the statement of this arch-criminal is corroborated by the facts, and that we have at last found a solution for a most astounding business. As the matter is eight years old, and as its importance was somewhat obscured by a political crisis which was engaging the public attention at the time, it may be as well to state the facts as far as we have been able to ascertain them. They are collated from the Liverpool papers of that date, from the proceedings at the inquest upon John Slater, the engine-driver, and from the records of the London and West Coast Railway Company, which have been courteously put at my disposal. Briefly, they are as follows:

On the 3rd of June, 1890, a gentleman, who gave his name as Monsieur Louis Caratal, desired an interview with Mr. James Bland, the superintendent of the London and West Coast Central Station in Liverpool. He was a small man, middle-aged and dark, with a stoop which was so marked that it suggested some deformity of the spine. He was accompanied by a friend, a man of imposing physique, whose deferential manner and constant attention showed that his position was one of dependence. This friend or companion, whose name did not transpire, was certainly a foreigner, and probably from his swarthy complexion, either a Spaniard or a South American. One peculiarity was observed in him. He carried in his left hand a small black, leather dispatch box, and it was noticed by a sharp- eyed clerk in the Central office that this box was fastened to his wrist by a strap. No importance was attached to the fact at the time, but subsequent events endowed it with some significance. Monsieur Caratal was shown up to Mr. Bland's office, while his companion remained outside.

Monsieur Caratal's business was quickly dispatched. He had arrived that afternoon from Central America. Affairs of the utmost importance demanded that he should be in Paris without the loss of an unnecessary hour. He had missed the London express. A special must be provided. Money was of no importance. Time was everything. If the company would speed him on his way, they might make their own terms.

Mr. Bland struck the electric bell, summoned Mr. Potter Hood, the traffic manager, and had the matter arranged in five minutes. The train would start in three-quarters of an hour. It would take that time to insure that the line should be clear. The powerful engine called Rochdale (No. 247 on the company's register) was attached to two carriages, with a guard's van behind. The first carriage was solely for the purpose of decreasing the inconvenience arising from the oscillation. The second was divided, as usual, into four compartments, a first-class, a first-class smoking, a second-class, and a second-class smoking. The first compartment, which was nearest to the engine, was the one allotted to the travellers. The other three were empty. The guard of the special train was James

McPherson, who had been some years in the service of the company. The stoker, William Smith, was a new hand.

Monsieur Caratal, upon leaving the superintendent's office, rejoined his companion, and both of them manifested extreme impatience to be off. Having paid the money asked, which amounted to fifty pounds five shillings, at the usual special rate of five shillings a mile, they demanded to be shown the carriage, and at once took their seats in it, although they were assured that the better part of an hour must elapse before the line could be cleared. In the meantime a singular coincidence had occurred in the office which Monsieur Caratal had just quitted.

A request for a special is not a very uncommon circumstance in a rich commercial centre, but that two should be required upon the same afternoon was most unusual. It so happened, however, that Mr. Bland had hardly dismissed the first traveller before a second entered with a similar request. This was a Mr. Horace Moore, a gentlemanly man of military appearance, who alleged that the sudden serious illness of his wife in London made it absolutely imperative that he should not lose an instant in starting upon the journey. His distress and anxiety were so evident that Mr. Bland did all that was possible to meet his wishes. A second special was out of the question, as the ordinary local service was already somewhat deranged by the first. There was the alternative, however, that Mr. Moore should share the expense of Monsieur Caratal's train, and should travel in the other empty first-class compartment, if Monsieur Caratal objected to having him in the one which he occupied. It was difficult to see any objection to such an arrangement, and yet Monsieur Caratal, upon the suggestion being made to him by Mr. Potter Hood, absolutely refused to consider it for an instant. The train was his, he said, and he would insist upon the exclusive use of it. All argument failed to overcome his ungracious objections, and finally the plan had to be abandoned. Mr. Horace Moore left the station in great distress, after learning that his only course was to take the ordinary slow train which leaves Liverpool at six o'clock. At four thirty-one exactly by the station clock the special train, containing the crippled Monsieur Caratal and his gigantic companion, steamed out of the Liverpool station. The line was at that time clear, and there should have been no stoppage before Manchester.

The trains of the London and West Coast Railway run over the lines of another company as far as this town, which should have been reached by the special rather before six o'clock. At a quarter after six considerable surprise and some consternation were caused amongst the officials at Liverpool by the receipt of a telegram from Manchester to say that it had not yet arrived. An inquiry directed to St. Helens, which is a third of the way between the two cities, elicited the following reply—

"To James Bland, Superintendent, Central L. & W. C. , Liverpool. —Special passed here at 4:52, well up to time. — Dowster, St. Helens."

This telegram was received at six-forty. At six-fifty a second message was received from Manchester—

"No sign of special as advised by you."

And then ten minutes later a third, more bewildering—

"Presume some mistake as to proposed running of special. Local train from St. Helens timed to follow it has just arrived and has seen nothing of it. Kindly wire advices. —Manchester."

The matter was assuming a most amazing aspect, although in some respects the last telegram was a relief to the authorities at Liverpool. If an accident had occurred to the special, it seemed hardly possible that the local train could have passed down the same line without observing it. And yet, what was the alternative? Where could the train be? Had it possibly been sidetracked for some reason in order to allow the slower train to go past? Such an explanation was possible if some small repair had to be effected. A telegram was dispatched to each of the stations between St. Helens and Manchester, and the superintendent and traffic manager waited in the utmost suspense at the instrument for the series of replies which would enable them to say for certain what had become of the missing train. The answers came back in the order of questions, which was the order of the stations beginning at the St. Helens end—

"Special passed here five o'clock. —Collins Green."

"Special passed here six past five. —Earlstown."

"Special passed here 5:10. —Newton."

"Special passed here 5:20. —Kenyon Junction."

"No special train has passed here. —Barton Moss."

The two officials stared at each other in amazement.

"This is unique in my thirty years of experience," said Mr. Bland.

"Absolutely unprecedented and inexplicable, sir. The special has gone wrong between Kenyon Junction and Barton Moss."

"And yet there is no siding, so far as my memory serves me, between the two stations. The special must have run off the metals."

"But how could the four-fifty parliamentary pass over the same line without observing it?"

"There's no alternative, Mr. Hood. It must be so. Possibly the local train may have observed something which may throw some light upon the matter. We will wire to Manchester for more information, and to Kenyon Junction with instructions that the line be examined instantly as far as Barton Moss." The answer from Manchester came within a few minutes.

"No news of missing special. Driver and guard of slow train positive no accident between Kenyon Junction and Barton Moss. Line quite clear, and no sign of anything unusual. — Manchester."

"That driver and guard will have to go," said Mr. Bland, grimly. "There has been a wreck and they have missed it. The special has obviously run off the metals without disturbing the line—how it could have done so passes my comprehension—but so it must be, and we shall have a wire from Kenyon or Barton Moss presently to say that they have found her at the bottom of an embankment."

But Mr. Bland's prophecy was not destined to be fulfilled. Half an hour passed, and then there arrived the following message from the station-master of Kenyon Junction—

"There are no traces of the missing special. It is quite certain that she passed here, and that she did not arrive at Barton Moss. We have detached engine from goods train, and I have myself ridden down the line, but all is clear, and there is no sign of any accident."

Mr. Bland tore his hair in his perplexity.

"This is rank lunacy, Hood!" he cried. "Does a train vanish into thin air in England in broad daylight? The thing is preposterous. An engine, a tender, two carriages, a van, five human beings—and all lost on a straight line of railway! Unless we get something positive within the next hour I'll take Inspector Collins, and go down myself."

And then at last something positive did occur. It took the shape of another telegram from Kenyon Junction.

"Regret to report that the dead body of John Slater, driver

of the special train, has just been found among the gorse bushes at a point two and a quarter miles from the Junction. Had fallen from his engine, pitched down the embankment, and rolled among the bushes. Injuries to his head, from the fall, appear to be cause of death. Ground has now been carefully examined, and there is no trace of the missing train."

The country was, as has already been stated, in the throes of a political crisis, and the attention of the public was further distracted by the important and sensational developments in Paris, where a huge scandal threatened to destroy the Government and to wreck the reputations of many of the leading men in France. The papers were full of these events, and the singular disappearance of the special train attracted less attention than would have been the case in more peaceful times. The grotesque nature of the event helped to detract from its importance, for the papers were disinclined to believe the facts as reported to them. More than one of the London journals treated the matter as an ingenious hoax, until the coroner's inquest upon the unfortunate driver (an inquest which elicited nothing of importance) convinced them of the tragedy of the incident.

Mr. Bland, accompanied by Inspector Collins, the senior detective officer in the service of the company, went down to Kenyon Junction the same evening, and their research lasted throughout the following day, but was attended with purely negative results. Not only was no trace found of the missing train, but no conjecture could be put forward which could possibly explain the facts. At the same time, Inspector Collins's official report (which lies before me as I write) served to show that the possibilities were more numerous than might have been expected.

"In the stretch of railway between these two points," said

he, "the country is dotted with ironworks and collieries. Of these, some are being worked and some have been abandoned. There are no fewer than twelve which have small-gauge lines which run trolly- cars down to the main line. These can, of course, be disregarded. Besides these, however, there are seven which have, or have had, proper lines running down and connecting with points to the main line, so as to convey their produce from the mouth of the mine to the great centres of distribution. In every case these lines are only a few miles in length. Out of the seven, four belong to collieries which are worked out, or at least to shafts which are no longer used. These are the Redgauntlet, Hero, Slough of Despond, and Heartsease mines, the latter having ten years ago been one of the principal mines in Lancashire. These four side lines may be eliminated from our inquiry, for, to prevent possible accidents, the rails nearest to the main line have been taken up, and there is no longer any connection. There remain three other side lines leading—

(a) To the Carnstock Iron Works; (b) To the Big Ben Colliery; (c) To the Perseverance Colliery.

"Of these the Big Ben line is not more than a quarter of a mile long, and ends at a dead wall of coal waiting removal from the mouth of the mine. Nothing had been seen or heard there of any special. The Carnstock Iron Works line was blocked all day upon the 3rd of June by sixteen truckloads of hematite. It is a single line, and nothing could have passed. As to the Perseverance line, it is a large double line, which does a considerable traffic, for the output of the mine is very large. On the 3rd of June this traffic proceeded as usual; hundreds of men including a gang of railway platelayers were working along the two miles and a quarter which constitute the total length of the line, and it is inconceivable that an unexpected train could have come down there without attracting universal attention. It may be remarked in conclusion that this branch line is nearer to St. Helens than the point at which the engine-driver was discovered, so that we have every reason to believe that the train was past that point before misfortune overtook her.

"As to John Slater, there is no clue to be gathered from his appearance or injuries. We can only say that, so far as we can see, he met his end by falling off his engine, though why he fell, or what became of the engine after his fall, is a question upon which I do not feel qualified to offer an opinion." In conclusion, the inspector offered his resignation to the Board, being much nettled by an accusation of incompetence in the London papers.

A month elapsed, during which both the police and the company prosecuted their inquiries without the slightest success. A reward was offered and a pardon promised in case of crime, but they were both unclaimed. Every day the public opened their papers with the conviction that so grotesque a mystery would at last be solved, but week after week passed by, and a solution remained as far off as ever. In broad daylight, upon a June afternoon in the most thickly inhabited portion of England, a train with its occupants had disappeared as completely as if some master of subtle chemistry had volatilized it into gas. Indeed, among the various conjectures which were put forward in the public Press, there were some which seriously asserted that supernatural, or, at least, preternatural, agencies had been at work, and that the deformed Monsieur Caratal was probably a person who was better known under a less polite name. Others fixed upon his swarthy companion as being the author of the mischief, but what it was exactly which he had done could never be clearly formulated in words.

Amongst the many suggestions put forward by various newspapers or private individuals, there were one or two which were feasible enough to attract the attention of the public. One which appeared in The Times, over the signature of an amateur reasoner of some celebrity at that date, attempted to deal with the matter in a critical and semi-scientific manner. An extract must suffice, although the curious can see the whole letter in the issue of the 3rd of July.

"It is one of the elementary principles of practical reasoning," he remarked, "that when the impossible has been eliminated the residuum, HOWEVER IMPROBABLE, must contain the truth. It is certain that the train left Kenyon Junction. It is certain that it did not reach Barton Moss. It is in the highest degree unlikely, but still possible, that it may have taken one of the seven available side lines. It is obviously impossible for a train to run where there are no rails, and, therefore, we may reduce our improbables to the three open lines, namely the Carnstock Iron Works, the Big Ben, and the Perseverance. Is there a secret society of colliers, an English Camorra, which is capable of destroying both train and passengers? It is improbable, but it is not impossible. I confess that I am unable to suggest any other solution. I should certainly advise the company to direct all their energies towards the observation of those three lines, and of the workmen at the end of them. A careful supervision of the pawnbrokers' shops of the district might possibly bring some suggestive facts to light."

The suggestion coming from a recognized authority upon

such matters created considerable interest, and a fierce opposition from those who considered such a statement to be a preposterous libel upon an honest and deserving set of men. The only answer to this criticism was a challenge to the objectors to lay any more feasible explanations before the public. In reply to this two others were forthcoming (Times, July 7th and 9th). The first suggested that the train might have run off the metals and be lying submerged in the Lancashire and Staffordshire Canal, which runs parallel to the railway for some hundred of yards. This suggestion was thrown out of court by the published depth of the canal, which was entirely insufficient to conceal so large an object. The second correspondent wrote calling attention to the bag which appeared to be the sole luggage which the travellers had brought with them, and suggesting that some novel explosive of immense and pulverizing power might have been concealed in it. The obvious absurdity, however, of supposing that the whole train might be blown to dust while the metals remained uninjured reduced any such explanation to a farce. The investigation had drifted into this hopeless position when a new and most unexpected incident occurred.

This was nothing less than the receipt by Mrs. McPherson of a letter from her husband, James McPherson, who had been the guard on the missing train. The letter, which was dated July 5th, 1890, was posted from New York and came to hand upon July 14th. Some doubts were expressed as to its genuine character but Mrs. McPherson was positive as to the writing, and the fact that it contained a remittance of a hundred dollars in five-dollar notes was enough in itself to discount the idea of a hoax. No address was given in the letter, which ran in this way:

MY DEAR WIFE,—

"I have been thinking a great deal, and I find it very hard to give you up. The same with Lizzie. I try to fight against it, but it will always come back to me. I send you some money which will change into twenty English pounds. This should be enough to bring both Lizzie and you across the Atlantic, and you will find the Hamburg boats which stop at Southampton very good boats, and cheaper than Liverpool. If you could come here and stop at the Johnston House I would try and send you word how to meet, but things are very difficult with me at present, and I am not very happy, finding it hard to give you both up. So no more at present,

from your loving husband,

"James McPherson."

For a time it was confidently anticipated that this letter would lead to the clearing up of the whole matter, the more so as it was ascertained that a passenger who bore a close resemblance to the missing guard had travelled from Southampton under the name of Summers in the Hamburg and New York liner Vistula, which started upon the 7th of June. Mrs. McPherson and her sister Lizzie Dolton went across to New York as directed and stayed for three weeks at the Johnston House, without hearing anything from the missing man. It is probable that some injudicious comments in the

Press may have warned him that the police were using them as a bait. However, this may be, it is certain that he neither wrote nor came, and the women were eventually compelled to return to Liverpool.

And so the matter stood, and has continued to stand up to the present year of 1898. Incredible as it may seem, nothing has transpired during these eight years which has shed the least light upon the extraordinary disappearance of the special train which contained Monsieur Caratal and his companion. Careful inquiries into the antecedents of the two travellers have only established the fact that Monsieur Caratal was well known as a financier and political agent in Central America, and that during his voyage to Europe he had betrayed extraordinary anxiety to reach Paris. His companion, whose name was entered upon the passenger lists as Eduardo Gomez, was a man whose record was a violent one, and whose reputation was that of a bravo and a bully. There was evidence to show, however, that he was honestly devoted to the interests of Monsieur Caratal, and that the latter, being a man of puny physique, employed the other as a guard and protector. It may be added that no information came from Paris as to what the objects of Monsieur Caratal's hurried journey may have been. This comprises all the facts of the case up to the publication in the Marseilles papers of the recent confession of Herbert de Lernac, now under sentence of death for the murder of a merchant named Bonvalot. This statement may be literally translated as follows:

"It is not out of mere pride or boasting that I give this information, for, if that were my object, I could tell a dozen actions of mine which are quite as splendid; but I do it in order that certain gentlemen in Paris may understand that I, who am able here to tell about the fate of Monsieur Caratal, can also tell in whose interest and at whose request the deed was done, unless the reprieve which I am awaiting comes to me very quickly. Take warning, messieurs, before it is too late! You know Herbert de Lernac, and you are aware that his deeds are as ready as his words. Hasten then, or you are lost!

"At present I shall mention no names—if you only heard the names, what would you not think!—but I shall merely tell you how cleverly I did it. I was true to my employers then, and no doubt they will be true to me now. I hope so, and until I am convinced that they have betrayed me, these names, which would convulse Europe, shall not be divulged. But on that day ... well, I say no more!

"In a word, then, there was a famous trial in Paris, in the year 1890, in connection with a monstrous scandal in politics and finance. How monstrous that scandal was can never be known save by such confidential agents as myself. The honour and careers of many of the chief men in France were at stake. You have seen a group of ninepins standing, all so rigid, and prim, and unbending. Then there comes the ball from far away and pop, pop, pop—there are your ninepins on the floor. Well, imagine some of the greatest men in France as these ninepins and then this Monsieur Caratal was the ball which could be seen coming from far away. If he arrived, then it was pop, pop, pop for all of them. It was determined that he should not arrive.

"I do not accuse them all of being conscious of what was to happen. There were, as I have said, great financial as well as political interests at stake, and a syndicate was formed to manage the business. Some subscribed to the syndicate who hardly understood what were its objects. But others understood very well, and they can rely upon it that I have not forgotten their names. They had ample warning that Monsieur Caratal was coming long before he left South America, and they knew that the evidence which he held would certainly mean ruin to all of them. The syndicate had the command of an unlimited amount of money—absolutely unlimited, you understand. They looked round for an agent who was capable of wielding this gigantic power. The man chosen must be inventive, resolute, adaptive—a man in a million. They chose Herbert de Lernac, and I admit that they were right.

"My duties were to choose my subordinates, to use freely the power which money gives, and to make certain that Monsieur Caratal should never arrive in Paris. With characteristic energy I set about my commission within an hour of receiving my instructions, and the steps which I took were the very best for the purpose which could possibly be devised.

"A man whom I could trust was dispatched instantly to South America to travel home with Monsieur Caratal. Had he arrived in time the ship would never have reached Liverpool; but alas! it had already started before my agent could reach it. I fitted out a small armed brig to intercept it, but again I was unfortunate. Like all great organizers I was, however, prepared for failure, and had a series of alternatives prepared, one or the other of which must succeed. You must not underrate the difficulties of my undertaking, or imagine that a mere commonplace assassination would meet the case. We must destroy not only Monsieur Caratal, but Monsieur Caratal's documents, and Monsieur Caratal's companions also, if we had reason to believe that he had communicated his secrets to them. And you must remember that they were on the alert, and keenly suspicious of any such attempt. It was a task which was in every way worthy of me, for I am always most masterful where another would be appalled.

"I was all ready for Monsieur Caratal's reception in

Liverpool, and I was the more eager because I had reason to believe that he had made arrangements by which he would have a considerable guard from the moment that he arrived in London. Anything which was to be done must be done between the moment of his setting foot upon the Liverpool quay and that of his arrival at the London and West Coast terminus in London. We prepared six plans, each more elaborate than the last; which plan would be used would depend upon his own movements. Do what he would, we were ready for him. If he had stayed in Liverpool, we were ready. If he took an ordinary train, an express, or a special, all was ready. Everything had been foreseen and provided for.

"You may imagine that I could not do all this myself. What could I know of the English railway lines? But money can procure willing agents all the world over, and I soon had one of the acutest brains in England to assist me. I will mention no names, but it would be unjust to claim all the credit for myself. My English ally was worthy of such an alliance. He knew the London and West Coast line thoroughly, and he had the command of a band of workers who were trustworthy and intelligent. The idea was his, and my own judgement was only required in the details. We bought over several officials, amongst whom the most important was James McPherson, whom we had ascertained to be the guard most likely to be employed upon a special train. Smith, the stoker, was also in our employ. John Slater, the engine-driver, had been approached, but had been found to be obstinate and dangerous, so we desisted. We had no certainty that Monsieur Caratal would take a special, but we thought it very probable, for it was of the utmost importance to him that he should reach Paris without delay. It was for this contingency, therefore, that we made special preparations— preparations which were complete down to the last detail long before his steamer had sighted the shores of England. You will be amused to learn that there was one of my agents in the pilot-boat which brought that steamer to its moorings.

"The moment that Caratal arrived in Liverpool we knew that he suspected danger and was on his guard. He had brought with him as an escort a dangerous fellow, named Gomez, a man who carried weapons, and was prepared to use them. This fellow carried Caratal's confidential papers for him, and was ready to protect either them or his master. The probability was that Caratal had taken him into his counsel, and that to remove Caratal without removing Gomez would be a mere waste of energy. It was necessary that they should be involved in a common fate, and our plans to that end were much facilitated by their request for a special train. On that special train you will understand that two out of the three servants of the company were really in our employ, at a price which would make them independent for a lifetime. I do not go so far as to say that the English are more honest than any other nation, but I have found them more expensive to buy.

"I have already spoken of my English agent—who is a man with a considerable future before him, unless some complaint of the throat carries him off before his time. He had charge of all arrangements at Liverpool, whilst I was stationed at the inn at Kenyon, where I awaited a cipher signal to act. When the special was arranged for, my agent instantly telegraphed to me and warned me how soon I should have everything ready. He himself under the name of Horace Moore applied immediately for a special also, in the hope that he would be sent down with Monsieur Caratal, which might under certain circumstances have been helpful to us. If, for example, our great coup had failed, it would then have become the duty of my agent to have shot them both and destroyed their papers. Caratal was on his guard, however, and refused to admit any other traveller. My agent then left the station, returned by another entrance, entered the guard's van on the side farthest from the platform, and travelled down with McPherson the guard.

"In the meantime you will be interested to know what my movements were. Everything had been prepared for days before, and only the finishing touches were needed. The side line which we had chosen had once joined the main line, but it had been disconnected. We had only to replace a few rails to connect it once more. These rails had been laid down as far as could be done without danger of attracting attention, and now it was merely a case of completing a juncture with the line, and arranging the points as they had been before. The sleepers had never been removed, and the rails, fish- plates and rivets were all ready, for we had taken them from a siding on the abandoned portion of the line. With my small but competent band of workers, we had everything ready long before the special arrived. When it did arrive, it ran off upon the small side line so easily that the jolting of the points appears to have been entirely unnoticed by the two travellers.

"Our plan had been that Smith, the stoker, should chloroform John Slater, the driver, so that he should vanish with the others. In this respect, and in this respect only, our plans miscarried—I except the criminal folly of McPherson in writing home to his wife. Our stoker did his business so clumsily that Slater in his struggles fell off the engine, and though fortune was with us so far that he broke his neck in the fall, still he remained as a blot upon that which would otherwise have been one of those complete masterpieces which are only to be contemplated in silent admiration. The criminal expert will find in John Slater the one flaw in all our admirable combinations. A man who has had as many triumphs as I can afford to be frank, and I therefore lay my finger upon John Slater, and I proclaim him to be a flaw.

"But now I have got our special train upon the small line two kilometres, or rather more than one mile, in length, which leads, or rather used to lead, to the abandoned Heartsease mine, once one of the largest coal mines in England. You will ask how it is that no one saw the train upon this unused line. I answer that along its entire length it runs through a deep cutting, and that, unless someone had been on the edge of that cutting, he could not have seen it. There WAS someone on the edge of that cutting. I was there. And now I will tell you what I saw.

"My assistant had remained at the points in order that he might superintend the switching off of the train. He had four armed men with him, so that if the train ran off the line—we thought it probable, because the points were very rusty—we might still have resources to fall back upon. Having once seen it safely on the side line, he handed over the responsibility to me. I was waiting at a point which overlooks the mouth of the mine, and I was also armed, as were my two companions. Come what might, you see, I was always ready.

"The moment that the train was fairly on the side line, Smith, the stoker, slowed-down the engine, and then, having turned it on to the fullest speed again, he and McPherson, with my English lieutenant, sprang off before it was too late. It may be that it was this slowing-down which first attracted the attention of the travellers, but the train was running at full speed again before their heads appeared at the open window. It makes me smile to think how bewildered they must have been. Picture to yourself your own feelings if, on looking out of your luxurious carriage, you suddenly perceived that the lines upon which you ran were rusted and corroded, red and yellow with disuse and decay! What a catch must have come in their breath as in a second it flashed upon them that it was not Manchester but Death which was waiting for them at the end of that sinister line. But the train was running with frantic speed, rolling and rocking over the rotten line, while the wheels made a frightful screaming sound upon the rusted surface. I was close to them, and could see their faces. Caratal was praying, I think—there was something like a rosary dangling out of his hand. The other roared like a bull who smells the blood of the slaughter-house. He saw us standing on the bank, and he beckoned to us like a madman. Then he tore at his wrist and threw his dispatch-box out of the window in our direction. Of course, his meaning was obvious. Here was the evidence, and they would promise to be silent if their lives were spared. It would have been very agreeable if we could have done so, but business is business. Besides, the train was now as much beyond our controls as theirs.

"He ceased howling when the train rattled round the curve and they saw the black mouth of the mine yawning before them. We had removed the boards which had covered it, and we had cleared the square entrance. The rails had formerly run very close to the shaft for the convenience of loading the coal, and we had only to add two or three lengths of rail in order to lead to the very brink of the shaft. In fact, as the lengths would not quite fit, our line projected about three feet over the edge. We saw the two heads at the window: Caratal below, Gomez above; but they had both been struck silent by what they saw. And yet they could not withdraw their heads. The sight seemed to have paralysed them.

"I had wondered how the train running at a great speed would take the pit into which I had guided it, and I was much interested in watching it. One of my colleagues thought that it would actually jump it, and indeed it was not very far from doing so. Fortunately, however, it fell short, and the buffers of the engine struck the other lip of the shaft with a tremendous crash. The funnel flew off into the air. The tender, carriages, and van were all smashed up into one jumble, which, with the remains of the engine, choked for a minute or so the mouth of the pit. Then something gave way in the middle, and the whole mass of green iron, smoking coals, brass fittings, wheels, wood-work, and cushions all crumbled together and crashed down into the mine. We heard the rattle, rattle, rattle, as the debris struck against the walls, and then, quite a long time afterwards, there came a deep roar as the remains of the train struck the bottom. The boiler may have burst, for a sharp crash came after the roar, and then a dense cloud of steam and smoke swirled up out of the black depths, falling in a spray as thick as rain all round us. Then the vapour shredded off into thin wisps, which floated away in the summer sunshine, and all was quiet again in the Heartsease mine.

"And now, having carried out our plans so successfully, it only remained to leave no trace behind us. Our little band of workers at the other end had already ripped up the rails and disconnected the side line, replacing everything as it had been before. We were equally busy at the mine. The funnel and other fragments were thrown in, the shaft was planked over as it used to be, and the lines which led to it were torn up and taken away. Then, without flurry, but without delay, we all made our way out of the country, most of us to Paris, my English colleague to Manchester, and McPherson to Southampton, whence he emigrated to America. Let the English papers of that date tell how throughly we had done our work, and how completely we had thrown the cleverest of their detectives off our track.

"You will remember that Gomez threw his bag of papers out of the window, and I need not say that I secured that bag and brought them to my employers. It may interest my employers now, however, to learn that out of that bag I took one or two little papers as a souvenir of the occasion. I have no wish to publish these papers; but, still, it is every man for himself in this world, and what else can I do if my friends will not come to my aid when I want them? Messieurs, you may believe that Herbert de Lernac is quite as formidable when he is against you as when he is with you, and that he is not a man to go to the guillotine until he has seen that every one of you is en route for New Caledonia. For your own sake, if not for mine, make haste, Monsieur de—, and General—, and Baron—(you can fill up the blanks for yourselves as you read this). I promise you that in the next edition there will be no blanks to fill.

"P. S. —As I look over my statement there is only one omission which I can see. It concerns the unfortunate man McPherson, who was foolish enough to write to his wife and to make an appointment with her in New York. It can be imagined that when interests like ours were at stake, we could not leave them to the chance of whether a man in that class of life would or would not give away his secrets to a woman. Having once broken his oath by writing to his wife, we could not trust him any more. We took steps therefore to insure that he should not see his wife. I have sometimes thought that it would be a kindness to write to her and to assure her that there is no impediment to her marrying again."

ALL ABOARD

Christopher Golden

That dreadful autumn, Sarah Cooper woke nearly every night in the small hours of the morning and lay in the dark, back toward her husband, the memory of their dead son filling the space between them.

During the day the tension did not weigh so heavily. Sarah and Paul wandered the house only dimly aware of one another, ghosts haunting their own marriage. Resentment and blame hung in the air like static building before a thunderstorm. Sarah knew that she ought to try to comfort her husband, but Paul did not seek her out, nor did she look for solace in his arms. Cruel and capricious happenstance had taken Jonah from them—a bacterial infection, a spiked fever, an ambulance too slow to arrive—but they had to hold someone responsible, and each found fault with the other, and guilt in the mirror.

They couldn't stay in this house much longer. Sarah would never survive it. Fifty-seven Brook Street existed now as a museum of sorrow. Jonah had bounced on the sofa, bumped his head on the coffee table, marched his walker across the kitchen tiles as a baby, and slept in his parents' bed almost as many nights as his own. The toys had all been packed away, but his room remained with its books and stuffed polar bear and the dinosaur border that ran along the top of the bedroom walls. Sarah kept that door closed, but could not bring herself to take down the pictures in the living room and the downstairs hall and from the bureau in her bedroom. Her hairbrush had brushed Jonah's hair. His Spider-Man cup hid at the back of a kitchen cabinet, waiting to be remembered; waiting to remind her.

How did Paul stand it? Sarah didn't know. They avoided the conversation most of the time. That seemed even worse because it felt like they were trying to pretend Jonah had never been there—that they did not grieve. But Paul made an effort to talk around the absence of their son, just as he usually avoided meeting her eyes.

By October, they spoke only when absolutely necessary.

When Sarah found the fuzzy Scooby-Doo costume she had bought Jonah over the summer, unable to resist even though Halloween had been months away, she crushed it against her chest and wept into the costume, brown fabric soaking up her tears. Then she put it into a box of Jonah's things that she planned to donate to the Salvation Army. She never mentioned it to Paul, and as Halloween approached, he never asked.

In the second week of October, she woke in the night with only the glow of a distant streetlamp filtering through the window. It must have been two or three o'clock in the morning. After so many weeks of such awakenings, she knew sleep would not be in any hurry to return so she lay and listened to Paul's rhythmic breathing.

The gulf between them had grown over the weeks since Jonah's death, expanding a little at bedtime every night. They hadn't had sex in all that time, though there had been times in the small hours of the morning when she had needed so badly to be held, to be touched, to be loved. But night after night they lay back to back, shoulder and neck muscles bunched with tension and expectation, and they edged further away, widening the gap between them.

Golden

A glow of moonlight draped across the shadows of their bedroom and the gauzy curtains billowed with the crisp autumn breeze. Sarah lay on her side and stared at the windows, at the curtains, and at nothing. The windows rattled with powerful gusts—the weather changing, winter drawing nearer—and she heard the skittering of dry leaves across the driveway and the front walk.

Then, off in the distance, the lonely whistle of a train.

Sarah had heard the sound every night for nearly two weeks. At first it had been barely audible, so that she had trouble determining its origin. Each night it seemed to become louder, though of course the train tracks couldn't be any nearer. In all the years she had lived in Dunston, she could not recall ever having heard the sound before, never mind seen a train. It must, she told herself, only run late at night when the town slept, when only insomniacs and grieving mothers might hear it.

She listened as the whistle faded and felt a terrible longing, wished she were on board that train, bound for destinations unknown.

When her tears came, she let them slide down to dampen her pillow. Her husband did not stir, but Sarah was not surprised. Paul had long since stopped being stirred by her tears, even in the light of day.

She slid nearer the edge of the bed and watched the moonlight and the billowing curtains and listened to the shush of the autumn leaves blowing across the lawn. In time, sleep would claim her again, tears drying on her face.

Sarah would hear the whistle of the train in her dreams, where she held her tiny son in her arms and rocked him, singing him softly to sleep on the way to his own extinguished dreams.

▟▙▟▙▟▙▟

The new offices of Sterling Software had been built just at the edge of town, near a narrow metal bridge across the Kenyon River. Window glass winked in the morning light as Sarah drove over the bridge, her travel mug rattling in the cup holder on the dash, spurting up a dollop of coffee.

The Kenyon River meandered southward under the bridge. In the spring it roared, but in autumn it remained a gentle whisper. She followed the road northeast on the other side, coming around a corner, all the while keeping the Sterling building in sight. It stood at the top of a hill that had been transformed into a mini-industrial park, complete with a Comfort Inn and a TGI Friday's restaurant. Sarah barely saw any of those buildings. In truth, she barely saw the road or the rich, harvest-hued foliage of the trees around her. Her focus was on driving to work, and she could do that with her mind on autopilot.

The dashboard clock read 9:12. Late again, and she felt badly about it. A tremor of discontent passed through her. Exhausted, she'd rushed to get ready, and the mirror had reflected both her tiredness—in the dark crescents beneath her eyes—and her haphazard attempt at fixing her hair and putting on makeup. *Get your life together, Sarah. You're dropping the ball.* But the advice sounded hollow. She couldn't convince herself that any of it mattered. Work. Sleep. Face. Life.

The car jittered over train tracks, causing her coffee to burble again.

Sarah frowned and tapped the brake, slowing down and glancing in her rearview mirror. She'd been over those tracks twice a day every day for more than a year, ever since Sterling had moved to the new location. There were no railroad crossing signs, no flashing lights, nothing.

Another few minutes won't matter.

She put the car in reverse and backed up, checking to make sure no other cars were approaching. At the tracks she braked again, pausing to peer both ways along the line. Grass grew up between the wooden ties. The rails themselves were dark with rust. In either direction the tracks curved away into trees and undergrowth that had begun to encroach over the years.

Sarah shook her head. No trains on this line. Not for years.

As she drove on, she could not help but glance at the mirror. The memory of the whistle from the late night train lingered, and led her to thoughts of Jonah and her dreams.

No. Work.

If she thought about Jonah, she would be useless at work. They had been more than kind, had offered her as much time as she needed to mourn. When Sarah had announced, after six weeks, that she was ready to return to her receptionist position, the office manager—Ellie Poole—had asked if she was *really ready*. Sarah had thought it a foolish question. How could she ever be ready to go to work, to put her loss behind her?

But at home all that awaited her was the museum of sorrow, the constant reminders. Her co-workers' sympathy made work little better, but at least she could find distraction there.

Sarah found a parking spot near the front of the building and climbed out. Dropping her keys, she swore as she bent to retrieve them, then slammed the door. With her purse over her shoulder and her coffee in hand, she hurried up the walk to the front doors. Inside the glass and chrome lobby, Martin stood at his security post, one earbud of his I-Pod in place and the other hanging loose. When he looked up and saw her, his face blossomed into a warm smile. The young guard seemed to be the only one at Sterling who could be genuinely happy to see her without his warmth devolving into pity.

"Morning, Sarah."

"Hi, Martin."

Behind the reception desk, a secretary named Laura Rossi gave her a grim look. Ellie had obviously shanghaied her to substitute until Sarah showed up, and the wide-bottomed, curly-haired woman did not bother trying to hide her displeasure. Sarah was almost glad that Laura didn't tiptoe around her.

"Let me guess—car trouble?"

"I'm sorry, Laura. The last time, I swear."

The woman got up from the reception desk and sighed, rolling her eyes, but she waved the apology away as though Sarah's tardiness was no big deal.

"It's fine. Martin's good company."

Martin grinned broadly. "I was serenading her."

Sarah managed a thin smile. Martin liked to sing, but softly, mostly to himself. She never minded, but she suspected that someone as generally uptight as Laura would be driven near madness by the man's musical mutterings.

The phone began to ring. Laura shot it a dark look, then turned her back and went through the door into the main offices. Sarah hurried over and picked up.

"Sterling Software. Can you hold, please?" She put on her headset, then took the caller off hold and transferred him to the northeastern sales manager.

"Some people can't seem to figure out how to use an electronic directory," Martin said.

Sarah nodded, but broke into a yawn.

"Don't do that," Martin protested, yawning in reply. "It's

contagious. No fair.”

“Sorry, just didn’t get nearly enough sleep last night.”

“Pretty much every night, isn’t it?”

His face and voice were kind. The question wasn’t an intrusion. Martin never intruded on her grief. If she didn’t want to answer, he would not mind. But Sarah found him warm and easy to talk to.

“I fall asleep all right,” she said, pushing her hair away from her face to meet his gaze. “But I wake up in the middle of the night and then it takes me an hour or so to drift off again. It’s weird what you hear at night, though, y’know?”

Martin removed the earbud and held the cord in his hand. “I do. The quietest noise seems much louder in the middle of the night.”

“Yes!” Sarah said. “During the day I can’t even hear the clock ticking, but at night it’s so loud. And now I hear the train every night. I almost listen for it.”

The security guard gave a soft laugh and a shake of his head. “Now you’re just fooling with me. That’s not nice, Sarah.”

She stared at him. “What do you mean?”

“Come on. The Three-Eighteen? I’m not falling for that old story. Didn’t believe it when my grandmother told it, either.”

A tractor trailer growled as it pulled into the parking lot and continued around past the building, headed for the loading dock in back. It distracted them both for a moment. When Sarah looked back at Martin, he was studying her curiously. She sat forward in her chair.

“What’s the Three-Eighteen?”

His eyes became narrow slits in his dark face a moment and then widened with sudden realization. “You didn’t grow up around here, did you? I forget sometimes.”

Sarah shook her head. “Nope. My family comes from

upstate New York. I moved here with my father when I was fourteen."

"Right, right. You've told me. Sorry. He worked at the mill, right?"

"Worked and died there," she said. "So what's this train thing?"

"Just a local ghost story. Most towns have a house all the kids think is haunted and I'm guessing we do, too. But the story that always gave me the creeps was about the Three-Eighteen. My grandmother used to talk about it and the counselors at camp used to tell it around the fire, along with the ones about Hatchet Mary and the Hook and that kind of thing."

Sarah frowned. "So, it's a ghost train?"

"That's the story. Passes by every night at 3:18 a. m. 'Carrying the ghosts of the ones folks can't let go of,' my Gram used to say. And it's only those folks, and people near dying themselves, who can . . ."

The words trailed off.

Breathless, Sarah stared at him. "Who can what?"

Martin gave her a sheepish grin. "Who can hear it. That's how all those old stories go, y'know? Supposed to creep us all out. That way if you hear a train whistle after dark or something that even sounds like one, you're supposed to think it's the Three-Eighteen come to collect you."

She dropped her gaze and stared at the marble tile beneath her chair.

"Sarah?"

His voice made her flinch. She looked up. "I hear the whistle every night."

Martin laughed and came over to her desk. He splayed one strong hand on the counter where people laid out their ID to be allowed inside.

"Sarah, come on. It's just a story. Whatever you're hearing, it's something else. Got to be some late night road work, smoke venting from the damn sneaker factory or something. But it's not a train, and it sure as hell ain't the Three-Eighteen."

She took a long breath and let it out with a small, self-deprecating laugh. Of course Martin was right. Sarah felt nauseous just thinking about the few moments she'd spent seriously considering the campfire tale as truth. Every town had local folklore.

"You okay?" Martin prodded. His wide eyes were full of concern. "I shouldn't even have mentioned it, but you brought up the train whistle and I just figured you were teasing me. This isn't the kind of thing you ought to be thinking about."

"I'm okay," she promised. How to explain the numbness inside and the gulf between herself and her husband? How to explain that the word 'okay' had entirely lost its meaning for her. Paul had always liked grim novels about the destruction of human society or the ecosystem or worse; he called it post-apocalyptic fiction. But Sarah was living a post-apocalyptic life. People who hadn't been through it couldn't possibly understand.

"You sure? It's only that you never seem like you're all here, if you don't mind my saying. Ellie Poole's been bitching about you coming in late and, well, looking kind of run down."

Sarah couldn't believe it. Ellie, who'd been so nice, was sniping behind her back after what she'd been through?

"Bitch," she whispered, glancing around at the doors that led into the main offices, just in case the bitch in question might walk in and overhear her. "Am I in trouble, Martin?"

"Not that I've heard. I'd have told you. But that could change."

Sarah nodded. Of course it could change. The second Ellie

figured that Sarah had had enough time to mourn Jonah's death that she couldn't file a wrongful termination lawsuit, the witch would come gunning for her.

With a sigh, Sarah sipped from her cooling coffee. "Guess this is the last late morning for me."

A Mercedes slid through the parking lot and into a space. Martin put the single ear bud back in place. He and Sarah both watched as a man stepped out of the Mercedes and started for the front door.

"Y'know, if sleep's the issue, you oughta get your doc to prescribe something," Martin said. "I took that one with the butterfly once. You know, the one in the TV ad. Worked like a charm."

Sarah straightened her top and smoothed her skirt, trying to look as professional as she could in spite of her state of mind. As the dark-suited man from the Mercedes opened the door, she glanced at Martin.

"I tried pills. They just make me more tired in the morning," she said.

Then she smiled at the visitor. "Good morning, sir. How can I help you?"

The man spoke and she barely listened, her thoughts still on Martin's suggestion. Sleeping pills would have been such a blessing, a respite from restless nights. But the few times she had taken them, they had interfered with her dreaming. And her dreams were the only time she could be with Jonah.

Nothing mattered more than that, including her job. Ellie Poole could go to Hell.

"Have you ever heard of the Three-Eighteen?"

Paul looked up from his plate—he'd made them a risotto that had once been a favorite for both of them, but now tasted bland to Sarah. Everything tasted bland to her now.

"You mean that old story about the ghost train?"

"Yes."

He shrugged. Even his indifference had sharp edges, cutting her with disdain. "Sure. When I was a kid we'd all talk about it. Go out to the tracks. One time I camped out down there all night with Jimmy Pryce—remember Jimmy?"

Sarah shook her head. She didn't. Paul was two years older than she was. She'd only been in high school with him for his senior year and then he'd graduated. But he'd lost touch with most of his old friends over the years. Whoever this Jimmy Pryce was, he hadn't sent them a card or flowers when Jonah died. The parade of faces at the funeral were a blur to her—she couldn't remember who had been there or not—but the cards and flowers she recalled perfectly.

"No? Jimmy thought you were pretty hot when you transferred in from New York." He smiled, and perhaps for a moment there was a glimmer of hope and life in his eyes, of happier times. It dimmed, as it always would, forever after.

"Anyway, we camped out down by the tracks one night. Spent the whole time scaring the crap out of each other with flashlights and telling ghost stories. When you're a kid you believe that stuff, deep down, even though you've gotta act like you're too mature to believe it, and too tough to be scared by it."

Sarah pretended to smile; a kind of peace offering. Then she went back to the flavorless risotto with Paul studying her closely. Their conversations had been infrequent in the past few weeks, and often tense. They talked around and above things and never addressed what lurked below.

Jonah would never hear the story of the Three-Eighteen. He would never camp out by the train tracks and tell ghost stories, never go trick-or-treating or have a friend like Jimmy Pryce, whose antics he would look back on fondly when fatherhood and dreaded maturity came along and the hard climb toward forty had begun.

Forty. At thirty-two, Sarah felt ancient. Sometimes she thought about what it would be like to be truly old and abandoned, stashed in some nursing home, all her passions diminished or taken away, waiting for it all to end. Waiting to die. This didn't feel much different.

"Why do you ask?"

The tone of the question, the awkwardness in his voice, put a chill between them. It should've had the opposite effect. Here he was, trying to have a civil conversation about something more than the weather or perfunctory work-related trivia, but it felt so forced that Sarah only tensed up further.

"No reason. I heard someone talking about it today and was surprised I'd never heard it before."

"You were fourteen by the time you moved here. Probably too old for ghost stories."

Again she forced a smile.

Paul took another bite of risotto and they descended into the sort of funereal silence to which they had become hideously accustomed.

Jonah had had his father's eyes.

Sarah managed a few more bites and then endured several minutes more at the table before allowing herself to rise and bring her dish to the sink. "I'll clean up later. I've been wanting a bath all day."

She'd been taking a great many baths of late. Paul had remarked on it only once, two weeks earlier, and she had told him tersely that she needed the alone time. He'd had no response for that. Once she might have confided in him, told him what she really did during those long evening baths with the radio playing up on the shelf—that sometimes she touched herself and tried to remember what it was like to be alive and in love and full of lust, and sometimes she used the edge of a razor blade or her tiny scissors to scratch and lightly cut her flesh, trying to discover if she had the courage to cut deeper and let herself bleed.

Either way, whether searching for passion or pain, she cried. With the water hot and steam rising, sometimes she even pretended to herself that there were no tears.

Her eyes snapped open and she inhaled sharply. Something had woken her, tonight. It took a moment for her mind to make sense of the thumping bass coming from a car passing by at the end of the street. God, that was loud. Some kind of post-modern blues-funk like Amy Winehouse, and it wasn't drifting off the way it should have been. The car had stopped for some reason.

Rubbing her eyes, Sarah slipped from beneath the covers and went to the window. She pulled the curtain aside and tried to peer out into the dark toward the end of the street. Not much breeze, but the night pulsed with the beat of that song. There came a laugh, the slam of a door, and then the car roared away. Some kind of mischief going on down there—the kind of thing she and Paul might have gotten up to, once upon a time.

Paul had left the window open wide and Sarah backed away and hugged herself tightly, shuddering. Even without a breeze, the night was cold. The weather had shifted again, but

New England was always like that.

With a frown, she realized she had been unconsciously rubbing the bandage on her forearm. She had gotten a bit carried away with the scissors in the bathtub tonight. *That's one way to look at it*, she thought, sleep still clouding her mind. Her arm ached where she'd cut it, and she hoped it had not become infected. If Paul noticed, that would be difficult to explain. Of course, that was an enormous 'if. ' He barely saw her anymore. She might as well be made of glass—a window where a woman used to be.

The clock ticked loudly on the nightstand. Once they had kept a baby monitor there and the sound of Jonah turning restlessly had kept her alert. But now there was only the clock and the soft breathing of the automaton who had taken the place of her husband.

Sarah watched Paul sleeping. He had mastered the emotionless mask that he wore during the day, but could not control his unconscious mind. His features were tight with sorrow and consternation. His dreams brought him the nightmares he spent the days attempting to evade.

Beyond him, the clock on the nightstand read 2:13 a. m. Sarah blinked and stared at it and the display clicked over to 2:14. She turned toward the window. The gauzy curtain seemed like a veil, now, but though she could not see as far as the Kenyon River from here, she did not want to look out across the town toward the river.

She climbed back into bed, sliding deep beneath the covers. On her side, she pressed her eyes closed and slid one hand under her pillow, an exaggerated pantomime, as though she could fool her body into thinking it was capable of falling right back to sleep. But experience had taught her better.

For fifteen or twenty minutes she lay there, stubbornly

persistent. When she surrendered to the inevitability of her insomnia, she opened her eyes at last and glanced around at the moonlit glow of her bedroom. Paul breathed softly beside her.

Sarah wanted to scream. If only her sleeplessness could have been made incarnate, turned into something she could kick and punch and claw. But it could not be fought. Especially tonight. Just as she had been pretending to herself that it would be possible to simply fall back to sleep, she had also avoided acknowledging the conversation she and Martin had had in the foyer of Sterling Software that morning.

Again, she glanced at the clock. 2:37, and Paul still sleeping, so peacefully.

Sarah slid from bed and grabbed her blue jeans, pulled them on. She'd been sleeping in a light blue t-shirt she sometimes wore to the gym and didn't bother with a bra, just pulling a fuzzy red sweater on over it. With another glance at Paul, she took a pair of socks from the drawer in her nightstand and went quietly downstairs.

She paused only once, while tying her sneakers, to wonder what exactly she hoped to accomplish. Her chest tightened with anticipation, a kind of giddy excitement that might have been hysteria. Then she went out the front door and pulled it quietly closed behind her. Her own car was parked inside the garage and the automatic door opener made a lot of noise, so she took Paul's Cherokee.

As she pulled out of the driveway, her hands were trembling. She didn't click the headlights on until she reached the end of the street and turned onto the main road. The dashboard lights cast an industrial gloom inside the car and the radio played low as she drove away from home, following the same course she took on her way to work.

The clock on the dash read 2:49.

Sarah hit the gas and the car lurched forward, speeding up. She couldn't be late.

She traveled as though she herself were a dream, gliding through the sleeping town in the small hours when night seemed darkest. Nothing else moved but the wind. In that surreal landscape, anything seemed possible.

At 3:11, her headlights picked out the old bridge over the Kenyon River. Sarah slowed as the car shuddered across the bridge, black water rushing past below. When she hit the pavement on the far side, she turned left and gunned it, tires squealing. All through the drive she'd managed a kind of Zen calm, complete with steady breathing and quick but even pulse. The sound of the tires broke her focus. Her face flushed with heat and she felt her heart pounding in her chest as she sped along the road that curved beside the river.

Without a railroad crossing sign or any other warning, she came up on the abandoned tracks too fast to stop. She rocketed over the tracks before hitting the brakes and skidding to a halt on the shoulder of the road.

3:14.

Sarah killed the engine and just sat there for a few seconds, hands on the steering wheel, listening to the car cool and tick and settle. If she gripped the wheel hard enough, her hands wouldn't shake. She felt her throat closing and her eyes brimming and she bit down on her lip.

Go home. Stupid girl. There's nothing for you out here.

Of course there wasn't. Why had she really come here? What did she expect, racing across town in the middle of the night, chasing ghosts? *You're losing it, kid*, she thought, grinning in the dark enclosure of the car. *Just losing it.*

But that was bullshit, too. She'd lost it the day Jonah died, and never gotten it back. Trying to pretend otherwise had been her sole occupation ever since.

With a shaky laugh she took the keys from the ignition and popped the door. The night wind gusted, whipping her hair across her face, crisp with the rich scent of autumn. From somewhere there came the smell of a wood-burning stove, carried on the breeze, and it made her realize that she was not the only one awake tonight. Not alone in the dark.

She slipped the keys into her pocket and shut the car door, then started walking toward the tracks. How many minutes left? Just a couple. Sarah stepped onto the tracks and looked in both directions. The moonlight only dispersed so many shadows, but enough to see that nothing about the tracks had changed. They were overgrown and unused, nearly buried in some places.

Closing her eyes, she raised her arms, imagining the 3:18 coming. Would it pass right through her, or run her down? Or might it, instead, pick her up and carry her away? Her eyes snapped open and she crumbled inward, wrapping her arms around herself. With a deep breath, she stepped off of the tracks, beginning to rub her thumb across the bandage on her wrist where she'd cut too deeply. Last night she'd almost been brave enough to join Jonah.

A long minute passed, and then another. Sarah glanced back and forth along the tracks, and then put her face in her hands, aware of how seriously she had deluded herself...of just how lost she had become.

Then she heard the whistle. It came softly a first, a distant, mournful cry. She caught her breath. It was the same sound she had heard night after night as she lay in bed, unable to sleep. Sarah pulled her hands away from her face. Still barely able to breathe, she turned to the left, staring along the tracks.

The whistle sounded again, moving closer, so much louder. Louder than she'd ever heard it.

"Oh my God," she whispered, shaking.

Unblinking, she stared along those tracks, but there was no sign of any train. She stood just at the edge, where the metal rail was sunk into the pavement. The whistle came again, this time so close that she winced at the sound. She could see nothing, but now she could hear the chugging of the train.

Mouth agape, Sarah took a step back.

The whistle blew, and the scream was so loud she covered her ears. Then the wind struck her, the hot blast of air displaced by the passing locomotive. Eyes wide, she stared at the place where it ought to have been, but saw only the road on the other side of the tracks and the trees on the riverbank beyond.

And maybe something else. The night air seemed to ripple, to have texture, just a hint of substance. Sarah glimpsed a face through a window. She blinked and other faces flashed by in the zoetrope flicker of passenger car windows. They streaked across the darkness in the space of seconds. Still there was no train, nothing but the night and echoes and the chuff and clank of a machine she could not see.

One of the faces was Jonah's.

A blink, only. There and gone in the fraction of a moment. The strength of her hope and grief could have summoned his image. But Sarah knew. She'd seen him.

"My baby," she said. And then she cried. "My baby!"

She fell to her knees beside the tracks as the wind from the passing train diminished and then subsided entirely, and the whistle grew distant. After a while she crawled forward and put her fingers on the old rail. The metal was so cold. Sarah lay down there in the road for a while, body across the tracks. A car might have come and run her down. The thought occurred to her, but she thought that wouldn't have been so bad.

Sometime before four o'clock, she staggered back to the Jeep.

▓▓▓▓▓▓

Paul let her sleep in. By the time Sarah rolled out of bed on Saturday, it was after ten o'clock. She took her time showering and getting dressed, then went downstairs and had a glass of orange juice. It had been a dreamless sleep, and when she'd woken it had taken her a minute or so for the mist to clear from her mind. When the events of the previous night came back to her, Sarah felt herself suffused with a profound contentment. Her soul had been empty for so long, but now it began to fill up again.

Jonah was gone from this house—from the world, even. But he was not out of reach.

The front door was open. Sarah went out onto the steps and saw Paul raking leaves in jeans and a New England Patriots sweatshirt. He looked so much like the old Paul, the one who'd loved her before he started hating himself. If only she could have stepped down onto the grass and by doing so enter the time before Jonah, when he would have welcomed an embrace on the lawn, when Paul had been playful and his eyes bright with possibility.

"Good morning," she said.

Her husband looked up. For a moment he smiled as though he'd forgotten all the loss and resentment, but then she saw it draw like a veil across his face. The illusion shattered.

"Morning, sleepy head," he said. Sarah appreciated the effort to be cordial. "You must've been up all night."

"Pretty much. After I woke up, around two, I couldn't get back to sleep until it started to get light."

He leaned on his rake, real concern in his eyes. "Honey, I'm sorry. You sure you don't want to start taking those pills?"

Sarah smiled. "It's Saturday. No law against sleeping in. Listen, I was thinking I'd make some chicken salad with the leftovers from last night. Some onions and celery. Sound good for lunch?"

"Yeah," Paul replied, still studying her. "Sounds great."

She still loved him, and she pitied him, and she hated him, just a little. Sarah did not really blame Paul for what happened to Jonah—that had been nobody's fault. But she wished that they could have found solace in each other. If only he could find some kind of peace in himself, he could stop pretending his heart had not been torn apart. He could have held her and cried, let her feel it was all right to cry with him.

But that time was past.

▦

After lunch, she told Paul she had some errands to run, and went to the cemetery. The leaves eddied on the breeze and rustled in whispers along the grass, red and yellow and orange. She parked her car on a narrow, paved path that separated the modern part of the cemetery from the earliest graves, which dated back to before the Civil War.

Sarah got out of the car and shut the door. Quiet and peaceful, the cemetery seemed beautiful to her. The sky hung bright blue above the rolling lawns and the trees full of autumn colors. Some of the crypts were marble and others granite, while a handful of the older graves were marked by statues of angels.

She took a deep breath and started across the lawn. Tree roots bulged under the soil like raised veins. Sarah brushed a hand against an old oak as she passed. On her way to Jonah's grave she made a small detour, stopping by the granite block that marked her parents' resting place. Her mother had been killed in a car accident when Sarah was very young, leaving her father to raise her. He'd been her whole world, until Jonah came along.

The family name—her maiden name—was engraved on the front in large letters. KOSKOV. On the back, both of her parents were listed, with their dates of birth and death.

Eli Josef Koskov

Teresa Annalise Koskov

Sarah ran her fingers across the engraved letters. "Hi, Daddy." She kissed the tips of her fingers and touched them to his first name.

Three rows further along she came to another. The cut of the stone differed, and instead of granite it had been fashioned of a blue-tinted marble. This one said COOPER. Sarah didn't walk around to the back. She had stared too long, too often, at the letters that spelled out her son's name.

She sat on the grass just to one side of the grave and sang to him the songs she had always soothed him with when he had trouble falling asleep. Billy Joel's "Lullaby." Harry Connick's "Recipe for Love." Melissa Etheridge's "Baby, You Can Sleep While I Drive."

Sarah had visited Jonah without her husband many times. But that afternoon was the first time she did not cry.

After dinner—a chicken cacciatore Paul had put together

while she was out—Sarah cleaned the house. It started with the dishes, but afterward she could not stop herself. Compelled to continue, she moved into the living room and dining room, then upstairs into the bedroom to wash the bathrooms and put away a week's worth of laundry that had lingered, folded, in baskets. Paul watched television on the sofa the whole time, calling to her every half hour or so to come and sit with him, to relax.

Sarah couldn't relax. She could barely stand still.

At bedtime, she slid beneath the sheets, bathed in the blue, flickering light of the television. Paul liked to have the news on while he fell asleep. He took comfort in the chatter, the monotonous drone of the voices. Sarah tried to tune them out. The news held no interest for her; it was nothing but a parade of tragedy. When Paul touched her hip, she thought he might want to make love. The idea startled her; it had been so long. But he only looked into her eyes.

"You all right?"

The question made her want to laugh and scream in equal proportion. Hadn't they both agreed that it was the most foolish question anyone ever asked someone who'd suffered a terrible loss? Of course she wasn't all right.

"Just tired," she said.

"Hope you get some real sleep tonight."

"Me, too."

But his eyelids were heavy. Already, Paul was drifting off, and Sarah didn't know if he'd even heard her.

As soon as he had slipped into a deep enough sleep, she got up again. The clock on the nightstand read 11:49. Pulling the covers up to make sure he wouldn't feel any draft, she left the bedroom. For an hour or so, she sat in Jonah's bed, surrounded by his things, holding a plush raccoon that had been his favorite—it had come with the name Sticky Fingers, but Jonah had mispronounced it as "Tikki," and afterward they had never referred to it any other way. She held Tikki close, rubbing it under her chin.

Sometime before one o'clock she went back into her room and changed into jeans and a sweatshirt. She'd never taken off her socks. After a visit to the bathroom, she carried Tikki downstairs and turned on the television, volume down so low she could barely hear it. Not that it mattered—she'd put on Cartoon Network and it was the visuals, not the sounds, that comforted her. Jonah loved any cartoon, no matter how old or how lame the animation. They had often curled up together and Sarah had stolen catnaps while Jonah watched. Tonight, Tikki watched with her, but there was no chance of Sarah falling asleep.

At two o'clock she set Tikki on the coffee table and turned off the TV. She laced up her sneakers and went out to the driveway. She'd left her own car out of the garage this afternoon. It didn't seem fair, somehow, to take Paul's Cherokee.

▦▦▦▦

The razor cut deep. Blood slid out over the palms of her hands, filling the lines first and then dripping from her fingers. In the chilly October night, the cuts felt like burns, yet she shuddered as she dropped the razor to the tracks.

Sarah grimaced, a strange satisfaction filling her. She let her arms dangle at her sides as she knelt on a wooden railroad tie, right in the middle of the tracks. She had half an hour or so before the 3:18 was due, so she had chosen a spot away from the road. On the off chance that a car came by, she didn't want to get run over. What terrible irony that would have been.

She let her head loll back and she stared at the stars. If she closed her eyes, she thought she might have been able to fall asleep. What lovely irony. It felt as if she'd been holding her breath ever since Jonah's death, and tonight, at last, she could exhale.

So she waited, and she bled. As the minutes ticked past she began to grow colder, not just on her skin but down deep in her bones. Her eyes fluttered.

It might have been that she closed them for a while.

The whistle startled her. Sarah blinked and caught her breath, staring along the tracks, searching for some sign of the train. That mournful cry came again, much closer than she would have thought. A terrible ache filled her and she felt weak from the loss of blood. Her body's instinct was to rise, to get out of the way, but that sluggishness gave her a moment to consider, and instead she stayed just where she was, content to wait in the path of the 3:18.

She stared down the tracks, narrowing her eyes. A light had appeared in the darkness. The more she focused, the more distinct it became, until Sarah realized that tonight, circumstances had changed.

The 3:18 was coming, and she could see it. The shape of the train hurtled toward her, just a hint of steam blurring the night above the engine. The sound filled the night, then—the whistle, the clank of metal, the chuffing effort of the furnace.

She smiled and her eyes moistened with tears.

The noise grew and the train hurtled closer, a phantom engine, only an intangible silhouette. But it was real. She had not imagined the whistle or the wind, and she swore to herself that she had not imagined Jonah.

Elated, she held her hands up as though to embrace the

3:18. What would happen when it struck her, or passed through her, Sarah could not be sure. But she knew what she wanted, what she had prayed for as she opened up her wrists. The cuts had started to scab but raising her hands tore them open again and trickles of blood ran down the insides of her arms.

She thought of what it had felt like to hold Jonah against her, to rock him to sleep, to watch him at peace.

Her breathing came in short gasps. She closed her eyes and threw her arms out wider.

The train hissed loudly and a blast of cold air struck her, blowing back her hair. She heard the screech of its brakes and opened her eyes to find the enormous locomotive slowing to a halt. With a kind of gasp, it came to a stop twenty feet away. Sarah stared at the 3:18. In the darkness it looked almost real, but she could see right through it.

An icy ripple went through her. A ghost. So close.

But then the truth of what was happening rushed in and she felt the smile blossom on her face, so wide that it hurt. Weak as she was, she staggered to her feet. She slipped in her own blood and nearly fell, but she ran for the train.

"Jonah," she whispered, under her breath. "I'm here, baby boy."

Sarah rushed alongside the first car, looking through the gauzy windows. Images floated within, faces that loomed up from a gray nothing beyond the glass. Some of them seemed to be in pain, while others only looked lost, their eyes vacant. The transparent figure of a little girl gazed out at Sarah with hope in her eyes. Sarah shook her head and ran on. She did not want to linger on any of those faces.

The second car gave her no answers and so she moved on to the third, wondering if she should have tried the other side of the train—wondering how long she had before the train began to move again and whether she should just try to get on board. Had enough of her blood been left behind on the tracks for that?

After the third car, she began to panic. Sarah ran.

"Jonah!" she called. "Where are you, sweetie?"

Halfway along the fourth car, she staggered to a halt. One hand fluttered to her mouth, smearing blood on her face. She laughed into her hand.

Jonah waved to her from the window. Then he retreated, as though getting up from his seat.

Sarah ran to the door at the end of the car. She could see through it to the trees on the other side and the river beyond, but the train itself had substance. It pulsed and gave off a strange luminescence, which might only have been the influence of the moon. The 3:18 was a ghost in and of itself, ridden by phantoms. But Sarah had not forgotten the story that had first brought her here. Near death herself, she could see it well enough.

Now she reached toward the handle beside the door, expecting her fingers to pass through the misty nothing of that specter. Instead, her bloody hand gripped cold metal.

"Oh, my God," she whispered. "Thank you."

She put a foot on the metal step below the door, and hoisted herself up into the open door at the rear of the car. Immediately, the train hissed and lurched, slowly starting forward once more. She could hear the clack of the rails and the breeze as it began to depart.

Sarah looked up and saw Jonah standing in front of her, on the platform at the back of the car. His precious face was just as she remembered, open and smiling, eyes full of love. Jonah reached for her. A shadowed figure loomed behind him, but she paid the other ghost no mind as she put out her arms to her son.

Strong hands snatched him backward, lifted him up and away from her.

"No!" Sarah cried.

The ghostly figure coalesced from the shadows, and she saw the face of the man who held Jonah.

"Daddy?"

He held Jonah against his chest. The boy wrapped his arms around his grandfather's neck, clinging to him, resting in that embrace.

Sarah's father stared at her, his eyes somehow more real than the rest of him, peering out at her from the gray realm of spirits.

"Stop holding on to us, honey. We're fine. The only thing that hurts us now is you not living the life we can never have. We'll see you again, when it's time."

Turning Jonah away from her, he reached out with his free hand—a gossamer thing, translucent and floating, a bit of nothing and shadow—and touched her face. He gave her a wistful smile, and then he shoved her.

Sarah tried to reach out and grab hold of the door frame, but her fingers passed through it like smoke.

She fell backward from the slowly moving train, hit the ground and rolled. By the time she looked up, she could hear it picking up speed, could feel the breeze of its passing, but she couldn't see it anymore.

The 3:18 had come and gone.

Sarah stared at the place where it had been until even the most distant whistle had disappeared, and all she had left was the memory of it. Somehow she knew that she would never hear the whistle of the 3:18 again.

For what seemed an eternity, she sat and waited to die. And when she did not die, she held her hands up in front of her face and looked at her wrists. The right still bled, though not much, and the other had begun to close already. Blood clotted and dried and crusted over. She had not cut deeply enough.

Sarah screamed, enraged that she still lived.

And then she cried.

So lonely, but alive.

In time she rose, weak and disoriented from blood loss, and followed the train tracks until she found her car. She managed to open the door and slid behind the wheel. Sarah wrapped her jacket tightly around her wrists, tangling herself up to stop any further bleeding, but could do no more. Unconsciousness claimed her.

Sometime later, with the sky beginning to lighten in the east, her eyes fluttered open. Her cell phone had been in her jacket pocket, and it was ringing. Freeing one hand, she managed to retrieve it.

Paul.

Sarah opened the phone and fumbled it to her ear.

"Hello?"

"Oh, God," he said, "you had me so scared."

"I miss Jonah," she mumbled.

He cried then, for the first time in a very long time, and Sarah knew that they had both bid farewell to ghosts that night.

BIOS

Amanda DeWees grew up in Atlanta listening to the sounds of trains at night and imagining faraway adventures. Now she writes Victorian paranormal mysteries and gothic romantic suspense novels, including *WITH THIS CURSE,* winner of the 2015 Daphne du Maurier Award for historical mystery/suspense.

Charles Dickens was an English writer and social critic. During his lifetime, his works enjoyed unprecedented popularity. He is now considered a literary genius because he created some of the world's best-known fictional characters and is regarded as the greatest novelist of the Victorian era.

Sir Arthur Ignatius Conan Doyle KStJ DL was a British writer and physician. He created the character Sherlock Holmes in 1887 for A Study in Scarlet, the first of four novels and fifty-six short stories about Holmes and Dr. Watson. The Sherlock Holmes stories are considered milestones in the field of crime fiction.

Christopher Golden is the New York Times bestselling author of *ARARAT, RED HANDS,* and many other novels. With Mike Mignola, he is the co-creator of *BALTIMORE, JOE GOLEM,* and other titles in The Outerverse comic book universe. As editor, his anthologies include HEX LIFE, THE NEW DEAD, and SEIZE THE NIGHT. Golden is also a screenwriter, producer, video game writer, and co-host of the podcast DEFENDERS DIALOGUE. Please visit him at www.christophergolden.com

Scott Goudsward is a slave to the cubicle world by day, and to the voices in his head by night. He writes horror primarily but has branched out to sci-fi and fantasy. His latest novel, *FOUNTAIN OF THE DEAD*, has been re-released by Crossroad Press. His short fiction most recently appeared in *The Final Summons*. The non-fiction book *HORROR GUIDE TO NORTHERN NEW ENGLAND* (co-written with brother David Goudsward) is now available from Post Mortem Press. He is a coordinator of the New England Horror Writers, spearheading numerous well-received anthologies, including *WICKED WOMEN* and the forthcoming *WICKED CREATURES*. Other anthology projects include *WOULD BUT TIME AWAIT*, co-edited with KH Vaughan, and *FRIGHT TRAIN* (which you are currently reading from), co-edited with Tony Tremblay and Charles R. Rutledge. Scott is currently working on a YA novel and looking for new anthology possibilities.

Bracken MacLeod is the Splatterpunk, Bram Stoker, and Shirley Jackson Award-nominated author of the novels, *MOUNTAIN HOME, COME TO DUST, STRANDED*, and *CLOSING COSTS* (from Houghton Mifflin Harcourt). He's also published two collections of short fiction, *13 VIEWS OF THE SUICIDE WOODS* and *WHITE KNIGHT AND OTHER PAWNS*. Before devoting himself to full-time writing, he worked as a civil and criminal litigator, a university philosophy instructor, and a martial arts teacher. He lives outside of Boston with his wife and son, where he is at work on his next novel.

Elizabeth Massie is a two-time Bram Stoker Award-winning and Scribe Award-winning author of novels, short fiction, media-tie ins, and more. Her novels and collections include *SINEATER, HELL GATE, DESPER HOLLOW, MADAME CRULLER'S COUCH AND OTHER DARK AND BIZARRE TALES,*

WIRE MESH MOTHERS, HOMEPLACE, NAKED ON THE EDGE, AFRAID, IT WATCHING, DARK SHADOWS: DREAMS OF THE DARK (co-authored with Mark Rainey), *VERSAILLES, THE TUDORS: KING TAKES QUEEN, THE TUDORS: THY WILL BE DONE, BUFFY THE VAMPIRE SLAYER: POWER OF PERSUASION,* and many others. She is also the creator of the *Ameri-Scares* series of spooky novels for middle grade readers. Massie lives in the Shenandoah Valley of Virginia with her husband, illustrator Cortney Skinner. She loves geocaching and the beach and can't stand cheese and mean people.

James A. Moore is the award-winning, best-selling author of over one hundred short stories, and forty novels, including the critically acclaimed *Serenity Falls* trilogy (featuring his recurring anti-hero, Jonathan Crowley) and his most recent novels, *BOOMTOWN* and the forthcoming *THE GODLESS*. He has been twice nominated for the Bram Stoker Award and spent three years as an officer in the Horror Writers Association, first as Secretary and later as Vice President.

Mikio Murakami is a Japanese-Canadian graphic designer. He specializes in cover art, T-shirts, logos, and drinking bad coffee. His design company SILENT Q DESIGN was founded in Montreal in 2006. Melding together the use of both realistic templates and surreal imagery, SILENT Q DESIGN's artistry proves, at first glance, that a professional for art is still alive, and that no musician, magazine, or venue should suffer from the same bland designs that have been re-hashed over and over. The evolution of artwork ranges both locally and internationally. **SILENT Q DESIGN** has commissioned work for Montreal and surrounding area bands such as Synastry, Endast and The Agonist. Likewise, SILENT Q DESIGN also boasts work for international musician Bob Katsionis (Toshiba-EMI / Lion

Music / Century Media) as well as Montreal Radio station 90. 3 FM's Sounds of Steel music program. Their works go beyond fantasy landscapes and surreal imagery, offering their customers personalized service. SILENT Q DESIGN prides itself on being a multi-faceted entity that can serve even the contemporary business world.

Lee Murray is a multi-award-winning author from Aotearoa-New Zealand (Sir Julius Vogel, Australian Shadows), and a five-time Bram Stoker Award®-nominee. Her works include the *Taine McKenna Adventures*, supernatural crime-noir series THE PATH OF RA (with Dan Rabarts), and debut collection *GROTESQUE: MONSTER STORIES*. Read more at leemurray.info

Errick Nunnally was born and raised in Boston, Massachusetts, and served one tour in the Marine Corps before deciding art school was a safer pursuit. He enjoys art, comics, and genre novels. A graphic designer, he has trained in Krav Maga and Muay Thai kickboxing. His work has appeared in several anthologies and is best described as "dark pulp." His work can be found in *Apex Magazine*, *Fiyah Magazine*, *Galaxy's Edge*, *Lamplight*, *Nightlight Podcast*, and the novels *LIGHTNING WEARS A RED CAPE*, *BLOOD FOR THE SUN*, and *ALL THE DEAD MEN*. Visit erricknunnally.us to learn more about his work.

Stephen Mark Rainey has been writing professionally for over thirty years. He is the author of numerous adult novels, including *BAPAK*, *THE LEBO COVEN*, *DARK SHADOWS: DREAMS OF THE DARK* (with Elizabeth Massie), *BLUE DEVIL ISLAND*, *THE NIGHTMARE FRONTIER*, *THE MONARCHS*, and others. Currently, he is writing novels for *Elizabeth Massie's Ameri-Scares* series for young readers, with three already in print and several more on the publication schedule. In addition, Mark's work includes five short story collections; almost 200 published works of short fiction; and the scripts to several *Dark Shadows* audio productions, which feature members of the original ABC-TV series cast. For ten years, he edited the award-winning *Deathrealm* magazine and has edited the anthologies *Deathrealms*, *Song of Cthulhu*, and *Evermore*. His short fiction has most recently appeared in *Borderlands 7* and *The Black Stone: Stories for Lovecraftian Summonings*. Mark lives in Greensboro, NC.

Charles R. Rutledge is the author of *DRACULA'S REVENGE* and *DRACULA'S GHOST*, and the co-author of three novels in the *Griffin & Price series*, written with James A. Moore. His short stories have appeared in over 30 anthologies. He is more powerful than a locomotive.

Jeff Strand is the Bram Stoker Award-nominated author of over 50 books, many of which have film adaptations in development. He has never had the opportunity to rescue a damsel who is tied to the tracks as a speeding train approaches, but he totally would, given the opportunity. He knows it's not a competition, but hopes you choo-choo-choose his story as your favorite in the collection. You can visit his Gleefully Macabre website at www.JeffStrand.com.

Tony Tremblay is the author of the Bram Stoker Award nominated novel *THE MOORE HOUSE*. He is also the author of two collections *THE SEEDS OF NIGHTMARES*, and *BLUE STARS*. Tony has also been a co-editor in the *Eulogies* series of anthologies, co-hosted a horror-related talk show, and is a co-founder of the NoCon Horror Convention. Tony lives in New Hampshire.

Mercedes M. Yardley is a dark fantasist who wears poisonous flowers in her hair. She is the author of *BEAUTIFUL SORROWS*, the Stabby Award winning *APOCALYPTIC MONTESSA AND NUCLEAR LULU: A TALE OF ATOMIC LOVE*, *PRETTY LITTLE DEAD GIRLS*, and *NAMELESS*. She won the Bram Stoker Award for her story *Little Dead Red* and was a Bram Stoker Award nominee for her short story "Loving You Darkly" and the *Arterial Bloom* anthology.

You can find her at mercedesmyardley.com.

www.ingramcontent.com/pod-product-compliance
Lightning Source LLC
Chambersburg PA
CBHW061617190726
48288CB00007B/2353